sweet baby
mine

sweet baby mine

a novel

Maria Daversa

DIVINE DOG

Copyright © 2022 by Maria Daversa

First edition June 2022
Printed in the United States of America

Cover design by Laura Boyle Design
Cover photo by Harvey Photography

ISBN 979-8-9861669-1-9 (paperback)
ISBN 979-8-9861669-0-2 (ebook)
LIBRARY OF CONGRESS CONTROL NUMBER: XXXXXXXX

Divine Dog Editions.

Visit www.mariadaversa.com for author information.

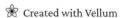 Created with Vellum

For my mother, for all mothers—for all women who still dream of living.

One does not become enlightened by imagining figures of light, but by making the darkness conscious.

~Carl Jung

1

ANA

Saturday, August 11, 2018

I failed my daughter once; like hell, I'll let her down again.

"So, why are you calling?" Tony's voice is strained. He's still angry about last night.

"I'm lost." I appeal to my husband's sense of compassion and hope he'll feel sorry for me, for the situation I've gotten us into.

"Mm-hmm."

"That's it?" Strands of disheveled hair spill across my face. I rake them behind my ears. "I'm out here trying to find our daughter," I say. "This is what you want, isn't it? A reconciliation?"

"Are you still taking your meds?" he asks.

"Why would you ask me that?" I am, of course, *not* taking my meds. The last thing I need right now is to feel dead inside. "Our daughter called us—"

"She called *you*."

"It's not a competition. Chloe's in trouble. Deep trouble."

"I know you, Ana. I know when you have something up your sleeve."

"Well, you're mistaken. That's not what's going on here."

"It'd be a first, then."

"How shallow do you think I am?—don't answer that." Tony's never appreciated how hard it is for me to step outside of myself, to see the real me in all my darkness. I want to do better, but it's not easy. I can see a way forward, but I don't know how to get there. Not yet. Sometimes, it's all I can do to get my head out of my ass.

"Fine," I say. "This time, it's not only about me."

I challenge the speed limit and sail under an information sign that hangs from an overpass. It tells me to slow down, that there's a flurry of construction ahead. Not that you'd know what's being constructed around here. When you're this far north along the A3, it doesn't take much to see you're not in Paris any longer. Certainly not the Paris of Shakespeare and Company, or Edith Piaf, or The Little Prince. No, this Paris is the other Paris, the one that exists on the wrong side of the Boulevard Périphérique. In this Paris, the highway drains of traffic, the breakdown lane chokes with hubcaps and plastic grocery bags, and the air stands dense with smog. Keep driving, and everything melds into a mélange of gunmetal, brick, and cement. A dead dog with a coat the color of midnight, rests amid the roadside trash. Its lifeless form suggests peace, but it's a lie. There's no peace here.

I dry my eyes and ease up on the accelerator. I approach the work zone and check my watch. Tony says something, but I can't hear him. "There's too much noise," I shout.

I dodge a pothole and stop directly in front of a road worker. He waves me forward, then motions for me to shift into the next lane. I tap the gas, and I'm about to move to the right, when another hard hat steps out from behind a dump truck. I hit the brakes, and my veggie burger flies off the passenger seat. Ketchup oozes all over the floor mat. For real, pal? A quick glance in the rearview mirror shows the entire highway is at an impasse—steam, smoke, and dust everywhere. The stench of liquid asphalt stings my nose, and I roll up the windows, but it doesn't help, and no one is going anywhere anytime soon.

I bang on the steering wheel. Shame bubbles up in my gut. What if Chloe thinks I'm not coming? What if she splits again, and I can't find her? What if she really harms herself this time?

"The last thing she said was to look for a street with a bunch of decrepit old houses." I choke up and stop talking. I don't want to cry again. I did enough of that last night. My eyes are so swollen they hurt.

"I don't know what you're so afraid of?" Tony asks. "You used to live in an abandoned building."

"Can you drop the asshole routine? I shared a loft in SoHo. In the '90s," I say. "It wasn't exactly Skid Row."

"Chloe asked for *you* last night." Tony's voice quivers. He can't understand why our daughter reached out to me, especially after the heartache I've caused her. "So, you're it," he says.

"We talked about this." My husband never listens. Magnanimity is not one of his strengths. He's a narcissist. He's selfish, egotistical, and requires constant admiration. It's the mask he wears to hide his self-hatred. Ordinarily, I'd cradle his damaged inner child, relieve him of his sorrow, but now is not the time. "We need to work together," I say.

"Maybe you should've thought about that before you gave her the letter."

"Damn it, Tony. I didn't give her the letter." I wait for him to dispute me again when the worker flags me on. I press the End Call button and hit the gas to make up for lost time. When

I find the right exit, I veer off the main road and search for anything that resembles a vacant house. Around here, though, all the homes are empty. Every structure is bruised, covered in graffiti, teeming with resentment. I aim for the curb, park, and kill the engine.

The street is quiet.

I free my phone from where it's mounted on the dash, and text my friend Adel.

My daughter is in trouble. Heroin. I'm out searching for her.

I burden her with my problems. I bombard everyone with my troubles, but my pain is too big to face alone.

She responds right away.

Sweetie, so sorry. You're a good mother. Find her!

If she only knew what kind of mother I was.

The car heats up fast without air conditioning. I dab at the moisture along my upper lip, then redial Tony.

He answers at once.

"Look," I say. "I don't want to fight with you again."

"Why don't you come home? We can go out again tomorrow and look for her together."

I'm taken aback by his abrupt pleasantness. "Where's all this coming from?" I ask.

"If you want me to help you, I will."

I futz with my shirt and sigh into the receiver. "What's up?" I ask. "Why are you suddenly being so nice?"

Tony clears his throat.

"I'm surprised, is all. This isn't the same attitude you had a minute ago. Did you have a change of heart?" My skin tingles. Maybe there's hope for our marriage, after all.

"This is about Chloe," he says. "There's nothing more going on here."

"Do you have to make it so crystal clear it's *not* about me?"

Tony sniffles into the phone. It's a quirk of his. He does it any time he's nervous or needs to buy some time before he responds. He mumbles something, but his mouth is too far from the receiver. Is he speaking to me—or someone else?

"Chloe asked to speak to me last night because I can relate to her," I say. "I know what she's going through." What's that fluttering sound in the background? I press the phone against my ear.

"Oh, for the love of—what makes you think you know our daughter any better than I do?"

"Because I *get* her." There it is again. What is that *sound?*

"Chloe and I have the same issues," I say.

"So, that's what we've decided to call them now? 'Issues?'"

Is someone with him? It sounds like sheets rustling in the background. Our bathroom door opening and closing. Now there's water running in the shower. There *is* someone in the apartment with him. My face is on fire. "She's there with you now, isn't she?"

"Who, Ana?"

"Fucking shit. Five minutes. You can't stop banging your whore for five whole minutes while we look for our daughter?" I hammer the console with my cell phone. "Why, Tony? Why?" I throw the phone. It strikes the dashboard and lands in the ketchup.

A group of kids in a faded silver Corolla drive by. Slowly. Algerian Raï blares from mammoth-sized speakers in the car's back window. Someone in the passenger seat takes note of me, but the car continues. The street is quiet again.

I clean off the phone and speed-dial Tony again. It goes straight to voicemail. "And don't forget about the dogs." The words wobble off my tongue. "Damn you, Tony."

I sit back and wait for the familiar itch; the feeling I get when my skin inflames, when I fear I'm being rejected and see myself alone, but it's not there. I was straight with Tony this morning. Seven years ago, I blew it, but I'm here for her now, and I can fix this. I'll find Chloe. I'll find her, and I'll bring her home if it's the last thing I do.

I get out of the car and make a beeline for the house on the corner. It's the only one that matches my daughter's description. I jiggle the doorknob, but it's locked. I bang on the front door and call out her name, but there's no response. I peer through the front plate glass. The place is empty save for a couple of light bulbs that hang from the ceiling. Trash litters the floor. I call out Chloe's name again; I use her childhood nickname. "Clover. Baby. It's Mom. *Allo. Est-ce que quelqu'un est ici?*"

Nothing.

I go around to the back of the house and find another door. I knock on this one, too. "*Je suis ici pour voir Chloé DiSalvo.*" I say I'm here for my daughter. Then I hold my breath and listen. Somewhere deep in the interior of the house kids laugh and a radio plays, but no one comes to the door. I spot another large window, but it's clamped shut. I search the dirt lot for a rock. I find one—a big one, and I pick it up and weigh it in my hand before I circle around to the front of the house again. I look to see if anyone's watching, then I hurl it through the window.

It shatters the silence. I duck as chunks of glass rain down on what's left of the lawn. I brush myself off, scramble across the debris, and grab on to the window frame. I check the yard one last time, but it hardly matters. I didn't come all this way to be shut out of my daughter's life now.

2

TONY

Sunday, August 5, 2018
Six days before Chloe's rescue

Ana breaks her chocolate cruller in half. She hands the larger of the two pieces to the small girl in front of her. My wife can't help herself. She has a soft spot for the most vulnerable among us. She is the patron saint of the marginalized and the defender of all who've been wronged.

It's a wonderful quality, but every now and then it'd be nice to enjoy my brunch without having to be interrupted by Ana's need to save the world. "Must you?" I ask.

"She's hungry."

"She is a vagrant."

"She's a little girl."

In all likelihood, she is an illegal immigrant and the progeny of one of the many nationalities that unlawfully enter this country every day. "We can hardly afford to feed everyone who sleeps rough," I say.

"It's a bite of pastry. Maybe you can be a little more accommodating."

My blood pressure rises. "She's not French. She's here to take advantage of our generous welfare system."

"Please, you have no idea if she's French or not, and if she's not, then she's most likely fleeing a dangerous situation at home—as are *most* of the women and children who come here."

"All right, you don't have to go all Gloria Steinem on me."

My wife rolls her eyes.

Honestly, who isn't running away from something these days? "We can't support them all," I say.

"*Quel est votre nom?*" Ana asks the child her name, but the girl shakes her head. It's clear she doesn't understand French. My wife requests again, in English this time, but she has no luck there either. The youngster points and carries on about what I can only surmise is her situation. She's found a friend in my wife.

If I had to guess, I'd say she can't be much older than five or six. She's dressed in a pair of shorts and a T-shirt, both of which are too big for her and belong to an older brother, who's probably soliciting money from the patrons of a café somewhere nearby. "It's against the law for children to beg," I say.

"I know what the law is." Ana surveys the mob of MacBook Airs assembled along the sidewalk this morning. She stoops to the girl's level and wonders aloud about where her family could be and why they aren't here with her. "I'm calling the center," she says. "Maybe they'll recognize her." She straightens the girl's shirt, then hunts through her purse for her cell phone.

My wife volunteers for an aid group that assists the homeless. She mostly mans the phones and answers inquiries about government benefits, but it requires a lot of time—time she happily gives them, even though it removes her from her family. It's not that I'm jealous, but we agreed to travel more once the girls moved out, and I don't see how this will happen with her having so many commitments, or more to the point, so many commitments to everyone except me.

"Someone *has* to be searching for her," she says.

While Ana may not agree with me, this child is savvier than either of us gives her credit for. I'm ready to explain this to my wife when a woman pops out of nowhere and takes the five-year-old by the shoulder, scoops her into her arms, and braces the girl against her hip.

"*Est-ce votre fille?*" My wife asks if she is indeed the mother.

The woman says nothing; she goes off in a huff. The girl watches Ana from over the woman's shoulder. Finally, the distance becomes too great. The child turns her head, and mother and daughter disappear into the crowd.

Ana waits another second, then she maneuvers her chair and sits across from me.

"I wish you hadn't done that." I check my email and scroll through messages. "These people are freeloaders."

"Tony, please."

She admonishes me, but it's nothing she hasn't heard before. I'm not a bad guy. I'd just like to see more of what I earn go into my paycheck rather than augment the multitude of benefits this country distributes at no cost. High taxes are the reason the French are in a world of debt.

My wife has said all she intends to say on this topic, however, and now occupies herself with her cell phone. Odds are she's reading posts from her Twitter friends. I don't tweet. It's an unreasonable undertaking. How does an intelligent person fit a coherent thought into no more than a few dozen characters?

She tosses the phone on the table, where it dings with an

incoming text. Ana taps the home screen, then taps the screen again. Her entire message board pops up.

I glance at it. I see my oldest daughter's name. For real? I look harder. Ana has a text from our *daughter*—correction, our *estranged* daughter? "Chloe sent you a text?" I reach for her phone.

Ana gets to it first.

My exasperation grows, and I lunge at it.

"Stop, Tony."

A white-haired duo seated several tables away turn and look at us.

"Why do you have a text from Chloe?" The tips of my ears are on fire. I extend my hand and wait for her to pass me the phone. I look like a despot, but I don't care. My wife has been in contact with our oldest daughter, and she's kept it from me.

Ana presses the phone to her chest.

We eye each other. It's a stalemate. I reach across the table again, but Ana lurches backward, and her chair crashes to the concrete. We're making fools of ourselves, but my wife and I are frozen in time, anchored in a perpetual battle that, while it may have subsided over the years, has resurfaced with the revelation my daughter has established contact with us—with *Ana*. I am beside myself. I sit back and shake open the *International New York Times*. My breathing is heavy, however, and the paper vibrates in my hands. I can't read a damn word of it.

I'm not good at confrontation, and I would happily keep my mouth in this type of a situation, but after years of silence, our oldest daughter has sent us a text message, and my wife won't let me read it. I have to say *something*. "Christ, Ana, can you at least tell me if she is all right?"

Ana picks up her chair, repositions it, and reseats herself. She sets her phone down directly in front of her.

I can't take my eyes off it. My wife has a text message from my daughter in that slimmed down hunk of metal, and I need to see it. I *will* see it. Right now, however, I could use another espresso, and I look around for our server—what the hell is his name? Eudes? Eudo? It's the kid with the gold stud in his tongue. Honestly, why would anyone do that to themselves? I peer inside the restaurant, but I don't see him. He's probably in the kitchen chatting up the other waitstaff. He's always nattering at someone.

I change position and cross my legs, left over right, then I flex my left foot upright. I rearrange the newspaper and flip straight to the business section. Late last week, China's Shanghai Composite Index went into free-fall faster than a penny tumbling off the Empire State Building, but I'm too distracted to read about it. It's hard to believe I can't even soothe myself with the financials this morning. I let the newspaper drop. "So, when did you plan on sharing this with me?" I ask.

Ana disregards my question. She's busy Twittering again. She finishes, then rubs her arms. It's a nervous habit, a tic, really. Whenever she's anxious, her skin itches. It's a result of the scars she carries; the self-inflicted wounds she made as a teen, a tactic she employed to help her survive the overly repressive symptoms of the borderline personality disorder that still haunt her today.

When I met my wife, I swore I'd do whatever was necessary to ensure her happiness. In return, she relinquished her entire world and followed me to Paris, all based on a promise —a flawed promise—that I'd love her unconditionally for the rest of her life.

It's a vow we've both come to regret.

I don't believe in unconditional love. Everything has a condition. It's a simple matter of economics. There was a time, however, when I thought if I could love Ana enough, I could heal all of her misery, but I've come to realize that's not the case. There's too damn much of it.

"You still blame me for why she left us," she says.

"She did not leave us."

"Call it whatever you like. Ditched. Dumped. Dispensed with. It's all the same. She *left* us."

"She did not leave *us*."

"What are you saying?"

Eudo's timing could not be more perfect. He sweeps through the restaurant's swinging doors and onto the sidewalk.

I catch his eye. "*Un express, s'il vous plait,*" I holler with more force than I intend. I pray I didn't offend him, since I would really like that second cup of coffee and insulting him will not help my situation. Eudo doesn't acknowledge me, but in a single motion, he sails back into the restaurant.

"Tony?" Ana asks.

I position the *Times* in front of me like a barricade.

"Tony." It's no longer a question. "Has Chloe tried to contact you?"

I drop the paper and attend to my croissant. I stab it with my fork and knife, then halve it.

My wife squirms in her chair. She fingers what's left of her doughnut. "She *has* tried to make contact with you."

I continue to slice up my pastry. I place a smaller section in my mouth.

"Tony." Her voice escalates.

I avoid her gaze.

"When?" she asks.

I look around and note the other patrons. "Let's not do this here," I say.

"Can you make it any more obvious?" she asks.

"It was a long time ago, An."

"How long?"

I carve up another bite-sized chunk of my breakfast. Blood pulses through my temples.

My wife sits back in her chair. She folds her arms across her chest.

"Fine." I set my utensils on the table. "Do you remember a few years ago when I withdrew a large sum of money from our savings account?"

"I do."

"And I told you the reason was because the interest rate on our mortgage had risen, considerably, and we needed to pay off as much of the principal as we could bear?"

"I said I remember."

"Well."

"Well?"

"We-e-e-l-l." I look over at her and grin. Sometimes it's these minor victories.

My wife raises an eyebrow. "That wasn't what you did with it?"

"No."

She raises both eyebrows.

I collect my silverware and hack off more pastry. "I wired it to Chloe." I stuff my mouth with it.

"You *what*?"

"She called and said she needed money." My mouth is full of croissant. I can barely get the words out. "A lot of it—"

"She *called* you?"

This conversation is beginning to feel like a cross-examination. I bring my cup to my lips and take a sip, but the liquid singes the roof of my mouth. I nearly dump it in my lap. I quickly place the cup in its saucer and pretend as if it didn't happen.

"Did you even question her as to why she needed such a large amount of money?" she asks.

"No, I didn't, but at the time, I asked a tech guy at the university to track down her IP address. He said the originator of the email had masked it, so he couldn't—"

"Masked it?"

"So, the only information I had from her was—"

"That our daughter needed a large sum of money and had no intention of telling you what she planned to do with it."

I ax off another portion of my pastry and shove it in my mouth. How can I tell my wife I didn't care *why* Chloe called, only *that* she called—and that she called *me*? All I cared about was that my daughter had reconnected with *me*, even if it was for five minutes and even if it was about money. My oldest daughter needed cash. I would've given her the world if she'd asked for it.

I look over at Ana. She's mangled her cruller. It's beyond recognizable. She ingests a portion of it. "You must be out of your mind." She chews and garbles her words. Bits of cruller spatter from her lips. "Our daughter is a heroin addict, and you go and send her an enormous amount of cash. That's brilliant, Tony."

"She communicated her needs to me."

"She stroked your ego is what she did."

"I couldn't deny her."

"Well, no, we wouldn't want that."

"You know what your problem is?" I amplify *my* voice now. "You were envious of my relationship with Chloe."

"Oh, please. The reason you had such a good relationship with our daughter was because you never said no to her. She couldn't do anything wrong in your eyes."

"Hell, she couldn't do anything right in yours." I slash at what's left of my crescent. I cram it on my fork.

"You have no idea what went on between Chloe and me." Ana proceeds to rip apart the last of her pastry. Crumbs fly everywhere. "You weren't home long enough to find out."

I shoot Ana a dirty look and turn away. My wife's go-to defense in any argument is my historical lack of physical and emotional availability.

"That's right," she says. "No comment." She deposits the entire mess of dough onto her plate. She brushes bits of it from her lap. "Don't shake your head. You'd change your tune if you knew half of what Chloe said to me that night. She insulted you, too, and only moments before she washed her hands of us. That's right, Tony. *Us.* She ran out on both of us."

I sit up and match her posture. "I may never know what happened between you and Chloe that night—"

"She rejected us, Tony." Ana hunches over the table. Her voice hardens. "That's what our daughter did that night. She snubbed us. Both of us. She rebuffed you as much as she did me."

"But what I do know is this." I bring my face right up to hers. "Whatever Chloe did, or said, she directed it at you and you alone, and you deserved every ounce of it."

"You will never see my side of this." She sits back.

I take another sip of my espresso, but it's cold. Acrimony flows out of me like hot lava, and I dump the cup in its saucer. I scowl at my wife. "It's because I know you, Ana. I know you'll do whatever it takes to get whatever you want, and you don't care who you abuse in the process. Even if that person happens to be your husband, and the thing you want to do is to sleep with another man." I sit back. Wow. Where did *that* come from? It's been twenty-three years since I thought about Ana's affair.

My wife's eyes fill up.

It's obvious, however, the violation I felt over her flagrant infidelity continues to seethe in my gut.

"That was twenty-three years ago," she says.

My wife is correct, but for me, it feels like yesterday. I thought I'd packed it away and buried it so deep I'd never find it, but it's obvious I can't erase the damage she did. It doesn't help that she's never once apologized, explained, or assumed responsibility for it.

Ana betrayed me.

She allowed another man to penetrate her—and barely a month after we wed.

Good God.

I loved my wife once. I truly did.

Maybe too much.

I look over at her.

Now she has a text from Chloe, and she refuses to let me read it.

I push out my chair, dig through my pocket, and remove a handful of euros. I plunk them on the table. Then I tuck the newspaper under my arm and step into the street.

Maybe once, I'll enjoy my brunch without my wife ruining it.

3

ANA

Tony trudges off without me. It's like the music's stopped, and I'm the last one standing without a chair. I try to remember some of the techniques Dr. Woodhouse taught me about how best to ground myself when we fight: things like taking deep breaths or holding something soft and plushy. But what's the point? After all this time, I still can't argue with my husband without agonizing over whether he'll leave me because of it—because of some awful thing I've said, or done. Or both.

I check my Twitter feed, then type out a tweet. "Why must hubz drag out the past whenever we fight?" I add a silly GIF of some kangaroos boxing and blast it out to the Twittersphere. I don't mention my own responsibility in any of this, like how I've kept so many secrets from him it's a wonder I haven't already obliterated this marriage.

I close out of Twitter and tap the Messenger app, but I can't deal with Chloe's text again. No, it's the memory of our last exchange I can't accept. I cringe whenever I'm forced to relive it.

It's not that I didn't want to be a mother. I wanted to be a mom more than anything in the world. It's just that I wasn't very good at it. I'm too greedy and insecure. My oldest daughter didn't leave home because she wanted to. Chloe left home because I *forced* her to. She left because when she'd discovered the truth—about me, about her—she'd threatened to tell Tony, and I had to stop her.

Desperate people do desperate things.

Don't get me wrong, if I could do it over again, I would, and I'd do it better. If only. If only. If only we could all live our lives free of regrets.

I should show it to Tony. I really should. Hiding Chloe's text will only make him mad. Why is it all the bad things we've done in the past never stay in the past? How come the misdeeds we engaged in during our youth always resurface? What if I'm not that same Ana anymore? What if *that* Ana was so hopelessly lonely that she couldn't help but fill the void in her life in all the wrong ways? At forty-five, should I still have to be defined by the mistakes I made when I was twenty-two?

The skin along my forearms irritates me, and I scrape at it with my fingernails.

What if Tony takes my phone someday, and he reads it when I'm not around? What do I say to him then?

Maybe I should password protect it.

No, that'll make him more suspicious. He'll think I'm having another affair.

I should delete it; that's what I really should do with it. I should get rid of it, so no one else in this family gets their hands on it, and so Tony *never* reads it. If he even had a hint of what happened between Chloe and me that night, he'd divorce me, for sure.

But I don't delete it. I can't delete it. It's a message from my firstborn, my eldest daughter, along with her favorite symbol of good luck—a four-leaf clover—because she wishes the best for me, even if I refuse. *Crap.*

I'll show it to him. I'm better than this.

No, I'm not. I'm a coward.

I stuff the phone back in my purse and step under a striped awning, grateful for the shade. I'm joined by a life-size stencil graffiti of a man in a tux playing the violin. Like a lot of the murals in Ménilmontant, it covers the entire wall of the building and is done by the likes of Blek Le Rat, Miss.Tic, or Jerome Mesnager. A vibrant, working class community that moves to a different beat, by day this *arrondissement* bustles with Tunisian bakeries, North African flea markets, and Senegalese bookshops, whereas by night its back alleys satiate with underground dance raves, avant garde jazz, and the imam's call to prayer.

Still, everyone we know moved away years ago, preferring to live in the city's more affluent districts. I've never understood it, except to believe they had grand delusions of how life ought to be. I don't suffer from that problem. I know how life should be, how it is. I glance over at the violin player again. I don't care for his disapproving eye, and I look away. I hardly need another critic this morning.

Tony proceeds along Rue du Château d'Eau. He embarks on the route home the same way he manages everything in his world: with grave determination. Yet, in the past few years, this ruthless drive to succeed has left its mark on him. At forty-nine, his six-foot-two frame rests in a perpetual slump. Frown lines circle his lips, and what was once a stunning head of auburn hair is now flecked with gray and cropped close in a self-conscious bid to hide a relentlessly receding hairline. The man is a ghost of his former self. Only his eyes have remained the same—they're an intense azure blue that's not unlike the color of compressed ice, or the tail feathers of a macaw, or the

Mediterranean in May as it laps against the walls of Antibes. They can still raise me up, high above the ocean's rolling surface, and keep me free from harm.

So, how did we grow so far apart?

I know losing Chloe hit him hard. Having her return would revive him, and I want to do this for him, I do, but it's just too much of a risk for me.

I gather my hair into a slipshod ponytail and catch up with him in front of the Hotel Aida Marais. A mixture of chocolate, poached salmon, and stewed kidney beans wafts through the open doors. Tony peers into the plate glass window. He brings his nose up to it and stabs at his cheek with his finger. He traces the slope of slightly sagging skin that dips below his jawbone. "Just once, maybe you could talk about *your* part in why you and Chloe had so many difficulties." He continues to mull over his reflection.

"*My* part?" I can't believe we're back to this. I know better than to respond. Of course, I had a part. A big part. A child's parents are her first cheerleaders. Children who have lots of support grow up to be happy and healthy and approach the world bursting with confidence. Children who have parents who ridicule them and make them feel bad about themselves, grow up believing they're not worth the shit they produce and spend the rest of their lives wishing they could disappear.

"Chloe was a drug addict." I redirect the conversation back to my daughter.

"No, she wasn't."

"Wasn't she?"

"She was a bit of a wild child, that's all." Tony yanks at the sleeves of his baby blue Oxford and rolls them up haphazardly, then he heads for the Place de la République: the road that rings Republic Square. He gets to the intersection, and the flashing man on the pedestrian crosswalk switches from green to red, but my husband doesn't stop. He parades into the road and forces a crimson red motor scooter to swerve into an adjacent lane so as not to hit him. The driver flips Tony off. My husband returns the salute and hops back onto the curb.

I step in front of him and violate his personal space. "So, what was it you thought Chloe was doing every time she told us she was sleeping over a friend's house, but we couldn't get anyone on the phone to verify it?"

Tony's eyes mist over. He glides his hand over the top of his balding head. "Chloe had a predilection for the unconventional, that's all." He sidesteps me and crosses the street. He circumvents the troop of sightseers on the other side who have stationed themselves in front of a bronze statue of Marianne, the champion of democracy, extinguisher of oppression, and opponent of the monarchy. Armed with their cameras, they capture for posterity a former, whiter notion of France.

I'm right on his heels. "Chloe sent this household wildly off track," I say. "She was the critical point in this family's complicated dynamics—"

"You can stop with the psychobabble. I'm not one of your clients."

"She was the fodder that fed our polarizing alliances."

My husband turns on me. "How is it that you've come to view yourself as the only one in this family who understands our interactions—our so-called unique *dynamics*?"

"Now, who's slinging the psychobabble?" The back of my neck is tight, and I squeeze it. "You need to think this through." I rotate my head to ease the pressure.

"I have thought it through." Tony enters the square and turns to face me. "Chloe never would've departed unless something bad happened that night and drove her away."

"Jesus, again with that night."

His jawline hardens, becomes more defined. "Show me her message," he says.

I wind my hand around the shoulder strap of my purse.

"I want to read it."

I pull the bag closer. Chloe's not even here, and Tony and I are entering our second standoff of the morning.

My husband yanks the bag out of my hands and bounds into the plaza. Pigeons balk and fan out in front of him. They scatter across the stones.

Panic presses against my ribs; my chest is so tight it hurts.

Tony runs across the square, then stops and fights for breath. He digs his hand in my pocketbook and pulls out my cell. He throws the bag to the ground and turns to face me.

I can't move my legs. Everything is closing in on me, and I'm afraid I'll crack. I comb the sky for a hole, some sort of break or moment of solitude so I can pull myself together.

What's wrong with you?

I hear my mother's voice. It reverberates in my ears like the bells of Notre Dame. Loud, resonant, and not to be questioned.

Can't you do anything right?

I can't escape it. It's with me everywhere; it glides along the parquet floors in our apartment, floats in the seams of my suits, and weeps through the grout around our tub. It's there whenever I eat, read, jog, or masturbate.

For once in your life, leave it alone.

I can't, though. I can't leave anything alone.

Tony and I are messy, but that's how it is with us. It's the way our disorders meld, it's how Tony's narcissism merges with my borderline. Tony contains me when I spill over, I indulge his emotional desert when he can't express it. Together, we lack boundaries, we can't corral our impulses. We're the juggling act of the psychiatry world. The yin and yang of the asylum elite. The high society of the looney bin. It works; we work.

I need to do something before I lose him—

I run headlong into the street.

A white Mercedes veers into an oncoming lane so as not to hit me. The car behind it slams on its breaks.

"What are you doing?" Tony yells.

I break out in a cold sweat and stand in the middle of the road.

The driver of the Mercedes yells at me and calls me crazy.

"That's right," I say. "I'm crazy. A real nutcase." I'll be whatever I need to be to stop Tony from reading that letter.

My husband rushes toward me.

I move further into the street.

The nine-six bus begins a sluggish climb in my direction.

The tourists stop snapping their pictures and watch. Busy Parisians slow their pace and stare.

I'm a spectacle, and it's all for an audience of one. I look over and make sure Tony sees me.

The bus driver steps on the gas.

I'm as still as a potted plant.

"Ana," Tony sprints across the plaza. The last few pigeons duck and cover.

I'm drunk, light-headed.

"Get out of the road!" he hollers.

"I'm sorry."

He quickens his step.

"I didn't mean to do it."

"Ana, please!"

But it's too late. I'm weightless. Free-floating. I'm hovering above the street.

The world goes silent.

There are no cars. No horns. No sirens.

There's no up or down. No left or right.

Then somebody shoves me.

The impact lifts me off the ground, and I reel across time and space, concrete and stone. People all around us shout and wave their arms; they direct us toward the curb. Someone leads me across the road, and we vault on to the sidewalk together as the nine-six grinds past us, its massive wheels close enough to touch. It blankets us in soot.

My husband wraps his arms around me, then he presses me against his chest.

He's still The One.

He'll always be The One.

Which is why he can never read Chloe's text.

4
TONY

Ana calms quickly in my arms. Her body odor is pungent. Or maybe it's my own underarms that are turning my stomach. Or maybe it's the fact that no matter where we go or what we do, my wife has to create turmoil, and I have to carry the brunt of it. It's wearing being her collateral damage. As I work to stop hyperventilating, I release her.

"I cut my knee when I fell." Ana points to herself. Her chin trembles, and her voice is faint. She sounds like a child with a boo-boo.

I follow her finger.

She spits on her sleeve and rubs the wound. Then she drops to the ground and sits cross-legged in the middle of the sidewalk. Her shorts hike up her thighs. I hone in on her creamy white skin.

With her bag still dangling below my arm, I sit beside her and position it on my lap.

Folks continue to come and go; they veer around us. Most work hard not to stare. Generally, I'm pretty self-conscious about strange people gawking at me. It makes me feel foolish, and I *detest* feeling foolish, but this event has sapped any last ego out of me.

"Remember how we were before we got married?" Ana asks.

Good Lord. We nearly lost our lives over her shenanigans, and now she wants to stroll down memory lane.

"When I had the loft, in that vacant building on Mercer Street." She eyes me. "You'd come over, and we'd hang out at CBGB's, then you'd spend the night," she says. "In the morning, we'd walk over to Battery Park and watch the sunrise over the Hudson."

Ana has a way of making past events in our life sound romantic, and I do remember them, but they happened so long ago, long before our marriage turned into a train wreck.

"We used to make love all the time." She resumes cleaning the cut on her knee. Her shoulder-length hair bobs crossways over her face and radiates with a blueish hue. It offsets her gray eyes, proving once more that my wife's beauty is undeniable.

I try not to look. I want to stay mad at her, or at least let her believe I am. It's the only weapon I have. She's right, however: I can't remember the last time we had sex—real sex, not the late-night business we generally engage in right before bed. Hell, I can't even remember the last time we were this *composed* with each other, let alone this erotic.

"We'd go at it all night," she says. "We didn't stop until we saturated our bodies with each other's sweat. When we were finally bleary-eyed, I'd lie beside you and picture myself crawling under your skin and disappearing behind your rib cage. It was the only place in the world I felt safe."

My wife's sentiment sends a tiny electrical charge straight through my center. It's a sensation I thought I'd suppressed a long time ago.

Honestly, can I suppress anything that relates to my wife?

I have been obsessed with Ana since the day I met her. It didn't matter where we went or what we did as long as we were together. Of course, it wasn't as if I had a lot of experience with women at the time. I didn't date during my high school years. I didn't join school clubs or attend school dances. I never crashed a party at the cool kid's house. I even missed my senior prom. Later, when I entered college, I reserved my university years exclusively for my academics. So, by the time I met Ana, although I'd matured physically, I'd never developed emotionally. I was angry, insecure, and frightened, and I had a rotten attitude. I believed the world owed me something, and I was determined to get it. Somehow—and I don't know how she did it—Ana saw through it all and fell in love with me.

I swore I'd never let her go.

That was then. Things were different between us. My wife wasn't trying to prevent me from reading my daughter's text message.

What if my daughter *does* want to come home? What if her intention is to reunite with us? I may not be good at expressing my emotions, but what I experienced the day she left brought me to my knees, and I promised myself I would never go through it again. I summon my nerve to confront Ana. "I want to know why Chloe—"

"Do you ever wonder what happened to that stray dog?" she asks.

For God's sake. We're back to our SoHo years again.

My wife dabs at her injury. "The one we snuck into the cab?"

"You mean the one *you* snuck into the cab," I say. "I wanted to keep our dinner reservation, remember?" The event Ana alludes to happened on Water Street under the Brooklyn Bridge back when DUMBO was an industrial park overcrowded with dodgy alleyways and dirty waterfronts. The dog was a stray. Ana had spotted it behind a dumpster. It was beyond skinny. On top of that, it was caked in mud and stunk of urine. I had wanted to leave it there, but Ana insisted we bring it back to her loft.

"We wrapped him in your coat," she says. "He was shaking. He was so cold."

I'll never forget that poor animal, or how appreciative it was after Ana sponged the dirt off its fur and fed it peanut butter sandwiches. It fell asleep on her futon. Unfortunately, I'd been the one to spoil the moment since it was also the night I told her I'd been offered a professorship at the Sorbonne— and that I'd planned to move to France in the spring. She cried at the news and begged me not to go. She pleaded with me to stay with her in New York. It was quite a scene with all her weeping and carrying on. It reminded me of the arguments my parents used to have. I couldn't take it. So, I did the one thing I could think of that would make her stop crying—and would give me peace of mind.

I asked her to marry me.

Don't get me wrong. It's not that I didn't love Ana. My love for her was ferocious. It was more that I should not have proposed to her right then and there. I should've waited, at least until I returned to the States. I never expected to stay in Paris for more than a couple of years and had envisioned using this professorship for nothing more than securing a position at a top-notch school in New York. I was nowhere near ready for what was yet to come, being married to Ana—and in a foreign country, no less. But I was her Captain America, and unfortunately, I would pay handsomely for it.

I watch her now, dumbfounded. "Is all this necessary? This recalling of our early years? You almost got us killed a minute ago."

"I didn't—"

"You stood in the middle of a main thoroughfare."

"You used to revel in my madness."

"Are you kidding?"

"What happened to you, Tony?"

"That bus could've hit us. We could've been—"

"There was a time when you couldn't get enough of my spontaneity."

She's right, but I continue to deny her assertions. I continue to tell her I have no recollection of engaging in any such behaviors with her. I even go so far as to claim she has me confused with someone else, another boyfriend perhaps, and I swear to her, repeatedly, how these memories she has in which she had fun with some unbridled and irresponsible man are not of me.

It's a lie, however, since all these memories *are* of me. I haven't forgotten one thrilling or zany venture Ana and I engaged in. How could I? Life with Ana was analogous to when I was ten and I went to Disney World with my brothers, and we discovered Space Mountain. There were no words for how it felt to ride the tram straight to the tippy top only to have it hurl you right back down again in a freefall of loops, spins, and rolls, and all of it done in the total absence of light.

My wife frowns.

Stress courses through my veins, and I'm filled with self-doubt. The little voice in my head says I'm a jerk for making her sad, and I seize Ana by the back of the head, pull her close, and plant one on her. It's a bit rough, but it's a good kiss. While I'm not one for public displays of affection, nobody can say I'm not zany and spontaneous.

Ana laughs and wiggles out of my grasp. She nabs her purse.

"What are you doing?" I ask.

"I knew it," she says. "You can't imagine your world without me." And with her purse pressed against her chest, she races down Avenue de la République. She stops once to see if I'm following her, then she's off again.

I can't get up fast enough. While I'm aware this is yet another of my wife's maneuverings, I also recognize there's a reward at the end of it if I can keep my mouth shut and play along.

Plus, she has the damn pocketbook again.

Ana doesn't wait for me. She zips through the intersection of Rue Oberkampf. This side of Paris is clearly her neck of the woods, so to speak. She knows this area like the back of her hand. In fact, her psychotherapy practice is right around the corner. Is she heading *there*? Christ, I hope not. That place gives me the heebie-jeebies, especially her office. She has too many scented candles, not to mention all the other bohemian devices she keeps there. I don't claim to understand half of what my wife does for a living. Most of it is suspect to me like this business of meditating with one's clients, or joining them on spiritual journeys, or assisting them in devising forgiveness protocols. Honestly, what in the devil is a forgiveness protocol?

My wife rushes by Le Crainte Café. I'm only a few footfalls behind her. As I pass the eatery, the owner calls out to me.

"*Bonjour, Monsieur,*" he says. "*Où est ta belle femme ce matin?*" He asks where my beautiful wife is this morning.

It's obvious he didn't see her skip by a few seconds ago. The man smiles and waits for my reply. He is enamored with Ana. The few times we've dined here, he's provided us with complimentary rounds of drinks and snacks and all because she charmed him with her laugh and the kindness she bestows on the working stiffs of the world—laborers like the sort that populate my family of origin.

Ana speeds past the record store, Zic & Bul, then she pauses in front of the African restaurant. She turns a second time to see if I'm still following her and tumbles heedlessly into a line of folding chairs. The server runs over. They exchange words, then laugh. How is he not angry with her? It's incredible the shenanigans she gets away with. Ana apologizes, sidesteps a motor scooter parked crosswise on the sidewalk, and stops. She faces me and lifts her shirt enough to reveal her lacy bra. "I love you, baby," she calls before she sets out again.

I gather speed and close in on her. At any moment, I expect her to slip into one of these stores, so we can continue our fun and games in there. It's how we did it when we were younger. We played an abbreviated version of hide-and-go-seek. I'd trail her until she eventually scooted into a pharmacy or a record store, then I'd chase her around the shelving units until I caught her. Sometimes, as we circled each other, she'd remove an article of clothing. We'd get so hot and horny that we'd have to dodge it into a closet or a storage room and do the dirty right then and there. One time I followed her into the men's room of a coffee shop and found her sitting on the edge of the sink with her Levi's unzipped and dangling around her ankles. With all the moaning and hollering she did, I thought for sure we'd get caught. My wife was wild back then, and I couldn't get enough of her. It was her personality disorder. It made her so damn sexy.

Ana now passes the Rexel-Ménilmontant, the best electrical supplier in this area. Then she trots past my dentist's office. Next, it's the bank where I deposit my checks from the university, which reminds me—

"Come on, Tony." She angles onto Avenue Gambetta.

I'll bet the farm she's on her way home, and she plans to cut through the cemetery. Good thing, too, because from this location it's the shortest route to our apartment, and while I don't want to think about it, I may be getting too old for this game. "I'm tired, Ana." My wife doesn't even bother to turn around to see if I'm all right. I could be having a heart attack, for crying out loud. Instead, she hurries through the open gates of the Père Lachaise.

I stop and wipe my forehead. Does she not realize that we're not in our twenties anymore, nor do we need to relive our earlier years when I chased her through Chelsea? I'm losing my head over my wife's nostalgia for our youth. I no longer want to have sex in public. It's not the way I choose to spend a Sunday morning at this stage of my life.

Ana darts down one of the cobblestone paths that divides this place into a grid. I pick up my pace so I can catch up with her and tell her I want to go home. The last thing I need to do is get lost in here. I've found myself off course behind these eerie walls before, and it's not fun. As I sprint past the more gothic mausoleums, I peek inside a few of them. These structures may have been a fine example of architecture once, but with all the dead brush and the overgrowth that now surrounds them, they give me the damn shivers.

I spot Ana, finally. She's heading straight for Jim Morrison's grave. Please tell me she doesn't expect me to screw her on top of that man's gravesite. Dear Lord, the place is a dump. People throw their beer bottles everywhere and spray paint the stones beyond repair. The maintenance crew can't keep up with the defamation. For Pete's sake, how can that guy still be popular? He sang songs for a living. He wasn't even that good. Yep, there she goes. My wife thinks we're going to have sex on his grave. A few more paces, and we could be home in our bed.

Ana hops the fence meant to keep the visitors out. She lies at an angle atop the dilapidated little garden of flowers in front of Morrison's headstone. There's barely enough room for her let alone the two of us. Christ, does she actually expect us to do this here?

I approach her and sit on the marble gravestone next to Morrison's plot. I have to work to catch my breath.

My wife strips off her shirt. Her skin glistens with sweat. It beads along her chest. She motions for me to join her. "This is so sexy, isn't it?" she asks.

I look around. Thankfully, no one else is here.

"It feels like old times," she says. "Wild was *so* our thing, baby."

My wife is right about one thing: wild sex *was* our thing. During those first few years together, our entire relationship was predicated on our shared interest in having sex that was kinky, boisterous, and violent enough to be rousing without being cruel. Sex is Ana's superpower. My wife has a talent for making a man feel desirable in the sack. Honestly, when it comes down to it, it's what's held us together all these years.

Don't get me wrong, I'm not a pervert, but I do like it a little rough. It's important to me. More to the point, it's important to me to do it this way with Ana. It's how my wife shows me she cares for me; it's how she apologizes for making me the object of her raging inner battles. It's the way she displays remorse for pulling me close, then pushing me away, then begging me not to leave her. Sex is the way Ana purges herself of her despair because it's the only time she lets down her wall and allows me to comfort her—it's the one time she allows me to be the one person in the world who can save her from herself.

I peer over at her again. Her half-naked body gives me goosebumps, and I want to take her in my arms, feel her thighs spread beneath me, and release her from her afflictions.

I scramble off the wall and crawl over to her. We assume the missionary position, and I run my fingers through her hair. "You're gonna want to hold on to something," I say. "It's going to be a wild ride."

"Promises, promises."

I tug at her bra and pull it down. I press my lips to hers.

Ana makes soft, seductive sounds.

It encourages me, and the urge to climax overwhelms me. I reach down her shorts and grope at her underpants. My movements are jerky, and I'm rougher than usual, but Ana doesn't complain. Her skin is damp, and she arches her back, so I touch her where she's wet until her breath catches in her throat. Then, I unzip my shorts, and I drive myself into her, but something is wrong. I'm losing my erection. I thrust some more, but it doesn't help. I can't sustain it.

"Are you all right?" she asks.

"I'm fine." I can't believe this is happening to me. I keep thrusting. "I want to make it last," I say.

"I've been a very bad girl," she says.

"You don't need to do that."

"Someone needs to teach me a lesson."

"I said you don't have to—"

"I know how you like it, Tony."

"Stop it, I said."

Ana wiggles and makes like she's struggling to free herself.

I don't admit this to her, but I *am* turned on, and now I'm also furious with myself for going soft. I pull her toward me, brace her calves on my shoulders, and start again expecting this to get me where I need to be, but it doesn't. Ana, however, is truly enjoying herself. She digs her fingers into the dirt and hollers out.

There goes the last of my hard-on.

I wait for her to stop carrying on, then I release her. I zip up my shorts.

"Did you cum, baby?" My wife pulls up her pants. "It didn't seem like it."

"What?" I stand and adjust my clothes. "Of course, I did."

Shame overruns me, and I scrunch up my face and make like she's the one who's confused. "You weren't satisfied?" Even I know this is an asshole remark.

She gives me an eyeful. It's not pleasant.

I pretend not to see it. Instead, I inspect the area. I look around like I'm checking for voyeurs when I realize her purse is still on the ground. She must have tossed it to the side when she got cozy in Morrison's pathetic garden. I snatch it up and hold it close. "She wants to come home, doesn't she?" I dig through it, but I can't find her cell.

My wife holds up her phone.

"Blast it, Ana!"

She stands and tucks it in her back pocket. She pulls on her shirt.

"She's my daughter. I have a right to read her text message."

My wife swipes the bag out of my hands. She brushes herself off and selects the path that's the shortest route home. "See you there," she says.

Ana may believe this conversation is over, but she's wrong. I will read my daughter's text message.

I don't know how I will do it.

Or when.

But I *will* read Chloe's text.

5
ANA

Tony swings open the door to our apartment to see Kookie and Dharma, our elderly German Shepherds, waiting for us in the foyer. My husband evades them and proceeds down the hall. After the morning we've had, he's beyond furious. Kookie, or Kooks as we call him, sniffs at Tony shorts, but Tony doesn't stop.

The dogs circle me now. They push and bump each other as it they were ten years younger than they are. The combat ends when Dharma finishes Kooks off with a head butt. It's the doggie version of a victory dance. It wasn't too long ago she would've tackled him like a tight end, but at twelve and laden with multiple physical ailments, it's not a maneuver she can do anymore. She becomes more brittle with each passing year. She's like an exquisite piece of Steuben glass; she needs a lot of love or she could break at any moment.

Kooks gives her space. He sits and patiently waits for me to love on him next. Although a year older than Dharma, and much larger in size, he's the more submissive of the two dogs.

He's really a gentle giant, a perpetual puppy in a big dog's body. His whole goal in life is to make everyone happy.

While no two dogs could be more different, they also couldn't be more alike, and this is in the way they express their need to love and to be loved. It's also here where I speak their language.

Tony returns with their leashes, and the dogs race each other for the door. It's a constant competition and a lot of effort to cross the street, but the Pierre-Emmanuel, a natural garden and a wildlife preserve, awaits them on the other side. It's a dog's dream.

Once everyone leaves, I head for the kitchen and patter down the hall to the rhythm of John Coltrane. It trickles in from our neighbor's apartment on the left—a lovely young couple who keep to themselves, preferring to spend their weekends getting high and listening to jazz fusion. We've tried to get to know them, but they're not the visiting type. It's fine. We're not complaining. Tony and I have it good here, and we know it. We've heard the horror stories about neighbors in other buildings, like how they play loud music at all hours or squabble over boundaries. We could have it so much worse. Really, we could.

"Meadow?" I call out. "Are you here?"

My youngest has been missing in action since the day she met her new boyfriend, Aurelien. No surprise there. Meadow is like a reed in a stream; she ebbs and flows and ripples her way through life. She's the family's flower child, the happy-go-lucky one, the mystical and spiritual heir to the DiSalvo name. Rather than give her opinion or ask questions about . . . anything, she'd rather roll with things. It's how she handles most everything, but I'm on to her. I've watched her do her hippie child routine since she was a preschooler. Which is exactly what it is. A routine. A schtick. It's how she pays no heed to the reality of life and exchanges it for a lighter version.

I pray I'm not the one who did this to her, that my unpredictable and combative behavior didn't make her this way. Or that my pressuring her to choose a side—my side—whenever Chloe and I went at it didn't result in her learning that the best way to manage conflict is to choose *no* side. I don't want to be the reason my youngest disconnects from the world, although I'm sure I'm the one to blame. I create chaos, and there's no way that can't affect a child.

I cross the kitchen and drop my purse on the counter. I pull my phone out of my back pocket and do a quick scroll through my Twitter feed, then go right to Cool Babes. This is a Twitter list I created for female therapists, most of whom I met at conferences and that I like to stay in touch with. I love these women. Each one's a badass who runs a private practice, drinks plenty of wine, and is as impulsive as I am. We like to tweet about life, love, and men, and they've become my go-to group for advice whenever I need it. They're my Tweeps. No, they're my awesomely *cool* Tweeps.

The first to respond to my earlier tweet about my husband is Jas. She sends a purple heart emoji for support. Jasmine Martin is the only one in the group with a medical degree, and although she's a psychiatrist, she never gives advice and tends to stay on the lighter side of things. She hails from Cairo and usually reacts to my tweets with Zen-type come backs. I copy her style and write, "Sweet friendship refreshes the soul."

Millie Beaulieu has also replied. She says I should explore what's under my fear of losing him, but I don't plan to do that. Nor will I tell her how I've spent years exploring what lurks beneath my emotions, and I have nothing more to show for it now than I did when I was a teen.

While Millie isn't one to share anything personal either, she's there for the rest of us when we need her, and I like that about her. She's also a dog lover like me, and she posts lots of videos of Sassy, her four-year-old lab. Today, Sassy is marching in place as they prepare for their morning walk. It's adorable, and I type out a response. "Good girl!" I add a red heart emoji.

I browse through the rest of my Twitter stream, but no one else reacted, so I send out another tweet. "I'm not the only one who fights with their family, am I?" It sounds more ominous than I'd like, but it's out there now. I scroll around a bit when I hear the jingling of keys in the front door.

"Everything okay?" I ask, half waiting to hear Tony grouse about how he forgot the poop bags again.

"Mom, it's me."

"Evelyn?" I look down the hall. "What's wrong? Why are you here? Didn't you get the check I sent?" At twenty-one, Evelyn recently completed her bachelor's degree, moved into her own apartment, and plans to return to the Université Paris Diderot this fall for her master's degree. When she finishes her education, she wants to move to the States, get her doctorate in psychology, and find work at a university there. Her ultimate goal is to examine the ways people develop personality disorders. She says it's a topic nobody understands yet. I say, if anyone has a shot at untangling it, it's my Evelyn. My middle daughter is smart. Real smart. She's definitely the one who got all the brains in this family. Honest to God, sometimes I have to wonder where she came from.

"I got it," she says. "I also got all the courses I wanted."

Evelyn goes straight to the cupboard where we keep all the munchies. She takes out an open bag of baked pita chips. I don't tell her this, but I keep them there especially for her.

"You and Dad went to the farmer's market this morning?"

She talks as she chews. She crosses the kitchen, opens the fridge, and takes out the orange juice. She drinks it straight from the carton.

"We did," I say. "I had planned on picking up some natural beef for dinner tomorrow night, but I didn't want to carry it around with me all morning."

"I can't believe Dad still drags you off to that thing every weekend. You hate people."

"I don't hate people. Why would you—? Oh, for crap's sake."

I act like I'm annoyed with her, but my middle daughter is right, well, *almost* right. It's not that I hate people; I hate what people do. When I'm around people I feel like I'm being judged or criticized, even though the one who does the most of the judging of me—and unforgivingly—is me. It's neurotic, I know, and it's one of the things about me my husband still doesn't understand. Tony thinks if you're a counselor, then you should have it all together. He can't get it through his big head that therapists are just as dysfunctional as anyone else. Earning a degree in psychology doesn't save you from getting tripped up on your own issues. Nor does it make you any less competent as a professional because you haven't yet learned how to face your own shit. It takes guts to confront your past. Not everyone can do it.

"Hey." I change the subject "Have you heard from Chloe recently?"

"*Chloe?*"

Evelyn's tone assures me she hasn't. Nor would she want to. Back when she and Chloe were kids and they shared a room, the sibling rivalry between them sometimes was lawless. I'd always figured that from Evelyn's perspective it was because someone had come before her, that I had loved someone prior to loving her. Of course, it didn't help that

Chloe looked exactly like me while Evelyn and Meadow shared Tony's looks. Then you toss in a few opportunities for Ev to catch Chloe doing drugs or just generally exploiting the household rules, and there you have it. A fractured relationship between sisters with no hope for repair.

"Why would I hear from Chloe?" Evelyn asks. "Better yet, why would Chloe call *me*?"

"No reason," I say.

What made matters even worse was that Evelyn was there the night Chloe and I argued. While she was just fourteen at the time, and it's possible she didn't grasp the broader implications of what had occurred, she *was* old enough to appreciate how the fallout would affect all of our lives. How it *did* affect all of our lives. And I'll never make up for that.

"Would you tell me if you did?" I ask.

"Why wouldn't I tell you?" Evelyn sounds surprised. She leaves the carton of juice on the table. "What's this all about?" she asks.

"I was wondering if you had, that's all. It's been a while, and I thought maybe—"

"Have *you* heard from Chloe?" She grills me with a voice that's protective, sage. "What's my brainless sister done now?"

"Nothing. No, I haven't heard from her, either." I force a laugh. I shouldn't have bothered her with this. "I'd be the last person she'd contact. You know what? Forget I asked."

Evelyn eyes me suspiciously. "Is everything all right?"

"Everything's fine."

She continues to size me up.

"Stop giving me the eagle eye," I say. "If something happened that you needed to know about, I'd tell you."

"Would you?" She chews her last bite of chips.

It amazes me how grown up she's become. It's like chatting

with a friend sometimes. I have to remind myself she's my daughter.

The front door opens again, and the dogs pick up on Evelyn's scent. They jog down the hall and straight into the kitchen. Evelyn greets them by making a huge fuss over them She gives them pets and snuggles and scratches them both behind their ears. The dogs are thrilled to see her, and they lap up every bit of it. These are the moments when I wish we could begin our lives over again, when I grieve for the way my children grew up so fast, and when I inevitably remember how I'm the reason this family disintegrated the way it did.

"Hey, Dad," Ev says.

Tony enters the kitchen behind the dogs and mumbles at Evelyn, then he gives her a peck on the cheek. My husband can only do one thing at a time. Like right now. He can't converse with his daughter and unleash the dogs, too. Kooks parades off with his leash stuck under his back foot while Dharma drags hers around behind her as she circles my daughter and sniffs for pita chips. Ev gets right to work and helps her father untangle everybody.

"Hey," Evelyn turns to me. "I'll talk to you later." And with that, the house becomes another chaotic free-for-all as the dogs, butts-a-wiggling and nails-a-clicking, follow her to the front door.

"Everybody pooped," Tony says.

When the dogs run back into the kitchen, I praise them both for their wonderful poops. Then I turn and retreat to the master bedroom. They follow me like baby ducklings— Dharma scoots off the carpeted runner and swerves around Kooks so she can get ahead of him. Her overgrown toenails scrape against the hardwood. Not to be outdone, Kooks stuffs his head into the crook of my arm, and I pet him, too, then the three of us file down the hall in a synchronous rhythm of eyes, ears, fingers, toes, and noses.

Situated on the fourth floor of an eight-story structure, Tony and I purchased this apartment when we learned I was pregnant and knew we'd need a bigger place. While it's a rare occurrence the times in my life that my father has come through for me, he did then. He sent us a check to cover the full price—for which we'll be eternally grateful. This is not something we could ever afford on our own. While it's an older structure and needed a lot of love, it had all the traditional aspects of Parisian architecture we wanted, and our initial plan was to restore it to its original charm with well-polished hardwood floors, fabric-backed wallpaper, and vintage reconditioned light fixtures. Yet none of this happened. Instead, secondhand oriental rugs disguise the hardwood, ivory paint turns out to be a viable substitute for expensive wallpaper, and the candelabras—well, we're still using the same antiquated wall sconces that were here when we arrived.

It's appropriate.

My husband and I are not people who can strip away the old of anything. Nor are we those who can create something new in its stead. When presented with any kind of challenge, we revert to old habits. We dress things up where we can, mask the wreckage where we need to, then flee the damage. It's not a solution since, in the end, it's all still there: the insults and the impasses, the stand-offs and the stare-downs, the explosions and the rebukes. The deadlocks and the dead ends. It's what make up the unforgivable and the not-so-forgotten that occur between a husband and wife and that fester below the surface until they eventually reemerge, though not without injury to both parties. But a marriage is like a well healed scar in that while the body has suffered a trauma, it's survived.

Dharma continues down the hall to the master bedroom

while Kooks and I stop in front of Chloe's old room. Kooks sniffs under the door, then sits and looks at me. He wants to go inside.

"You're right," I say. "It's like ripping off a band-aid." But the hairs on my forearm stand on end. Since Chloe left, I haven't gone in her room for anything more than to dust and vacuum. I wrap my fingers around the doorknob, count to three, but stop at two and push. The door opens wide, but it's anticlimactic. There's nothing to see.

The room is darker than I remember, and I grope at the wall for the light switch, but it does nothing to ease the gloom. So, I cross the floor and separate the curtains, but this only magnifies it. The sheetrock has buckled, and the cracks have bled through the walls. It looks like an early Warhol in here. How could we have let it get this bad?

Kooks enters, circles twice, and winds himself into a ball on the area rug in front of Chloe's old bed. A twin oak, it coordinates with the two bureaus set against the far wall. It's a set, a gift from Tony and me for her twelfth birthday. Now, it's all that's left of my eldest daughter's childhood.

I run my fingers across the top of the taller bureau, then down the front of it. A swarm of psychedelic butterflies still camouflages several of the drawers. Threadbare and missing parts of their anatomy, what started as a lovefest between my daughter and these wacky stickers became an embarrassment in her later years. Strange how something so dear to us at one moment in our lives can become so abhorrent at another.

"C'mon, bud," I say.

Kooks rises from the floor, and his front legs shudder. He shakes it off.

"Good boy, buddy." I shower him with encouragement— that and a regimen of pain meds is the best I can do for him.

He accompanies me to the end of the hall, where we enter

mine and Tony's bedroom. Dharma lounges on the Persian rug
in the center of the room. She lifts her head and peers at us.
Kooks goes over to her, pecks at her with his snout, then lies
beside her. He does a big doggie stretch. It's a full four-legger.

Tony comes in behind us, drops his phone on the bed, and
places his iPad beside it. He takes off his shorts and sets these
on the bed as well. He smooths out the wrinkles—an action he
repeats over and over. It's a behavior someone diagnosed with
obsessive-compulsive disorder would understand. Tony likes
things to be clean, organized, and symmetrical. He relishes
routine. A slim man with an exterior tighter than the binding
of a textbook, he lives in a world where rules prevail against
chaos and rituals must be respected.

Once he completes the process, he pokes through his
laundry basket until he finds an old pair of gym sweats and
puts these on. He trundles off down the hall where he emits
archaic yet comforting sounds from the kitchen. The refrigerator door opens and closes; bowls clink on the counter; water
rushes into the sink. A piece of flatware falls to the floor, and
Tony swears at it. While his voice is no longer youthful, it still
carries the rumbling, full-bodied pitch of a cello. Or, if not a
cello, surely an instrument with the quality of a baritone. It's a
sound that emanates only from the intimate and devoted relationship that exists between such a distinguished apparatus
and the gifted musician who masters it.

I sit on the bed and relish the peace. Dharma sighs and
stretches her own feeble legs. Alloy wind chimes tink-a-tink
outside the window and welcome the wood-warbler that's just
landed in my railing planter. Kooks gets up and goes over to
investigate it. The French call these birds *pouillot siffleur*—
whistling squid. Although I've never understood the squid
reference, I do know these birds are all about the song. They
have a voice, and they will be heard. Vibrant and full of life,

they inundate Paris every spring, stay through the summer, and fly south for the winter. I'm surprised this one is still here. It should be halfway to Namibia by now.

Kooks is completely taken with these peppy little birds. The poor dog befriends them every spring, then cries every August when they leave.

I leave him to his bird friend and sprawl out across my grandmother's silk quilt, a gift from a woman I've never met and who died before my mother, Barbara Storm, née Sutton, was old enough to drink. While anyone's memories of the woman would be hazy, it doesn't stop my mother from reminding me how much I'm like her, and not in a good way. I love my mother, deeply, but I'll never understand how to make her happy, or love me back, or at least in any way I need.

In her defense, she was the one who found me the first time I cut myself. It was a disaster. I hit a vein by mistake, and she wasn't too happy about it. It must be difficult having your kid slice herself to shreds. Then, once I was admitted to the hospital, she had to go home and clean up the mess all on her own. She still reminds me periodically how much blood stains. It's her way of expressing her love for me—pointing out the ways she's been kind to me, how she went out of her way to care for me.

She's not a bad person, my mother. She wants what we all want—to be someone important. She wants to be someone other than who she is as if that person isn't good enough. She wants to be Someone with a capital S as if this one simple modification will make her life more meaningful. It was my job to transform her into that special Someone, but I failed, and unlike my father, Charles "Chuck" Storm, I couldn't leave her. Not in the flesh, anyway. It's no wonder I jumped at the chance to go to Paris with Tony. Nobody moves four thousand miles away from home unless they're groping for a geographical solution to their pain.

The problem is we're too much alike. My mother and I brutalize everyone around us, then we call it love. We selfishly cling to others, frightened they'll abandon us if we let go. We're like amoebas—sliding, crawling organisms without shape or structure. It's a sickness, a madness, really, and it flourishes like purple loosestrife on my mom's side of the genealogical tree. It afflicts at least one woman in every generation, one of its main features being this need for constant love and reassurance from the people closest to us, and we'll badger and bully them until we get it. We have to; it's what reaffirms our sense of self since, without it, we don't have a self.

I hop off the mattress and cross the room, then remove the lid from the cedar chest that sits at the foot of the bed. This bamboo trunk has accompanied me for every move since I was eighteen. I use it now to store a portion of the decades' worth of gifts I've received from all three of the girls. I run my fingers across the top layer of their crayon-colored drawings, their plaster coasters, their quilted pot holders. I can still remember the day I received each nature print, paper spider web, and story stone. Each construction paper animal. Every greeting card.

I hover over the chest and dig through it for any and all correspondence I've received from my eldest, and I'm in awe. It's as if I'm seeing them for the first time. Each one of Chloe's cards is more dazzling than the next. The artwork is inventive; the penmanship is exquisite. Open and boundless, it's free of constraints with letters that arc and dip across the page in a natural rhythm and sentences that run into and over each other as if the rules of language, of anything, were devised for everyone but her. Her handwriting exudes a sense of entitlement and raw sexuality—a unique blend of strength and vulnerability that makes people want to be around her.

It's nothing like my own script. The way I craft words onto a piece of paper has never exuded anything sexual, nor has it ever made anyone want to stay with me, even though it's the one thing I've craved my entire life.

Tears sting my eyes. I love my daughter, but no good will come of her reestablishing contact with us. Chloe was diagnosed with the same disorder as me—BPD. She suffers from the same recklessness, the same limitations, and the same compulsions I do, and there's not enough room in this family for two erratic and volatile women.

I stuff everything back inside the chest and close the lid. I slog over to the nightstand beside the bed, fiddle with the drawer until it opens, and comb through its contents, but I don't see it. I give the compartment a good shake, and the joint rolls to the front. I grab it, along with the lighter and my cell, cross the room, and throw open the window. Then I light up. The sickly-sweet smoke tastes good, and I let it swaddle my inner child like a newborn's pearly white blanket.

Years ago, I promised Tony I'd quit. We'd gone to a dinner party, and I got drunk and high and ended up flirting with the host. Who was married. *He* didn't mind, but his wife wasn't too happy about it. Neither was Tony. It wasn't the first time I'd made a fool of myself in front of his colleagues. So, I swore to him, and I made him a promise: it would never happen again. I'd stop all of it—drinking, smoking, messing with my meds, if he'd forgive me this one last time.

What can I say? I tried, I really did. Sometimes it's the best-laid plans . . .

I give Twitter another check to see if anyone else replied to my new tweet about fighting with your family. Adel has. She tells me to "be cool" and reminds me how Tony and I have fought with each other for a long time. "It'll take time to resolve your differences," she says and adds the hashtag #Self-Care. In her fifties, Adel Berger is the oldest member and the self-proclaimed grandmother of the group. She fits the bill, too. She refuses to cover her gray, says it's a symbol of her wisdom, and she reacts to tweets with suggestions like how we should center ourselves around the deeper questions, or that it's good to forgive ourselves for the things we did in the past. It's all sage advice, although it's not guidance she herself follows. I don't think anyone would say trolling your ex-husband on social media is *sage*.

I close out of Twitter and call her. I could really use a listening ear right now, and Adel's the only one in the group I've spent any quality time with outside of hanging at a hotel bar and getting stinking drunk at an expensive psychiatry conference.

I draw another hit off the joint and wait for her to answer. The smoke wafts into the alleyway across the street, then drifts skyward. It grazes a full-length fresco of Camille Claudel. I look into her eyes and wonder if things would've been different if she were alive today? If she'd had her affair with Rodin now? What most people don't know is that back then, while Claudel was frolicking around with her so-called mentor, she was also busy being a sculptor in her own right and that when their tryst ended, only she was the one who was defiled. Only *her* career was the one that was toast. That's when she suffered a breakdown, withdrew from the world, and died alone in a mental asylum. As if she was sick, or mad, or insane.

As fucking if.

Some people say Rodin betrayed her. Others say it was because she lived in a misogynistic society. I say, it didn't help that her mother was cold and disapproving. I gaze at the image again and wonder whose family is more messed up, hers or mine.

Mine. It's definitely mine.

"Chloe sent me a text." The words are out of my mouth as soon as Adel picks up. I shouldn't have bothered her, and I wouldn't have if Tony and I hadn't fought about it this morning. The whole thing has left me raw and confused. Like I suck as a mother.

"Did you think you'd never hear from her again?" she asks.

"No, of course not," I respond with indifference, but I'm annoyed with the question. I *did* think I might not see her again, and not in a bad way. Somewhere in the back of my mind, I'd harbored this romanticized notion that I was the martyr in this situation—the anguished mother whose daughter ran away from home and abandoned her.

"You sound like you believe if Chloe reenters the picture, she'll spill the beans on you."

I inhale again, draw in deep.

"Maybe it's a good time to tell Tony the truth," Adel says. "The *whole* truth about your affair."

"You mean fling." My frustration increases. "It was nothing more than a roll in the sack. Okay, a couple of rolls." I stub out the last of the joint on the windowsill and drop it. It lands in the shrubbery.

"Does he know about the argument you had with Chloe that night?"

I don't want to lie to Adel, but I'd rather not have to explain how I've kept this a secret. How *this* is the reason Chloe left home. I look for the joint, but I don't see it. Why did I do that? What if some little kid finds it?

"Is Tony aware that Chloe read Géraud's letter?" she asks. "And that she confronted you with it?"

The obvious answers are no and no. It was never a

conversation I'd expected to have with my oldest—then or ever. She'd caught me off guard. It was the first time in weeks I didn't have to work late, and I had high hopes for a quiet evening at home. Tony had a late class, and the girls were at their respective after school activities—with only Evelyn due to be home soon, but not yet. I'd planned on having a quick sandwich for dinner, then reading the paper without interruption. The last thing I expected to find was my daughter on the floor of my bedroom, surrounded by years' worth of memorabilia. *My* memorabilia. Keepsakes from my past she'd delved into without my knowledge. Or consent. Old cards, dried flowers, and childhood photos she'd excavated from out of my closet and had strewn around the room. She was searching for something, and judging by the look on her face, she'd discovered far more than she'd bargained for.

"What's this?" She had the letter in her hand.

My heart stopped.

"You had sex with another man?" The word *sex* dripped from her lips like bile. "You're a whore," she said.

I walked over and slapped her. Just like that. I regretted it, but it was too late.

The force of the blow had knocked her to the ground.

"Don't speak to me like that," I said. "I'm your mother."

"My *mother*? Since when have you stopped drinking long enough to be anyone's mother?"

"I'm warning you, Chloe."

"Maybe the truth hurts." She dragged herself across the floor. She couldn't put enough distance between us. "If you don't like it, then you should try acting normal, for once."

Normal. The word hit me like a closed fist. It was a gut punch, and a reminder of every failed dream and fruitless goal I'd ever attempted. It split me open. I couldn't stop myself.

No mother should ever tell their daughter the things I said to mine that night.

No mother should do *anything* I did to my daughter that night.

Chloe bolted into the kitchen. She got her cell phone out of her bag. "I'm telling Dad!" she shouted.

I was right behind her. I caught her by the hair and wrenched the phone out of her hand.

My daughter wrestled herself away from me. She ran down the hall and straight into my closet and tore it apart. She flung clothes on the floor and emptied the shelves. She took my old shoeboxes—emptied of shoes and filled my most treasured mementos—and hurled them at me. Then she wept and called me horrible names.

I wish I could say I don't remember the rest of that night, or how with its mixture of shock, guilt, and revulsion, it was forever lost to time, but that would be lie. "Your father knows." My voice shook, and the words were out of my mouth before I'd considered the consequences. "He knows you're not his biological daughter."

Chloe stopped short. "Liar," she said.

"I told him when I found out I was expecting."

She held her hands over her ears.

"He couldn't wait for me to get pregnant again so I could have *his* child."

"Shut up!" she cried.

It was the biggest lie I ever told, but it hardly mattered. My only goal was to save my marriage. Then I blew into her room like a tropical cyclone, stuffed everything she owned into a garbage bag, and dumped it at her feet. "Now get out," I said.

There's no doubt I did indisputable harm to my daughter that night, but what choice did I have? I couldn't let her tell

Tony what she'd discovered. I did what I had to do to save my marriage.

No, I did what I had to do to save *myself*.

"You mean, Tony has no idea you told Chloe she was conceived out of wedlock?" Adel asks.

"You make it sound so easy, like I can just sit him down and tell him what happened."

"Who needs to be sat down and told what happened?" Tony stands in the doorway.

6

TONY

"You'll damage the molding if you keep that up." Ana ends her phone call.

I'm standing in the doorway of our bedroom. I'm dangling from the antique ornamental door frame and swishing around on the balls of my feet. It's one of the few reckless behaviors I engage in. There's a hint of smoke in the air. It has a familiar aroma to it. Was Ana smoking pot—

"You remember what happened the last time you did that." She is motionless.

Dharma pokes at my calf with her muzzle. I angle to the side and let her pass. Per usual, Kooks schlepps in right behind her. I let go of the frame.

Having had a small snack while I was in the kitchen, I came in to ask Ana about the Buliers' party tonight—about what time we were expected to be there. I would have liked not to speak to her at all this morning, but I want to plan out the rest of my day. "Who was that on the phone?" I ask.

Ana fiddles with her cell, which for her means scrolling through her beloved tweet tide. "My *mother*," she says.

That answer is plenty good enough for me. I don't need to know anything more.

"I'm not in the mood to deal with the Buliers tonight." She continues Twittering.

"When *are* you in the mood to deal with the Buliers?" I extricate myself from the frame and sag against the door jamb. Chace and Médée Bulier have been our friends since Ana and I moved into our first apartment in Belleville. It was during a chance meeting on the stairs one morning when Chace and I bumped into each other and ascertained we were both newly appointed faculty members at the same university. That was all it took. We introduced our respective partners to one another, and our pairing as a foursome became accelerated and robust. It was the Parisian experience my wife had hoped to find here. In those days, Chace, too, lived with his betrothed, Médée, prior to marriage, and Médée, like Ana, was eager to settle down and raise a family. The four of us were similar in nearly every shape and form.

Unfortunately, as the years progressed, things between us became less rosy, especially between Chace and me. It seems we were destined to be rivals. While I've spent the bulk of my tenure at the Paris School of Economics engaged in instructional pursuits, Chace shot to the top of the institution's political circle like an M-80. It's served him well, however, since he now directs the school's wealthiest and most distinguished research center, even though I suspect his appointment had more to do with his diplomatic networks than his work ethic. It was this advance that did the most damage to our relationship—that and how he became my boss.

"I'm not sure I can go through with it," she says.

"Go through with it?"

"The night. The party. There are too many issues weighing on my mind." My wife rolls onto her side.

I pretend I don't hear her and snap my fingers like I'm calling over the dogs. Neither one moves. Dharma looks at me, then closes her eyes. "Issues?" I ask.

"Chloe?"

My head hits the wood.

"Do you have any idea what this could do to us, to our marriage?" she asks. "If our daughter came here—even for a visit?" Ana drops her phone. She sits up and supports herself on one elbow.

A tsunami of adrenalin courses through me. It's been seven long, lonely years since my oldest left home. Now, for reasons unknown, she's contacted us, and I can only presume it's to offer us an olive branch. I don't want to fight with Ana again, but it's obvious if my wife has her way I won't have any say in this at all, and I'll never see my daughter again. I stand straighter and prepare for the confrontation.

"You may not remember what it was like back then," she says, "but I do."

I exhale, loudly. The sound is more inflated than necessary.

"She tried to come between us."

"That's ridiculous."

"I couldn't take it if something happened to us."

"This is our *daughter* we're discussing." I look at her. "What in God's name are you so afraid of?"

"Things went off the rails when she was here."

I shake my head. "Chloe's the last person in the world who could wreck our—"

"She had too much influence over you," Ana says.

"Oh, for Christ's sake." The veins in my neck feel like a pulled parachute cord on descent. I glide down the door jamb until my butt hits the floor. I stretch my legs, press my toes against the post on the opposite side of the doorway, and force them against the wood until the balls of my feet hurt. I keep pressing. "Chloe made the first move," I say. "It makes for an excellent opportunity to reconcile."

"Reconcile?" Ana bolts upright and swings her legs over the side of the bed. The box springs sound like a fisher cat at midnight. She chides me with her eyes.

I shrug my shoulders to release the tension. The muscles in my neck and shoulders are tighter than a runner's shoelaces.

"Where's all this coming from?" Ana asks. "Your sudden interest in reconciliation?"

"My wish to re-establish a relationship with my estranged daughter is not sudden."

Ana squints at me. "With everything she put us through, you'd have to be nuts for even thinking about it."

"I deserve the name-calling?"

"It's not name-calling. It's what it is. You're nuts, my friend. Nuts."

I realized long ago that every conversation with my wife has the potential to tap into her explosive volatility, and as a result, I've learned to censor my communications. This particular argument, however, is one I refuse to suppress, and I will finish it no matter the outcome. "If my goal to reunite with our estranged daughter makes me nuts," I say, "then so be it."

"Well, count me out because I can't do it."

"You mean you *won't* do it," I say.

"I won't simply let bygones be bygones, if that's what you're suggesting."

"You're her mother." I roll my head in her direction. The fireworks should begin any minute now.

My wife doesn't react to my comment, however. She bounces off the bed, crosses the floor, and stands in front of one of the two burled walnut bureaus positioned at the other end of the room. "Is this about how you're going bald?" she asks. "Are we back to that again?"

"For Pete's sake, Ana." My voice cracks more than I intend. The battle has just gotten underway, and I'm giving up too much ground. I scramble to my feet, reach for the frame again, then think better of it. I stuff my hands in my pockets and knock my shoulder against the door jamb. "Okay," I say. "Consider this. What if the three of us could clear the air and brush off the past? What if me, you, and Chloe could establish a neutral ground with which to reconstruct our family? A place where we—where the whole family—could reconnect?"

"Stop saying that." Ana creases her brow. "Stop talking about reconciling and reconnecting. *Jesus.*"

I cross my arms in front of me. I emit another over-the-top huff.

Ana digs her hands into the top drawer of the dresser. She holds up a handful of garments. They're all black. "So, how is it that you've arrived at this conclusion?" she asks. "This idea of reconnecting with our daughter?"

I brace my head against the column.

"I'm not being difficult," she says. "I'm trying to understand your thought process."

"You just said it," I say. "It's because Chloe is our daughter. It's irrelevant what happened between the three of us. She will always be our daughter. Period. That's it. That's my entire thought process."

Ana chooses a shirt from the smattering in her hands. She eyes me and waits for more.

"And because I'm getting old."

"Oh, for fuck's sake," she says. "We're all getting old." She propels the garment across the room. It lands on the floor. She leaves it there.

"For crying out loud," I say. "I'm trying to communicate with you about my thoughts on aging, about how I'm having a difficult time becoming middle-aged, and this is how you respond?"

"We're all becoming middle-aged, Tony. Everyone is having a difficult time." Ana now excavates a skirt from the same drawer. What a surprise; it's also black. "You think you're the only one growing old, but you're not." She hurls this piece of clothing across the room as well. It also lands on the floor. Days from now, if she decides not to wear either one of them, I'll find them in the same position—on the floor, where she left them.

"Good God. I can't keep doing this with you."

"*This*?" she asks. "What is 'this?' What do you mean when you say, 'you can't keep doing this?'"

"This," I say. "Whatever you want to call it. This here. *This*. This thing we do with each other. How I share an important aspect about myself, and you pooh-pooh it. I tell you I'm struggling with growing old and all you want to do is insult me."

"I want to know what you meant by 'this.' You said 'this.' What is 'this?'"

"I told you. *This*. How we bicker and squabble. I can't do *this* anymore."

Ana drifts over to the other dresser. A Tibetan wooden box sits on top of it. She opens the box and removes a slim, sapphire bracelet. Offset by diamonds, the blue gemstones are set into seventeen platinum prong settings. It's an exquisite piece of jewelry. I should know; I bought it for her.

My wife runs her fingers over the gemstone-encrusted links. She drapes the bracelet across her wrist and approaches me. The stones clatter gently against each other. "Get this for me?" She holds out her arm.

I fiddle with the clasp until it clicks. Then I give it a gentle tug for good measure.

"You gave this to me for our first wedding anniversary." She lays the bracelet across the back of her hand.

"Yes, I did."

"We were window shopping in Cannes." She pads over to her dressing table.

"Darn thing cost me three months' salary."

The light dims in her eyes.

Why did I have to say that? I knead my neck again and pull the statement back. "But you were so charmed by it. How could I say no to you?"

"If I remember correctly," she says, "it was the first time we set foot outside our hotel room." She sits on a small, upholstered bench and contemplates herself in the mirror. "We were too busy screwing each other's brains out to do much of anything else." Our eyes meet in her reflection. She removes her shirt and drops it on the rug. Bones protrude along her spine. They interface with the various defacements and blemishes that scar her body.

It's not attractive, but I can't take my eyes off her. I want to, but I can't.

Ana senses this, and she toys with the lacy material on her bra. She manipulates each bra cup until, one at a time, her breasts liberate themselves and tumble out.

Perspiration builds along my back. My wife still has the points of a twenty-five-year-old.

"Let's try this again," she says.

Is she kidding? I couldn't get it up this morning. What makes her think I'll do any better with round two? I contemplate the carpet and concentrate on its ornamentation.

"We're home now," she says. "You can take all the time you need." She stands and unhooks her bra.

What is she up to? She wants to have sex twice in one morning?

Is she *trying* to humiliate me again?

Or is this her way of convincing me to deny Chloe a visit home? *Christ*, she will stop at nothing to get her way.

Ana fingers her breasts.

I'm not looking at her. Instead, I take stock of the rows of plaster half-moons that cover the ceiling, but it's as if my eyes are out of my control, however, and I watch her out of the corner of them. I need to know what this is about.

She prods at her lacy underpants.

I wish she wouldn't do this.

She eases them over her boyish hips and steps out of them. Then she struts into the middle of the room. Naked.

I glue myself to the doorpost. I can't stop ogling Ana's exposed pubic hair. It takes everything in me not to grab my balls. I refocus my attention on the ceiling. How do you like that? The pattern's arc resembles an ocean swirl. What if I *did* try it again? Could I maintain an erection this time?

My wife comes closer. She takes my hand and places it against her chest.

The top of my head prickles. My fingers tingle, and—I let my hand go limp.

"Asshole." She strikes out at me.

I catch it, but not before it clips my bottom lip. We tussle, and I hold her by the wrist. I can't help but become aroused. My wife's comment about me in the cemetery was on the mark. I can't get horny without a little aggression being involved.

Ana stops fighting me. "I know you," she says. "I know what you need."

If I could press myself any further into this wooden beam, I would.

"Rough sex makes you feel invincible."

I groan. Who wants to hear their deepest fears said out loud?

"That's right, baby. You remember."

I cover my head with my hands and slither down the wooden frame. Ana's referring to when we were first married, and I enjoyed a good bout. We both did. What started as a role-play about domination and submission quickly turned into something else altogether, since Ana and I couldn't help but take it to the extreme and act out our twisted and disordered aberrations on each other. It was a deviant game in which I took charge, Ana surrendered, and we both got off on it—the swinging fists, the ripped clothing, the way I pinned her beneath me, how her chest swelled against mine. I'd never experienced anything so primal.

We were perfectly paired, perfectly disturbed.

"Take me. Right here," she'd say.

And I would, right there on the kitchen floor.

It was a pattern we'd repeat again and again because Ana made me feel like a man, a *real* man, a *man's* man, and for a kid who grew up with an overbearing authoritarian for a father, it was a boon to what smattering of self-respect I had at the time. Whatever way Ana wanted it was how I gave it to her because the most important thing to me was having Ana want me. I would've done *anything* to have Ana want me. Without her, I was like a dead fish, gaping and vacuous, dumped on the dock.

Sweet Jesus, I can't be that person again.

Ana advances in my direction. "Touch me." She stoops to my level, takes my hand, and places it between her thighs. "Show me how a *real* man does it."

My wife's comment sends me off the deep end. Can she be any more divisive? I don't want to have sex, I want to read Chloe's text. I struggle to my feet and shout at her. "Where's your damn cell phone?"

7
ANA

Tony's face is bright red. He barrels over to the bed. "What did you do with it?" He strips off the comforter, but the phone isn't there.

I look around the room. Where *is* my cell?

My husband scopes out the bedroom. "I want to see Chloe's text message. *Now.*"

I retrieve my shirt and cover myself. I slip into my panties. "All right. Calm down," I say. "There's no need for dramatics."

"In fact, I want to see *everything* you've hidden from me," he says. "All of it." He turns in my direction. His eyes bore into me. "You're always keeping secrets, and I'm sick of it."

I'm paralyzed. Tony's already cross with me, and I don't want to do anything to place myself further in his line of fire.

"Where do you hide it all? I know there's more."

"I have no idea what you're talking about." I am *so* lying. I've been gaslighting him for years, and about all sorts of things, but I do it for his own good.

My husband storms over to the same bureau from which I just retrieved my outfit. He opens a drawer, gathers up a handful of my sweaters, and throws them on the ground. He rifles through the rest of the drawer and proceeds to the next one.

I want to run over and stop him, but he's too worked up. For a man who prides himself on being rational and composed, he has a hair-trigger of a temper, and I know better than to interfere when he's in this state.

"Where is it?" he asks. "I bet you have decades' worth of stuff I've never seen."

"What's all this about?" My voice cracks. My mind is reeling, and I can't think straight.

"Don't play me for a chump, Ana. I want to know where you keep it all, all your *precious* mementos—all your *billets-doux* from your former lovers." His eyebrows pucker as he works himself into a snit.

"This is ridiculous," I say. "How did we go from discussing Chloe's text to you wanting to read my old love letters?"

"Are they in the closet?" he asks. "Is that where you've stashed them?"

My husband knows I've saved every letter from every lover I've ever had. I debated tossing them out when we got married, we even talked about it, but I couldn't part with them. Tony said he understood. He said he didn't care. He assured me his ego was stronger than a bunch of old missives. He convinced me he was secure in the knowledge he was the most important man in my life.

He lied.

He rushes into the closet now. He snaps up a handful of my suits and dresses and pitches them to the floor. I hurry in after him and return the garments to their rightful hangers. He ignores me, hops onto a step stool, and roots around on the shelf above the closet rod. It's the shelf that holds my old shoeboxes—the ones with my special remembrances. He slides one forward, but he's too hasty, and it crashes to the rug.

He leaps off the stool and dumps the box upside down. A montage of outdated cards, photos, and napkins swirl around us like a lost river in the Amazon. He rejects my pleas to stop this ridiculousness and scours through the jumbled mess until he finds it: my bundle of old love letters. My husband yanks at the faded, rose-colored ribbon that holds them together and the collection erupts. Letters scatter across the rug.

I dive into the pile along with him and pray I find it before he does—the letter from Géraud.

"Ha!" Tony waves it at me. It's obvious he remembers the man's name. "So, what have we here?"

The thing is in pretty bad shape. It's been scotch-taped in so many places, it's almost unreadable. It's the way Chloe and I left it. The sight of it in Tony's hands rattles my intestines, and I think I might shit myself.

He separates the letter from the envelope. His eyes narrow. He thinks Géraud tried to make a play for me and win me over. But what the letter actually says is the man refused to believe the child was his and that even if it was, he wanted no part of it. He'd got what he wanted, and he was done me.

"Tony, don't." I swipe at it.

He raises it so I can't reach it. He pays me back for the stunts I pulled with my cell phone this morning. His eyes shift back and forth across the page as he reads it. Then his posture stiffens, and his breathing becomes weightier. "I can't believe you kept this," he says.

I make one last attempt to get it away from him. "I can explain," I say.

"Sweet Mother of God," he lowers it. His face fills with red blotches. "Did Chloe read this? Is *this* what the two of you fought about the night she left?"

I can't look at him.

"Holy hell," he murmurs. "She *did* read it."

"I never meant for—she wasn't supposed to read it." Can I really justify my way out of this one?

"Chloe understands she's not my daughter." His chest balloons, and the lines along his cheekbones harden.

"I can explain." Desperation hemorrhages from my pores and pools at my feet. I've lied about my daughter's paternity for the past twenty-three years. How do I even begin to undo this?

I don't. I can't. Tony has me dead to rights, and it only takes another second for me to descend into that place where chaos fuses relationships, doubt forges unions, and madness fosters stability. It's a state of mind I'm familiar with, my ground zero. It's where down is up, right means left, and I can make it so nothing you believe makes sense anymore. I'm the seller of snake oil, the mistress of spinning plates, the queen of the spider web, except this sovereign has finally slipped from her silken net.

My husband rips the letter into pieces. He shreds these into even smaller fragments letting bits fall to the rug. When he's done, he drops to his knees, collects what he can, and pummels it all into one vicious mass. Then he hurls it at the wall.

The impact brings the dogs to their feet. Dharma flattens her ears and runs for her bed. Kooks slinks in right behind her. All futile acts because there's no place for any of us to hide.

"You never listen to me." I crawl around and gather up what's left of the letter.

Tony gets down on all fours and scuttles around after me. He looks like a cartoon figure. He steals back what few bits I've recouped, and he shakes them at me. "How did Chloe get a hold of this letter? I want the truth."

"I'm *giving* you the truth." I spit tiny particles of saliva.

Why is it the one time I'm honest, my husband doesn't believe me? "She went through my things, and she found it."

Tony's nostrils flare like a prizefighter in the final round of a bout. He holds up his fist, clenches the last snippets of Géraud's correspondence. "Son of a bitch, Ana. Stop. Lying."

"Tony, please. Hear me out."

"You're lying!" he shouts. "She didn't find it. You gave it to her."

"I messed up, all right?" My legs go weak. Beads of sweat form along my hairline.

"I've heard this line too many times."

I catch his sleeve. "Wait, I can explain." I form the words, but it's my mother's voice that rings in my head—the way she begged my father to stay, how she clung to him long after the marriage ended and despite how he'd abused her. I can still hear her wailing into the floorboards.

"We can make this work, baby. I know we can." My father had bloodied her bottom lip and forced her face into the hard-wood, but she was so terrified to be alone, she didn't care what it took to keep him. She still wanted the man who repelled her, even if it meant she had to forsake the daughter who was lost without her.

Over and over, it happened.

Time and again, she chose him over me.

Did she ever love me at all?

Does anyone?

Tony flicks me off like a speck of dust. An insignificant bit of waste.

I can't be alone . . . "Baby," I cry. "Please don't give up on me."

My husband puts up his hands to ward me off. "Good Lord," he mutters. "You've genuinely outdone yourself this time." He turns toward the door.

"Where are you going?" I scrape my arms with my fingernails. Ugly, red marks appear.

Tony keeps walking.

Dear God, tell me I haven't destroyed this marriage beyond repair. Terror sticks in my throat, and I can't swallow, and I can't speak, and I can't breathe, and I can't breathe, and I can't ... breathe.

I scan the room. A ceramic birdbath sits on my nightstand. A small red bird perches along the edge of the basin. I grab hold of it and press the bird's tail against my jugular. "I'll do it," I say.

Tony stops. He turns. Our eyes meet.

I gouge myself with the statuette and sob like an infant.

Dharma lurches into the middle of the room and barks. She wants us to stop this madness.

I want to stop it, too, but I don't know how. Nothing I've said or done this morning has brought out my husband's tender side. Something is very wrong between us, and I can't put my finger on it. He hasn't run over and removed the ceramic dish from my hand, or rubbed my back to calm me, or told me I could rest my head in his lap until I stop crying.

"You need help." His words burn with a long-simmering irritation.

My face crumples. I know what he means, but I'm not going to do it.

"Call Dr. Woodhouse," he says.

"No."

If looks could kill. I turn my head. "I don't need therapy," I say.

"Can you see yourself?" He hollers at me.

"You don't know what it's like, the humiliation of having to bare your soul about your childhood, about—" I don't finish the sentence.

My husband shakes his head.

"What if I don't?" Dread sets in. My palms are damp.

Tony makes for the door.

I throw the figurine and chase after him. I ambush him from behind.

My husband stumbles, regains his footing, and peels me off like a piece of decaying painter's tape.

I collapse to the floor. "I'm hanging here by a thread," I shout.

"All the more reason to call him." There's a tone in his voice; it's uncompromising. "I said I was tired, Ana."

"Tired of what? What does that mean?" I wait for a response. Some word from him that says I'm on the wrong track, that he'll hang in there with me again, and we'll see this through together, again. "Are you saying you'll leave me over this?" I ask.

My husband looks me in the eye, then turns and walks out of the room, taking with him all assurance that I'm a person who deserves love. Or forgiveness. Or respect.

He leaves me with nothing.

"She's not even yours," I say.

8

TONY

"Honestly, I would rather not discuss it." I am on my BlackBerry with Didine Fidéline—Didi. She is my lover, or what the French call *ma maîtresse*. I prefer their term to the American description. It's sexier. Didi and I have been seeing each other for the past four years, and it gives me the greatest of pleasures to know that my wife is completely ignorant of our relationship.

"Ana and I argued again." It's an understatement, of course.

Didi listens attentively. She always listens intently. At forty-eight, Didi is a native Parisian of African descent, and while she doesn't talk about it much, she grew up in Paris because her parents emigrated here from the Côte d'Ivoire in 1962 to avoid that country's unrest. She's tall, a snappy dresser, and wears her hair in cornrows that she keeps pulled back in a pony-tail. It's sophisticated and no-nonsense, like her. She's also highly educated, having received her Juris Doctor from Stanford. Later, when she returned to France, she quickly became a titan in the field of Competition Law, not only here but within the whole of Europe. It's quite an accomplishment and a greater accolade than any I've ever acquired. Yet, above and beyond all of these wonderful attributes, the quality I love best about Didi is her drive and determination. She's a mature woman who knows what she wants, and within months of co-teaching a class with me on the theory of finance, she made it clear she wanted me.

Go figure.

Suffice it to say, she is the complete antipole of Ana, and it's such a joy to be with a woman who revels in herself. She transports me to a different world when I'm with her. I'm no longer that working-class kid who came from a broken home, had a father who laid asphalt for a living or a brother who lived on the street.

Of course, it doesn't absolve me from being a cheater and an adulterer. This may be an excuse for my behavior, but I'm lonely. Like everyone else, I want to be loved. I deserve it, and I don't find it at home. My wife says she loves me, then she abuses me both verbally and physically until she gets her needs met.

I'm worn out.

So, why don't I divorce her?

How do I explain I'm as fucked up as Ana is? How do I describe that, on some dark, dirty level, her needs satisfy mine?

Besides, the last thing I plan to do is confront my wife and upset the status quo. It's not a road I care to go down anymore. It's easier to be silent. At least, I know what to expect. I've found all the potholes, and I've learned how to avoid them. Besides, the longer I fume, the more it upsets her, and the better chance I have to get what *I* want—and right now, I want to read Chloe's text message.

"I've hit my breaking point," I continue to complain about this morning. I'm hopeful Didi will show some compassion for my situation. I could use it right now. Didi is divorced, so she's keen on the battles that ensue between husbands and wives. Of course, this also means she has little interest in hearing about them. It's fine with me. More and more, I find when Didi and I are together, I don't want to talk about Ana. I want to talk about us.

"How about you?" I change the subject. "You have some very special guests staying with you this weekend." I flatten the palm of my hand against the wall.

Didi has two beautiful daughters. Both live away from home, and they both plan to visit their mother this weekend. Charlotte, her eldest, graduated from Harvard Law this past spring, while Sarah starts classes at Princeton in the fall. Sarah has been away most of the summer living with friends on the Jersey shoreline. She's a bit of a party girl. I've explained to Didi that Sarah is young, and that's what young people do, but Didi is ruthlessly ambitious, and this sort of behavior from one's child is unacceptable to her. I dare not tell her about mine and Ana's trials with Chloe. It's best I keep my mouth shut. What do I know? I won't be receiving any Father of the Year award any time soon.

Didi switches topics and rails about her immature and unreliable ex-husband. Although they finalized their divorce two years ago, he continues to find reasons to embed himself in their family unit. Didi says he suspects she's dating some- one, and this is the reason for his renewed interest in her and the girls. Based on my limited knowledge of him, I'd have to say he's *that* type of guy. The kind who takes no interest in his family until he's certain they are about to move on with their lives without him.

"I don't expect Ana back until later this afternoon." Honestly, judging by her condition when she ran out of here, she won't be back for hours. "How soon can you get here?" I shift position and check the digital display on my watch.

Didi bullets through her schedule and provides me with an expected time of arrival.

"An hour is great." I love her predictability. "I'll make us a couple of sandwiches. While you're here, we can go over our paper on how anti-competitive practices affect markets. I have some fresh thoughts on our data set."

Ever the lawyer, she agrees, but not without representing her case.

I can't dispute her. It's futile. Although, I do have one sure way to win. "Right," I say, "I would be happy to address your questions, but only if we're naked."

She laughs. It's a wholehearted chortle.

I do, too. "I'll see you in an hour then."

I set my BlackBerry on the table, reconsider, and shove it in my back pocket. I stretch my arms above my head and wiggle my fingers. Then I retrieve my tablet from where it sits on the kitchen counter and check my email. There are a dozen messages from frantic students upset about their summer grades. I neglect them all. I have no time for their petty grievances right now. My *maîtresse* is on her way over, and I'm about to get lucky. For real this time.

I head down the hall, through our bedroom, and into the master bath where I place my tablet on the toilet seat cover. Kooks enters behind me with his favorite green squeaky ball clenched between his jaws. He squeaks it at me. Then he squeaks it again, and again, and again. Then he squeaks it some more. One thing I've learned from my previous toy excursions with him is that if I don't acknowledge him, he'll squeak the darn thing until my brain stops working. I take the ball, and I squeak it for him. He plops his butt on the floor. It's a polished sit, and I hand him back the toy. He seizes it and lies across the tiles with it. He takes up most of the bathroom floor. He drops the ball between his paws and rests his chin on top of it.

I pat him on the head, return to my tablet, and tap on the *Wall Street Journal* app. The front page of the newspaper fills the screen. I peruse the headlines, but there is still no news on China's currency rates. So, I probe my likeness in the antique mirror above the sink, but all I see is a baldheaded, middle-aged man, and I can't help but ask the following question.

What am I doing with my life?

This is not the question of what in the world am I doing with the various aspects of my life, such as my career, or my marriage, or my affair with Didi. This is the much bigger question of what in the world am I doing with my life as a whole. It is *the* question, the big enchilada. It's the What in the Name of Pete Am I Doing with My Fucking Life question. It's the question each of us must ask ourselves at some point in our pointless and puny lives, and it sends me into a tailspin whenever I do. Every. Single. Time. Because each time I ask it, I come up with the same answer, which is the following.

I have no idea.

I have no way to answer whether I've actually made any difference in this stinking world, and it's supposed to be the whole reason we're here. It's the barometer of our adulthood, the underpinning of our legacy. It should be the way we culminate our precise worth on this rinky-dink rock. It's what we expect to leave behind for the next generation.

But what happens when you sit back, examine your life, and realize you've fallen short? When you recognize that what you've amassed for future cohorts is not enough? Or not good enough? Or not meaningful enough? These are all good questions, to which I would again answer with the following.

I couldn't even begin to tell you.

I peel back the shower curtain and hop into the tub. My lower back constricts and reminds me again how I'm aging. It doesn't help that my ankles creak every time I climb a flight of stairs, my knees vibrate whenever I go for a run, and my shoulder pops out of place each time I lift a heavy object. All of which causes a considerable amount of internal hysteria and convinces me that the nip in my joints is arthritis, each burp is an ulcer, and every headache is an ischemic stroke. Even the slightest amount of tension behind my ribcage is enough to convince me I'm suffering from acute heart failure.

It's like a bad dream, and I can't wake up.

A year ago, I developed a nodule on the tip of my nose, and I swore on my mother's grave that it was cancerous. I Googled everything I could find about carcinogenic lumps, bumps, and protrusions, then I organized it all and saved it in a confidential file on my desktop. Not less than a dozen times a day, I opened it, studied the pictures, and weighed them against what I observed on my own knob until I determined that what I had, beyond the shadow of a doubt, was indeed a cancerous polyp, and I would die. I lived with this horror for months until I couldn't tolerate it any longer and decided I'd share it with my wife. So, one night, after we'd clicked off the bedroom light and crawled into bed, I blurted it out. "I have cancer," I said.

Then I waited. I waited for Ana to provide me with comfort and support for what had become my short and doleful existence. I expected her to reassure me that we would get through this dreadful ordeal together. Instead, she launched into a diatribe about how I spend way too much time consumed with my demise, branded me with obsessive compulsive personality disorder, and scolded me for twisting the whole lot of it into a catastrophe.

I ruminated about it for weeks. I refused to speak to her. I pacified myself with the knowledge that, when I eventually received the news that I had cancer—oh, and I *would* receive a diagnosis of cancer—my indifferent and insensitive wife would be wracked with so much guilt that it would send her straight back into the bowels of her own disorder and leave her there for good. The thought that I was right and she was wrong filled me with such glee I was practically giddy the day of my appointment. Then the dermatologist stepped into the exam room, diagnosed it as a mole, and promptly sliced it off with a single-edged razor. I hung my head. I was mortified.

I turn off the shower and climb out of the bathtub. I collect my towel. It hangs next to Ana's towel and reminds me how I've spent the last quarter-century with a woman who presents with more than her share of deep-seated psychological problems and who regularly makes me her target. While it is accurate that Ana and I are two sad, lonely people who will stop at nothing in our quest to beat each other down with the same old arguments and the same old condemnations, nevertheless, I'd rather do *anything* other than face the reasons why I'm still married to my wife.

I tie the towel around my waist and line my toothbrush with toothpaste. Yet, on top of so much unhappiness, I now have a chance to reconnect with my daughter—a child who gives me profound joy. A daughter who can only be explained as a unique prodigy who makes me want to be a better parent; she made me want to be a better father. Chloe's latest communication presents a golden opportunity to reconnect with her after so many years of silence. It's the kind of occasion that doesn't come around often, but when it does, it makes life worth living.

I refuse to let Ana take it away from me.

I spit in the sink and pat my mouth with the corner of the towel. I tap Kooks on the head again. He lifts his chin, and the squeaky ball comes loose and rolls leisurely across the floor.

Yet, rather than head into the bedroom to dress, I pick up my iPad, close out of my inbox, and fire up my Space Galaxy app where I mount my very own customized space ship and begin to annihilate alien ships at breakneck speed.

I am the most valiant ruler of the galaxy.

I am the divine lord of the universe.

It is for this reason that I *will* see Chloe again.

9
ANA

I wedge the sports coupé into the last available spot on the street. The front tires straddle the curb, then plunge back down onto the pavement. I jam the vehicle into first and wrench up on the emergency brake. The afternoon sun beams through the windshield and floods the front seat with white light. It burns my eyes, but I won't cry because this is how it starts. This is how it works its way into your soul, with big, blubbering tears. What happened earlier was a glitch in our marriage, that's all. I didn't mean for all that stuff to happen . . . that nonsense with the birdbath and whatnot. I still have time to put everything back the way it was—back when life was normal, and sane, and ordinary.

Tony's wrong. I don't need therapy.

I'm not calling Dr. Woodhouse.

I get out of the car and double over. Does he mean it? Will he actually *leave* me over this?

This is more than a glitch, and for once in my life, I don't know how to repair it.

I don't even know where to begin.

I sit on the curb.

What time in our lives am I trying to get back to? It's been years since Tony and I were intimate—truly intimate. It's been too long since all we cared about was being with each other. You promise each other it won't happen to you, things won't change, you won't let it, but life infiltrates in ways you'd never expect. In no time, your relationship takes a back seat, and you become ignorant to the lack of attention you're giving each other. Pretty soon, it falls off the schedule completely, and you turn a blind eye to it all entrenched in the belief that the connection you've built is so wonderful, so sound, that you fail to notice your own carelessness.

Yet it does happen, and it spreads like a virus let loose on an unsuspecting world. You can't stop it or slow it down. Soon, your priorities change. You begin to focus more on whether one of your cars needs repairs, *again*, or whether the mechanic will blindside you with another astronomical repair bill, *again*. You even ruminate about whether you should buy a new one, except you have two, three, maybe four more years of the girls' tuition yet to pay, and you can't do it all. You agonize over whether to pay off the credit cards or reduce the balance, at least, so you could invest in a used car. Something to get you around for a while.

You worry less and less about whether you've gained weight, or shaved your legs, or trimmed your pubic hair. You don't think about what to wear to bed, or whether it's sexy enough, or flattering enough, or whether it's even suitable until it occurs to you that you can't remember the last time you had sex. But who has time to fret about it since the laundry still has to get done, and your daughter has that thing at school and she needs her favorite green shirt for it? And that comes first. It has to.

Oblivious and undaunted, by this point you're so deep in

the indifference it's extended its tentacles into the rest of the household. It inhabits the everyday chores around the apartment. It's part of your most mundane conversations. Like the inquiry of who's going to make dinner because neither of you cares to cook anymore. You can't even bribe each other to use the Cuisinart, or the sous vide, or the panini press. Not without an argument or an outright brawl, at least, because no one wants to clean up after these useless machines.

Then there are the weekends which come along with their own shipload of questions like how long has it been since you went dancing on a Saturday night? Particularly since it used to be the highlight of your weekend. There was a time when you couldn't imagine anything better than spending a late night at some hip jazz club downtown, someplace where you had a few drinks, maybe even a few more, then you tottered home, toppled into bed, and screwed each other until you were wrecked. Now, the most exciting thing you both do is rent a DVD, uncork a cheap bottle of wine, and get drunk in front of the television. You still topple into bed afterward, but it doesn't have a damn thing to do with sex.

Adel once said that if you could count on your significant other to pick you up when your car broke down, your relationship was solid. I don't know. Seems like your husband's commitment should be worth more than what you expect from your Uber driver.

I look over at Dharma. She's sitting up in the back seat, watching a bird peck at something in the street.

I hug my knees.

He didn't mean what he said this morning . . . did he? Would he really walk out on me? Or divorce me? Over this?

Crap. The *this* being I fucked him regarding Chloe's text.

He's only asking me to call Dr. Woodhouse, to work out

some shit I'm still hung up on. How bad could it be? I like Dr. Woodhouse. I wouldn't have to spill my guts. He knows everything about me, anyway.

Mostly everything.

I glance at Dharma again. She remains fixated on the bird.

I can't do it. There has to be another way to save my marriage without involving Woodhouse.

I stand and return to the car. Dharma becomes consumed with me now. She wants out. Such a good and patient girl. I open the door, and she hops onto the sidewalk and sniffs at the congested air. She's trying to determine what's changed since she was here last. She probably understands better than me how new businesses keep cropping up along this alleyway. When she's satisfied, she crosses the empty street and waits for me in front of my building. I follow her, hold the door for her, and she sashays into the main waiting room. She barks at Naitee Lal, my office assistant.

"*Bon-jour*, Dhar-ma!" Naitee sings out her name, then she hops off her stool and meets Dharma in front of her desk. She offers the dog a bone-shaped cookie—she keeps a bag of them on hand for the occasions when my dogs come to visit. I get it. It's hard not to indulge such debilitated animals.

I smile and drop my purse. Dharma brings over her new biscuit to show me before she chews it on top of my bag. Crumbs and spittle fly out of her mouth.

Nait returns to her desk where she surrounds herself with stacks of multicolored manila folders. Three months shy of twenty-seven, Naitee is a slight woman who works with me part-time until she decides on a career and goes back to school. Even though she shares an apartment with her mother in La Chappelle, or what's considered Little India, she's hardly a *rêvasseur*, or a daydreamer. She's your typical Parisian Gen Z-er

—determined, hip, and smart. She plans to study photography and wants to apply to either the Paris College of Art or Spéos Paris within the next year. Neither school is far from here, and I'd love for her to stay on after she gets accepted, because she *will* get accepted to whichever one she chooses.

She gets up and follows me to my office. As we walk together down the hall, she entertains me about her most recent adventures with her new boyfriend. When she gets to the funny part, she tosses her head back and laughs. Large, gold hoop earrings sway in her earlobes. The earrings are pretty, and they complement the line of diamond studs in her right ear. We enter my office to see that Dharma has made herself comfortable on the overstuffed dog bed I keep here for her and Kooks. She has a hot pink stuffed pig pinned between her front paws. She's got it by its neck, and she's gnawing on its ear—a reminder of how, despite her sweet demeanor, she's still a predator at heart. I scratch her head. While it's such an ordinary gesture on my part to bring her here, it means everything to her to come. Of course, Nait's cookies aren't too bad, either.

I unload the stack of folders I'm carrying, and they scatter across my desk. Some end up on the floor. Then I flip open my laptop and check my email for any messages from my clients. There's one from a woman I recently started treating who needs to reschedule again. I'm not surprised. She works sixty-five hours a week while raising five kids, all under the age of six, and all on her own. She has a husband, but he's no help.

While it's my job to motivate my clients—like her—to learn how to resolve their emotional issues from the past, and face the difficulties that prevent them from advancing in their lives, sometimes it's a tall order. Confronting past trauma requires a lot of hard work. It's not easy to forgive someone who's mistreated us. Especially when it's someone we love.

Ask me. I've yet to meet a grudge I didn't lust after. Other times treatment is simply not the right answer. Like with this woman. She needs someone to help her resolve her living situation, and that's not me. I'm her advocate. I'm the professional who's supposed to help her sort through her issues so *she* can decide what to do, except one day soon I'll end up telling her to get the hell out of there, and once that happens, she'll stop coming in altogether. Then I'll beat myself up over it because it's excruciating to think that I allowed her to leave therapy the same way she entered—with nothing. It makes me feel useless.

Years ago, I thought if I touched one person's life, if I helped even one individual to be the best version of themselves, it would have been enough. I would've shown the world I'd done some good. It would've proved I'd lived a good life. Unfortunately, the older I get, the more I realize that for every individual I affect, hundreds slip through my fingers, and there's nothing I can do about it.

I make myself a note to call her and reschedule, then I scroll through the rest of the messages. Evelyn and Meadow have both sent me emails—Meadow's sent me two. I open Evelyn's first. She asks again if I've heard from Chloe and offers some new information about borderline personality disorder as a way of speculating about her older sister's long-standing symptoms of craving love, then rejecting anyone who gets too close to her. It's not the first time Evelyn's wondered about the mental health of her older sister.

I type out a reply, then I delete it. I want to commiserate with her, but I don't always know where to draw the line. It's tempting to have a conversation with her about Chloe, but it's a bad idea. Chloe is Ev's sister, and I'm their mother, and I shouldn't make Evelyn my sounding board when I'm feeling overwhelmed.

I open Meadow's email next. My youngest explains that

she and Aurelien plan to drive to Marciac this weekend, a town that's in the middle of a three-week-long jazz festival. Meadow says Aurelien scored tickets for Sunday's performances, and he's booked hotel rooms for them. I stop reading.

Meadow's email makes me want to go home and pull the covers over my head. Mostly, because she doesn't *ask* me if she can do this. She *tells* me she's doing it. It's appropriate, I guess. She's nineteen. But she's still my baby. When did we come to the place in our relationship where she no longer needs my permission? For anything? Including going away for the weekend and having sex with her boyfriend? It's hard to see her in this light. It wasn't that long ago she was playing dress-up in my old business suits.

Nait picks up the folders on the floor and lays them out on my desk. Her hair is done up in a bun this afternoon, and a small gold hoop bobs from her left nostril. She has on a pair of ripped jeans, and a cropped vintage T-shirt with the words "Led Zeppelin World Tour 1977" written across the front. She wilts across my desk, and her shirt hikes up and shows off her belly, and along with it, her tattoo. It's a school of Japanese koi fish that swim the full length her body from her ankle to her neck. It's a stunning piece of body art and not at all like the home-made tattoos I used to carve across my skin when I was younger. Words like "Help" and "Death" that cost my father a small fortune to have removed. While my mother had her way of commanding my father's attention, I had mine.

"You are at work early today, yes?" she asks. "Did you and Tony not enjoy your cafés this morning?" She stands straight, shifts her weight, and checks her nails. The koi fish go into hibernation.

I don't answer. She's too happy with her new boyfriend. Why should I be the one to tell her what marriage is really about? Like how my husband ransacked my closet this morning and found an old love letter, or how he tore it up in my face and screamed about family values, or how I paid him back by depriving him of his daughter's paternity. "It wasn't a good morning," I say. "For either of us."

I grab my phone and check Cool Babes, see if there are any more responses, if anyone else has shared anecdotes about their family fights. Kat writes, "Good to keep your emotions in check," and she adds the smiley face with the smiling eyes emoji. She also adds the hashtag #LetterToMyInnerChild. Kat Davis is the other member on the list who is American. We've swapped stories about what it was like to grow up female in the US, and our experiences are pretty similar. While Kat was born and raised in LA, rearing a girl in this society is the same no matter where you live. It's sexist, and it warps a woman's mind. It fills her with falsehoods about what she can and can't do in the world, and by the time she realizes it's all crap, it's too late.

Sky Robert also replied. The youngest member of our group, Sky lives in the UK and finished her master's degree in counseling psychology this past spring. Although she wanted to be a writer, her folks paid for school and weren't too keen on the idea, so they steered her away from it. She chose psychology because she didn't think she could do anything else, and once she got her degree, never even bothered to pursue a job in it. At present, she works as a bartender and says she enjoys it. She makes a boatload of money, and she gets to *act* like a therapist: without all the headaches and bureaucratic paperwork. What's not to love? She tells me to hang in there and adds three chocolate chip cookie emojis.

I close out of Twitter and call Adel again. If I plan to rescue my marriage, I'll need a lot of help doing it, and that's where she comes in. Rescuing waifs is somewhat her specialty.

Adel's phone rings on the other end. "*Allo?*"

"I'm so glad you're there." I put her on speaker, place my cell on the desk.

Nait hands me a pen, then stuffs her hands in her pockets.

I gesture at her to pull up a chair and sit down. I supposed this is as good a time as any for her to learn about long-term relationships. She goes to the back of the room, grabs a folding chair, and drops it in front of my desk.

"I'm having a bad day," I say.

"You didn't sound good earlier," Adel says.

"Things went straight downhill after we talked." I remove a file from the stack and check to see if all the summer invoices are inside.

"Tony knows about Chloe's text, and he wants to read it. I don't know what to do."

"I wish I had an answer for you," Adel says. "This would be a lot for any family to deal with. When was the last time you saw her?"

"Seven years ago. When she packed up all her belongings, stuffed them in the back of her drug-dealing boyfriend's Citroën, and moved out." What must this sound like? They're probably asking themselves why I didn't stop her.

Nait shifts in her seat. She coils a loose strand of hair around her finger. She can't take her eyes off me.

"Our house was a living nightmare." I sign the first statement in the folder. "Chloe had a way of dividing and conquering us all."

"Children learn to do that," Adel says. "Especially if they're given the opportunity, if they sense their parents are not in agreement."

"Chloe and I never got it right." I can't look Nait in the eye. I'm opening the wrong can of worms if I allow Adel to raise questions about my parenting techniques. I need to turn this around and take the attention off me, put it back where it belongs: on my daughter.

"Did something happen between you two?" Adel asks. "Like, early on. Was there some disagreement that kept you from connecting with each other?"

"You mean besides how she snuck into my closet, snooped through my things, and discovered I had an affair?" This should vindicate me. No way my daughter should've gone through my belongings. I caught her red-handed that day. I sit back in my chair.

Nait stops toying with her hair. "You had an *affair*?" she asks.

My cheeks burn with regret. I shove the stack of invoices back into the folder. "It was a long time ago," I say. "It never should've happened."

"Oh, honey," Adel says. "No one's blaming you. We've all done things we wish we could erase. We learn from them and move forward."

Not all of us.

Nait kicks off her shoes and braces her feet against my desk. She's all ears now.

"It was stupid." I concentrate on her toes. "Tony and I had been married only a few months, and we were having problems. Serious problems. So, when I was invited to this charity event, I got hideously drunk, and . . . I cheated on him."

Adel is quiet, and I can't read Nait's face. Should I finish my story? I could really use a friend right now, someone who's willing listen to *my* side of things and understand what *I* went through. "Then, I got pregnant," I say.

"Pregnant?" It takes Nait a whole five seconds to put two and two together. She's too astute to let this get by her. "So, this child you had with this man, this is your daughter Chloe?"

I finger the next folder in the pile. "I don't know," I say. "Maybe. I think so."

"Wait a minute. I thought you were certain about this?" Adel asks. "You told me Chloe was *not* Tony's child."

"I *think* it's true." My voice quivers, and I sit up straight. "All I know is I wanted to have a baby, and Tony wasn't ready, and when I found out I was pregnant, there was no way I wasn't having it." I don't know how to explain to them that I also thought becoming a mother would make me normal, that I actually believed giving birth would change me into a person who didn't suffer from a personality disorder. That it would make me more like other women. Compassionate. Nurturing. Less of a fuck up.

"What did your Tony think when he discovered you were pregnant with another man's child?" Naitee's voice is soft, gentle.

"He didn't know about it." I pick at the corner of one of the folders. "Until this morning."

Nait's head jerks back a teeny tiny bit.

"Was he furious?" Adel asks.

"How did he find this out?" Nait asks.

"He tore through my stuff this morning and discovered an old letter from Géraud in which he'd *claimed* the baby wasn't his." I gather up the folders and push them to the other side of my desk. "It was the letter Chloe read," I say.

"That's awful," Adel says. "I'm so sorry, Ana. It sounds as if you two had quite a blow-out this morning."

"On top of it, he made it sound like I *wanted* to drive her away." I can't look at either one of them. Of course, I wanted her out. She knew too much. What kind of mother does that? The answer is the *worst* kind. "Tony insists I showed it to her on purpose."

"*Did* you?" Adel asks.

"No, I didn't."

"I don't understand why you saved it," Adel says.

"I didn't *save* it," I say.

"But you still had it?" Nait asks. "Right?"

"Yes, I still—" My arms feel prickly, and I scratch them. "Okay, maybe I did save it, but I hid it. It was tucked away in an old shoebox. It wasn't meant for anyone else to read but me. I never expected Tony would read it."

"But it held information about whether or not Chloe was his daughter." The tone in Adel's voice shifts. It's more accusatory.

"It was an old souvenir from my past, that's all. One I wasn't ready to throw away." I wait for Adel to speak, to tell me how she's kept old mementos, too. I wait for her to absolve me of my wrongdoing. She does neither.

Naitee's chair squeaks as she sits straighter.

"Maybe it was wrong." I pick at my cuticles. "But my daughter shouldn't have been rummaging through my closet. It was obvious she was looking for something. When I caught her, I let her know it."

"What did you do?" Adel asks.

"I did what any good parent would do in that situation. I reprimanded her, and she didn't like it." My lies multiply and circle me like feral kittens in an alleyway.

"She must have been so upset," Nait says. "When she learned about her father."

"She was devastated. She threw a fit and accused me of still seeing him. I tried to convince her the relationship with Géraud was long over."

"Affair," Adel says. "You mean the *affair* was long over. You just called it a 'relationship.'"

"No, I didn't."

Naitee's toes squirm against my desk.

"You did," Adel says. "You used the word 'relationship'."

"Why would I say that?" I look down at my desk. "It wasn't a *relationship.*"

"Did you love him?" Adel asks.

"No, I didn't *love* him." My face feels hot. I've set myself on fire, and I don't know how to put it out. "Why are you two interrogating me this way?" I argue like a child who can't get her way. I slide the folders toward me, then I hurl the whole bunch of them into the bottom drawer of my desk. The wood groans under the abuse.

Naitee takes the hint. She jumps up from her chair and heads for the door. On her way out, she wiggles her fingers at Dharma; she spurns all eye contact with me.

"Nait, I'm sorry."

"What happened?" Adel asks. "What's going on over there?"

I take Adel off speaker. "I can't do anything without making a mess," I say.

"It's good you brought this up," Adel says. "I can help you with it."

"No," I say. "I need to figure this one out on my own." Then I tell Adel I'll call her later, and I tap End.

I snap up my purse and root around for my knife. I take it out and wrap my fingers around its obsidian handle, and my skin fuses to it like a high school science project gone awry. Suddenly, I'm fourteen again, hiding in the bathroom, doing shots of tequila, and spilling blood. My blood.

I don't care what you call it; self-harm, self-injurious behavior, or self-mutilation. It's all the same to me. It's skin-cutting, and we've been doing it forever. Our forbearers tattooed, branded, and scarred themselves into oblivion. They used it to describe their social status, enhance their beauty, and prove their valor. While I wish I could say I did it for the same reasons, I can't. When I cut, it's with a single purpose in mind: to end the drumbeat in my head that tells me I'm defective.

I don't want to lose Tony.

But I won't go back into therapy.

10

TONY

"You're here."

"*Je suis ici.*" Didi sings this. She stands in the open doorway. This afternoon she has on a dark skirt and a white T-shirt. While her hair is still braided, it hangs loose along her back. It's quite the informal look for her.

"It only took you forty-four minutes," I croon at her and squeeze her shoulders. "Traffic was light this afternoon."

Didi smiles. It is convivial. I can count on her to admire my penchant for exactness. It's so unlike my wife, who finds it annoying.

I reach for her tote bag. Visible are the bindings of three hard-cover books. One bears the title, *Competition and Legal Thinking in a Modern France*. Didi and I co-authored this textbook the year we started sleeping together. I suppose you could call it our foreplay. Several manuscripts are stuffed in between the books. "I believe you wanted to revise our most recent paper," I say.

"If I'm to get naked with you, then I would expect you to make it worth my while."

"Come in, come in." I titter at her erotic response and usher her into the foyer.

Didi takes my face between her hands. She offers me an open mouth and lips that taste like peppermint candy and burnt café au lait.

I drop her bag. I kiss each of her open palms, then I kiss her lips. Then I ease myself out of her embrace. I don't want to appear too eager. "Would you like something to drink?" I also don't want to let her go, so I take her by the hand, and like a pair of high school sweethearts, I lead her into the kitchen where I motion for her to sit at the table. Then I procure a glass from the cupboard. "We have coconut water, herbal tea, oh, and last week I picked up a nice chai at Carrefour. And we also have some pomegranate juice in the fridge."

"The pomegranate juice, please."

I place the juice on the table, then sit opposite her.

Didi takes a sip. She sets the drink down and arches an eyebrow. "Do you want to tell me about your fight with your wife?" she asks.

I offer a lackluster smile. Didi knows little about my family other than how Ana and Chloe had a problematic relationship that culminated into a major disagreement that caused my daughter to run away from home. I haven't had any reason to share much more than this. "It's a good thing you're seated," I say.

She doesn't crack a smile. Didi doesn't tolerate much baloney.

"My eldest daughter decided to contact us," I say. "My *estranged* eldest daughter. It's provoked quite the brouhaha around here." I hold back on Ana's revelation about Chloe's parentage. I'd rather not dredge up this level of family dirt yet. We'll appear too unseemly. This is not the kind of scandal Didi has ever experienced in her family.

Her expression turns frosty, and the lines on her forehead crease. Didi's forehead is a complex expanse of canvas and a tribute to her wide range of emotional expressions. It's the main area on her face I look to whenever I seek reassurance that I haven't done something thoughtless and ignorant, activities that tend to happen far too often for me and that Didi is all too astute to point out.

I slouch in my seat and slide my feet further under the table. The tips of my toes jut out beyond the other edge. A cookie crumb lodges itself against my left heel and pinches my skin.

"This sounds serious." Didi fiddles with her glass of juice.

"Oh, it's major." I chuckle, but it has a spiteful undertone to it. My bitter feelings toward my wife are still acute.

"In the four years we've been together, we've had few discussions about your oldest daughter."

"Yes, well. I didn't think—"

"It was important enough for us to discuss?"

"We have no secrets." Honestly, right about now I'll say anything. I can't face another woman's grievance today.

Didi has more juice. She places the glass on the table; it lands hard. "Please," she says. "I've had my own ration of chaos this week. I'd rather not have to listen to your mumbo jumbo again about why you choose to stay with your wife."

"Mumbo jumbo?" I didn't know Didi knew any American colloquialisms. I sit forward and plant my elbows on the table. The crumb presses against my foot. It hurts like a mother.

"Everything about your situation has to do with Ana," she says. "Ana, and your reasons for staying with her. If we wait long enough, it will return to her."

I want to dispute her, but she's right, and I would rather not admit it. So, I go on the offensive. "You're the one who generally initiates any conversation we have about my wife," I say.

"Don't you mean the forsaken child you married and for whom you must perform feats of heroism to maintain?" she asks.

"I don't even know what that means."

"It's an explanation of the myriad of ways you rescue your wife—particularly from herself."

"Well, somebody has to do it. She can't—"

"Have you ever allowed her to fail?" Didi wheels the glass between her palms.

"Ana won't succeed on her own."

"Of course not," Didi says. "Not when she can count on you to succeed for her."

"I told you. Someone needs to do it." I clasp my hands together and twirl my thumbs.

"Why must it be you?" she asks.

I twirl my thumbs faster.

"Or, perhaps, you *enjoy* saving her," she says. "Perhaps you have a fetish about needing to be seen as her hero."

I sit straighter in my chair. The crumb juts deeper into my heel.

"What am I saying?" she mumbles. "I find this marriage dubious, at best."

I nod. There was an afternoon, early in our affair, when Didi discovered the varying shades of bruises peppered along my arms, legs, and abdomen. When she learned Ana had caused them, she was appalled.

"Yet you remain with her," she says.

I nod again.

"So, is it pleasure that you take in being her savior? Or is this about your need to dominate her?"

"Dominate her?" My head spins. How could Didi know this about me?

"You are the reason she is unable to achieve anything in her life. You enable her. In a sense, Tony, you victimize your wife."

"Victimize her?" My pulse quickens. "If anyone is being persecuted around here, it's *me*."

Didi eyes me. She's calmer than a cup of chamomile tea. "Sometimes, I think you encourage it."

"What?" I sit squarer for emphasis. The crumb impales me. "That's absurd. Now you're talking crazy."

"Okay," she says. "So, what do you see as the crux of your dilemma?"

I look away. This conversation has become more intense than I was prepared for this afternoon.

"What did she do that made you so angry?" she asks.

This is not an issue I want to broach right now. What I want is to alter my position and free myself from the jaws of this crumb, the dang morsel is stabbing me like a dagger, but I'm afraid to move. The silence between us becomes pronounced, and all I can hear is Kooks. He stretches his hind legs, and his tail sweeps across the terra cotta tiles.

"There is so much more to your marriage than what it presents on the surface," Didi says.

My palms sweat, and I rub them together.

She taps her empty glass with meticulously manicured fingernails. They knock against it as if they were tiny switchblades. "Would you like to know what I think?" she asks.

I give up. I slump in my chair and throw my hands up in the air.

"I think you are still emotionally connected to Ana," she says. "In fact, I believe you are *too* emotionally connected to her."

Didi's observation zaps me with a shock of electricity so great it could take out half of Australia. I emit an audible groan.

"Ana yearns for you. She wants you to be her hero. She longs for you to continuously rescue her, and for your part, you enjoy it. Her need for you to save her appeals to your ego."

"Is that such a bad thing?" I look at her. I've never heard it stated in such a derogatory manner. I cross my legs, left over right, left foot flexed upward, and at last, the cookie piece dislodges itself. I visualize the underside of my foot. It's bloody and raw, and I want to cry at the carnage. "I thought men were supposed to rescue women," I say. "It's in our genetic makeup."

Didi stands and strolls across the kitchen. "For heaven's sake, Tony. We're not cave-dwellers," she says. "We are not the sum of our biology. How you respond to your wife is a choice, and the way I see it, Ana's need to be perpetually protected meets a comparable condition in you to be her champion. It's quite irrational."

I whirl around in the chair and face her. "What are you saying?" I ask.

Her forehead pinches. It becomes a series of vertical lines.

I don't want to make Didi any angrier at me than she is, but with all her talk about how I'm pretending to be Ana's hero, something in me snaps. "You have no idea who I am." I stand for emphasis. I plant one hand along the back of my chair and lodge the other on my hip. "Here I thought you were the one woman who *got* me, but I can see I was wrong. You don't understand me at all."

"Oh, please. Do not kid yourself."

"No. No. You think you know me, but—"

"You want to know what I *get* about you, Tony?" she asks. "What I *get* about you is the tragic way Ana longs for you, the way she can't live her life without you or your approval, and how you love it. What I *get* about you is the way Ana works this marriage to maintain her grip on you, and how all of this together gratifies a rival need in you—a *perverse* one. You may not want to admit it, but it's the actual reason you refuse to leave your marriage. It's why *you* continue to maintain your hold on *her*."

Didi's words cut into me like a meat cleaver. "That's a load of nonsense." I shove the kitchen chair. It scuffs up the tiles, but not enough to do damage. Kooks stirs, but he doesn't bother to inspect the commotion.

Didi crosses her arms over her chest. "So, why don't you ask her for a divorce?"

"Because."

"*Because?*"

"I can't." What a useless explanation, but I can't give Didi a better one. I wilt back into my seat. I'm no fool. If Didi knew who I *really* was, she'd leave me in a second. If she so much as suspected that my consuming need to subdue Ana, to subdue all women, is as perverse as she surmises, she would never tolerate it. How can I tell her that all of our kinkiness in the bedroom is more than fun and games for me? She can label it however she likes, but I only feel important when I'm holding all the cards.

I will not admit this.

"Because I don't like change." I flail my arms, confident the gesture will lend more weight to my argument. For the most part, however, I'm just flailing. "The slightest deviation in my day-to-day routine paralyzes me," I say. "I can't handle anything new. I need a routine, a schedule, and I'm unwilling to disrupt what I've established here. There. I said it. Are you happy now?"

Didi is quiet. She sets the glass on the counter.

"Is that what you wanted to hear?"

She leans against the tile countertop.

"I don't know who I am anymore without this marriage. Hell, most days, I don't know who I am, period. I'm interned in my life. It's pathetic." This is probably the most honest statement I've made all afternoon. I massage my foot where the crumb lacerated my skin.

"Thank you. This is all I ask for."

"Why are you even with me?" I ask.

"Oh, Tony." She laughs. "We have no formal commitment to each other. While I enjoy spending time with you—"

"You like bonking me."

Didi smirks. "This is correct," she says. Her displeasure with me eases. "The point is that either one of us can terminate this relationship at any time."

"Terminate?" My paunch does a backflip. "Are you breaking up with me?"

"No, Tony. I'm saying I'm happy with the way things are between us. If you are not in an emotional space where you're strong enough to let go of your marriage and create a more permanent relationship with me, then so be it. Our affair will eventually run its course and—"

"Run its course?"

"I do not require you to leave your wife." She hoists herself onto the counter and swings her feet. She settles her eyes on me. "Nor do I plan to convince you into having a more serious relationship with me. While I would like to be in a more committed relationship someday, I want it to be with a man who wants to be with me."

Years ago, if someone asked me if a woman like Didi would ever care for a man like me, I would've guffawed. Yet it sounds like Didi could, maybe, love me? Honestly, is it possible a woman like Didi might actually fall in love with a man like me

—a man with the kind of faulty engine under his hood that I have?

"I will not fool myself into believing I have a committed relationship with someone when I do not." Her voice is wholly devoid of its earlier caustic tone. Her eyes shine. She doesn't need me. Honestly, Didi doesn't need any one. She is an island unto herself.

"I can be that man for you." My legs wobble. No greater lie has ever been told.

She crosses the kitchen and places her hands on my shoulders.

It's selfish, and I don't deserve it, but I need it. I need to hear her say she wants me. I want her to reassure me how much she needs me. It's all that will alleviate my fear that I'm not the man I could be—or should be. "How do you put up with me?" I ask.

She laughs. It's robust.

"You could do so much better than me."

"I know."

"Hey, that's not the right answer."

She grins and embraces my hands in hers. She wants to do the dirty, I can tell.

Man, so do I.

I lead her down the hall to mine and Ana's bedroom. I've waited the entire afternoon for this moment.

Didi enters and goes straight to the bed. She sits on the edge of it and removes her shirt, revealing a white strapless corset. Or, more to the point, what could pass for a corset. It barely covers her nipples.

I lie beside her, arms and legs outstretched like a man who's survived an inquisition.

Didi straddles me and plants a kiss on my forehead. Next,

she kisses my cheeks, then my lips. It's hard to believe a kiss could be so sinful yet so wholesome at the same time.

I wriggle out of my clothes as fast as possible, thankful for the Viagra I popped before she got here since I anticipate the vigor with which we will do it today will be intense. While I may not understand all the reasons this woman likes to be with me, what I do know is she loves having sex with me, and I reverse course and take the lead.

When we've both climaxed, I monitor her forehead for any aftereffects from our earlier conversation, but there are none. Her expression is soft, so I don't pull out. I linger longer than usual, and in no time, I'm aroused again. I hedge my bets Didi is not tired either, and I shift my hips slightly and hope I'm not wrong.

Didi intensifies her grip on me and, with this one simple gesture, reassures me about . . . everything.

It's enough, for now.

11

ANA

"Hey, Nait?" I shout.

Dharma opens her eyes.

Naitee pokes her head in the doorway. She smiles at the dog but continues to avoid all eye contact with me.

"Can you watch D for a little while?" I smile in case she looks over. "I'd like to go for a run. You know, clear my head."

"Of course, Ana." She enters, crouches in front of the Dharma, and scratches the fur under the dog's chin. "*J'aime cette petite fille,*" she says to her.

Dharma lifts her head. She shifts her eyes from me to Nait, then back to me. You can't fool a dog. They know when something's up.

I open my desk drawer and take out the extra gym clothes I keep there. I change in the bathroom at the end of the hall, return to my office, and deposit my street clothes in the top drawer of my desk. I sit on the floor and lace up my sneakers, and before I stash my bag in the drawer with everything else, I remove a credit card from my wallet and tuck it in my sock.

Then I stand, stretch, and give Dharma a pat on the head. I rush down the hall, past Nait, and trot out of the building. I cross Boulevard de Belleville and duck behind a moving van parked on the sidewalk. Then I look back to see if Naitee is watching me, but she isn't. So, I hail a cab, hop into the first one that stops, and tell the driver to drop me off anywhere along the Boulevard de Clichy—a stretch of road that passes through the infamous Red Light District of Paris.

I don't know why Tony is suddenly making demands on me now. I should've showed him Chloe's text, and Géraud's letter, and I definitely should've told him about the fight I had with Chloe that night, I get all that, but to force me to go back into therapy? Or, what? He'll leave me?

Fuck that.

Fuck *him*.

The driver pulls up to the curb, and I hop out and dart across the street. I find a bar right away: the Bière et Beautés. Its façade is dark and dreary, and it's constructed mostly of old wood paneling. A dull, burgundy awning hangs over the front door. It's off-putting, but as soon as I step inside, the scene changes. There's music and laughter, and why not? This area of Paris is the Place Pigalle. In some ways, it's still the *belle époque* of the Moulin Rouge. It's the one spot in the entire city where you can find whatever you're looking for, so long as what you want are porn shops, peep shows, and strip clubs.

So long as what you want is sex, and right now, sex is *exactly* what I want.

The room is smaller than I expected, and the bar is in the back. I cross the room, ignoring the so-called entertainment on the stage. The sticky hard-wood floor creaks, and the stench of stale beer and cigarette smoke hover heavy in the air. A deafening stream of '80s R&B hits me. Each song melds into the next, and they're all bolstered by a continuous, pounding base.

The place is one big, thumping stew of hedonism and self-indulgence, and it reminds me of the bars I frequented in college, minus the strippers, of course, and *before* I met Tony. Places I haunted when I needed someone to hold me, and fuck me, until all of my pain liquified, and all of my broken parts healed. Places I visited when I needed someone to make me believe I was the only woman in the world who mattered, even if it was only for the rest of the afternoon.

I tuck my wedding rings into my shorts pocket, and I hop onto an empty stool. I shout over the music, "I'll have an Old Fashioned."

A grungy man in a maroon T-shirt stands on the other side of the bar. He holds a lit cigarette between his thumb and forefinger and skims a copy of yesterday's *Le Parisien*. He doesn't look up from his paper.

I'm ready to repeat myself when a good-looking man with trim muscles and thick, brown hair sits beside me. I figure him for an Italian, probably twenty-four, twenty-five years old. He's dressed in beige khakis and a button-down, and his tailored abs and biceps press against the seams of the shirt. Maybe he's a banker, or an advisor with an investment fund. He's definitely someone who can afford a periodic weekday lunch at a strip club.

Instantly, I picture us having sex. Then I imagine having to explain it to Evelyn. What would she think knowing her mother was here? Drinking in a bar in the middle of the day? With a man her own age? In the Red Light District, no less? Except the very idea of it—sex, and more to the point, anonymous sex—makes my belly go all jittery. It's faint, but I can feel it. I glance over at him.

He raps his knuckles on the bar and refers to the unkempt man by his name. Rob. He asks Rob to bring him a German beer.

Rob lays his paper down, stubs out his cigarette, and sets a Heineken in front of my new friend. He turns to me next. I tell him I'd like an Old Fashioned, and he places a water glass in front of me and pours a generous stream of bourbon into it. More than generous.

The Italian salutes me with his Heineken. I smile and do the same with my bourbon. It goes down smoother than an electric guitar string, and I should know. I was raised on it. Bourbon was my mother's drink of choice. It was what soothed her, especially after my father left. It was the sole thing that altered her mood and transformed her into the kind of mother a daughter could love.

And vice versus.

The Italian checks out the stage, so I turn and have a look as well. A topless young woman jives and churns around a dirty silver pole, and a group of businessmen seated in front of it ogle her. The filthy pole doesn't bother them. All they care about is the way she grinds her backside against it. The song switches, and so does the dancer. This new one boogies out wearing nothing but a thong and four-inch-high stiletto heels. She, too, vogues and postures and gyrates her backside against the greasy pole. Both women can't be much older than sixteen —Chloe's age when she left home.

Did my daughter dance naked in a bar while she was on the run?

Was she forced to have sex with strangers to survive on the streets?

I swallow more bourbon.

I check my phone and scroll through Cool Babes, but the list is quiet today. So, I fire off another tweet to the group. Nothing important, a few words to keep us connected. I don't explain where I am or how I plan to get busy with a cute stranger in a bar. I'm not sure they'd understand. Kat might. A while ago, she confided in me that she slept with a hand model on their first date. It didn't sound odd at first until she explained that the whole time they did it, he wouldn't touch her with his hands because he said he had to protect them. She didn't care. He did some pretty amazing things with his tongue, so she was happy.

The Italian signals the bartender that he'll have another, then he tries to strike up a conversation with me. He says something, looks into my eyes, and waits for an answer.

The music is too loud, and I don't hear what he said, but the bourbon is already clouding my brain, so I end up giggling at him for no reason. It comes across more flirtatious than I intend.

He doesn't seem to mind.

"What's your name?" I shout.

"Michael."

I lie and tell him mine is Val, then we talk for a bit before we order another round. When it comes, we toast again, and we gauge how much of our soul we're willing to surrender to get what we need from each other. It's not the way I did it when I was twenty-five, but I get it. It's the way you do it when you're older, when you've been burned more times than you care to remember, but you still want someone to touch you. It's the price you pay when you look for tenderness in a bar.

We keep drinking until we both get really tipsy, and we start toasting to stuff like France winning the World Cup, and the fate of Guevara the university sit-in dog, and in the midst of all this toasting, Michael's hand drifts across the bar and he touches my fingers. Then he strokes my wrist with his thumb, and it feels like I'm back in junior high at that Friday night dance, with the guy I really liked who took me by the hand, and led me to the back of the cafeteria, and held me in the dark. It was dangerous but thrilling.

When Michael is done holding hands, he nudges his beer out of the way and kisses me. A familiar heat settles below my gut. It's been a long time since a man other than my husband paid attention to me, and it emboldens me. I hold his eye contact and stir my drink with my finger, then I play with the ice at the bottom before I make a production of licking the bourbon off my finger.

His eyes widen, and he grabs my thigh. I move in closer, and we kiss again.

By the time we stumble through the door to the ladies' room, I'm breathless. Michael asks if this is all right, and I respond by unbuttoning his shirt. But he can't wait, and he strips it off and throws it on the floor. He removes mine next. It also goes on the floor. While our actions have the makings of a bad porno flick, I don't care, and I remove my bra and drop it in the sink.

He moves close and fingers the bones in my neck, he caresses the scars on my abdomen. He doesn't ask how they got there, or why I cut myself when I was a kid, or the reasons I took lit cigarettes and burned holes in my stomach, then poured drain cleaner over them so they couldn't heal.

He just goes to his knees and kisses them.

If there's an ideal definition of ecstasy, this is it.

While he's down there, he tugs at my shorts, but I'm too sweaty, and the material sticks to my skin.

I try to help, and I yank at my clothing, but I'm overzealous, and my wedding band falls out of my pocket. *Crap.* It bounces several times and rolls across the floor before it strikes the opposite wall.

The bathroom is silent.

The Italian stands. He looks me in the eye. "You are married," he says.

I nod.

"Why did you agree to do this with me?" he asks.

"I wanted to have sex."

"But you are not single."

"Does that bother you?"

"It upsets me that you have a husband."

"I thought Italian men did anything for sex." I fix my shorts.

"This is not true for all men of my culture."

"I guess not." I slouch against the sink.

"How do you expect me to love you when you are sworn to someone else?"

"It's called anonymous sex," I say. "People do it all the time."

Michael's face relaxes. He shakes his head. "Why must *you* do it?"

His questioning turns real, and I cover my chest with my arms. He thought I was one of the *good* ones. Now he sees I'm not, and he can't come to terms with it. I study his face. "Because I like it, and I'm good at it," I say.

He smiles. "No, you are searching for something."

"I *was* searching for a meaningless romp in the hay, and I was hoping you would provide it for me."

Michael laughs. It's unrestrained and sincere. "No, that is not all of it," he says. "You expect something from me. Something other than sex."

I look away.

"No one wants to have sex with someone they don't know. We all would like to be with a person who cares for us, with whom we can be our honest self."

Leave it to me to find the one stranger in all of Paris who'd rather counsel than screw me. "I never show my real self." Even *I* can hear how sad those words sound, but how do you explain to someone that the last time you looked inward, you were twelve and all you found there was a cauldron of toxic waste?

That's what happens when your mother turns her back on you.

Deceptions are like that; they're not clean. They sting everyone the same. Love gets lost, animosity goes unchecked, and emotions like shame, disgust, and resentment assume Biblical dimensions. It doesn't matter who betrays you, whether it's your best friend, your lover, your spouse. Your mother. Being the victim of such dishonesty plays with your head because, while you may not have the words for it, somewhere inside, you understand that when people love you, they protect you, and if your mother won't do that for you, then it must be your fault. You must've done something terrible to make yourself so unlovable.

Tony's wrong. No therapy will cure me of this. Only sex will cure me of this. Someone to *love* me will cure me of this.

I had such high hopes for today.

I pluck my bra out of the sink. "Do you even find me the least bit attractive?" I ask.

Michael laughs again. Hard. He even snorts through his nose. "Come here." He pulls me toward him and grinds his hips into mine. His chest is hot, luxuriant, and his skin smells like persimmon wine. He takes my bra and returns it to the sink, then he whispers something in my ear. It's in Italian.

The one word I understand is *bellissima*. Beautiful.

"I am sorry someone broke your heart." He walks his fingers through my hair and massages my scalp.

It feels nice, and I don't pull away.

"This is such a cool song, yes?" He loops his arms around my waist and lets his breath dust the top of my shoulders. Then he rocks me. He rocks me like I'm a Kadupul flower, or a Sekai Ichi apple, or the Pink Star diamond. He rocks me like I'm someone's firstborn child, and every moment of my life is meant to be commemorated. He sways to the music, and he rubs himself against me. He's hard.

I search out his lips. I expect this will be our final scene, a quick peck good-bye. Instead, Michael's kisses me with passion. He kisses me with desire.

He's changed his mind.

I don't know why or what it means. Nor do I intend to ask. I don't feel the need to get his phone number or his address, and I have no plans to pester him about whether we might meet again. I don't say anything as I let him in . . . and in . . . and in, and for the next few minutes, I surrender.

12

TONY

"**B**onsoir Ana. *Bonsoir* Antonio." Chace welcomes us to his home with arms extended.

Chace Bulier is the lone person in this world, besides my father, who insists on calling me by my birth name. He gives my right hand a good shake, and air kisses me on both cheeks. Then he envelops Ana's hands in his and does the same, only he plants solid kisses on her. My wife turns to me and scoffs.

"How is life in the enchanting village of Ménilmontant?" he asks.

I don't answer. Chace couldn't care less about our enchanting little village. It's been twenty-four years since he and Médée moved away, and I can count on one hand the number of times they've returned for a visit—and it's not for the lack of an invitation on our part. As soon as the Buliers had the opportunity, they bolted from Belleville. They moved in with Chace's father, Guy Bulier, who owned an apartment in the sixth *arrondissement*. Chace cared for the older man until he passed away at which point he and Médée inherited the place.

Soon afterward, Chace clipped his Fabio Lanzoni hair, married Médée in a brief civil ceremony—to which neither Ana nor I were invited—and commenced their real lives in the sixth: Paris's most expensive and fashionable district, and the home of Saint-Germain-des-Prés. It's where the Haute bourgeois of Paris reside, and it's where Chace and Médée believed they belonged.

Ana nudges my arm.

I hand Chace the box of German chocolates. It's a dinner gift from us. I wouldn't want the Buliers to deem us impolite. He takes it without looking at it, then encourages us to follow him into the living room. As we proceed down the hall, I scout out the other rooms hoping to find someplace quiet where I can read for a while and pretend I'm not here. I already know how the night will go—Ana will get drunk and create a scene, I'll blame Chace for providing her with too much liquor and God knows what else since I know someone will have drugs here, and my wife and I will return home knee-deep in a heated argument. And this is the woman who wants to convince me she *doesn't* need therapy?

We enter the living room to the sound of Miles Davis spinning on Chace's expensive Clearaudio turntable. Nothing but the best for my old friend. Several other guests mill about the room. A particularly attractive couple chat among themselves near the fireplace. Both look in their early seventies, and I consider them to be friends of Chace's dad. The woman has on a '40s style pillbox hat. It tips forward and sits on her forehead, British style. A feather bobs off the back. It's quite refined.

I look around at the other guests. *Everyone* looks refined. No one here resembles my family in any way. Nobody looks as though they have children hooked on drugs, or progeny who dye their hair blue, or a daughter who blames them for everything bad that happens in the family the way Evelyn blames me. What the hell happened to us?

Christ.

I block it from my mind and scan the end tables for snacks. Not the type to skimp on food when they give a soiree, the Buliers have put out their usual array of hors d'oeuvres. I score a handful of tarts, and while I'm not sure what's in them besides tomatoes and a green sauce that looks like pesto, I pop one into my mouth. Meh, it's okay. I've made better.

"I miss you both so much." Chace massages my wife's neck. "You are still the most passionate American woman with whom I am acquainted, my dear Ana."

"Right." I gorge myself on another tartlet. "Too bad it comes at such a great expense to those around her." I sound like an overindulged infant and immediately regret the comment.

"For some people," Ana says, "they're willing to pay the price."

"For some—"

"For some people," Chace adds, "they simply discover they are better suited to the intellectual rigor of science than the emotional complexities of human relationships. This is the way it is with my good friend Antonio, yes?"

In the early days, I used to rip into him about my name. But here we are decades later, and it's as if he never heard me.

Ana chides me again and mutters about me being sullen and hostile.

"I am not sullen," I rebut with a mouth full of bruschetta.

"Maybe 'secretive' better explains it?" Ana asks.

A chill goes through me, but Ana has no knowledge of Didi, so I assume she's referring to the money I sent to Chloe years ago. "Well, if that's not the pot calling the kettle a likeminded match." I prepare another retaliatory remark when Médée sets her dainty and flawlessly pointed foot between us. She places a perfumed smooch on each of my cheeks and fidgets with my collar. Prior to meeting her husband, Médée had trained as a ballerina and received a spot in a major dance company. For reasons that were never made public, she left the company within a year. When the four of us began meeting for drinks, she was in the process of studying for a degree in finance. I knew enough about her even then to understand it didn't matter which profession Médée chose—she had sharp elbows.

"I am not sullen," I repeat.

"No." She grins at me and twiddles with my shirt. "You are not a sullen American."

"For the love of Pete," I say, "Ana and I aren't here ten minutes, and we've had to be separated twice."

Chace catches my shoulder and winks at me. "Ah," he says. "This is why the good Lord created mistresses, yes?"

Médée smirks at her husband and finishes meddling with my collar. She mentions what a pleasure it is to see us both again, then she takes Ana by the hand and leads her into the kitchen, where they join a select group, an influential clique, I presume, of women.

I don't take my eyes off them. I attempt to assess the nature of their conversation. Of course, I'd do a much better job if Chace stopped chatting me up. He continues to pepper me with questions about my present venture, even though he can't remember the name of it. It's produced quite a number of academic papers for me, which is something of a big deal, as I haven't written much in the past few years.

"I am sure you have everything well managed." He positions himself in my line of sight. "It would be so unlike you if you did not."

I peek around him. Ana takes no notice of the other

women. She is riveted by the Twitters on her phone. "It's going well," I say. "Quite well."

"I am pleased you have once again decided to devote your energy to your research." He lightly sweeps at longer, lengthier hair that's no longer there. "Are you able to meet your budget this academic year, particularly with the administration's latest round of cuts?" he asks.

"Yes, well, I assume that I will, but it remains to be seen." I take a gander at the huddle of women again, but Ana is no longer among them. "It's all going quite well," I say again. Where is my wife? I inch my way toward the living room and look inside, but I don't see her there either. "Many thanks to you and all your support, Chace."

"Ah, Antonio. No need to thank me." He smiles widely and points me in the direction of the living room. "Please, there's a fresh plate of hors d'oeuvres waiting for you in there. It has your name on it, I am certain."

I don't need a golden invitation. I rocket through the room and proceed straight to the bar. If Ana is anywhere, she's there. Although undersized, a full bar with a line of top-shelf liquor is a staple at any Bulier affair. What's also a staple? The location; it's set up directly in front of their enormous picture window so as to maximize the views of both the French Senate and the Jardin du Luxembourg, which are nothing less than spectacular at this hour of the evening. In this way, their guests are allowed to both enjoy their beverages and bask in the beauty of the palace's twinkling lights.

I spy my wife at the bar, and I make a bee-line for her. She is busy doing what *she* does spectacularly: captivating Frenchmen. She gestures at one while she hangs from the arm of another. It doesn't take much to understand that neither man is interested in the particulars of her anecdotal tale. They're riveted with the curve of her bustline, which is spilling out all over the top of her black silk dress.

What in the blazes is she thinking?

I approach the group and give a nod to the man tending bar. A dowdy man of medium build, René Martin is Chace's friend from his university days—although it's hard to believe, since no two men could be more different. Legend has it, however, that while they were at university, they were both involved in a theatre troupe. Later, after graduation, each man went his separate way. Chace pursued a career in education and finance, while René prevailed in the arts and has since staged numerous productions, including Ionesco's plays with the Théâtre de la Huchette. I swear, no two men could be less alike.

"A Kronenbourg," I say.

René removes a cold one from a large bucket of ice behind the bar and hands it to me. I can see it's the only Kronenbourg in the container, and more than likely, it's the only Kronenbourg in the entire apartment. I take it and position myself next to my wife if for no other reason than to prove I'm her husband and she's with me. Then, like a true neanderthal, I place my arm on her back and rest my thumb along the base of her spine. I wait for the sparks to fly.

Ana molds her body into mine.

What is this behavior?

"Do you still remember that time, Tony?" She brings a glass of deep red wine to her lips and empties it. "When we rode the Eurail into Spain and spent the night in that teensy-weensy village right outside of Barcelona? Oh, what was the name of it?"

While Ana and I have traveled extensively throughout Europe, we have never toured Spain. Nor have we stayed the night in some undersized village near Barcelona.

"There was a sleazy bar, way off the main road," she says, "where we played pool with the locals and drank too many glasses of Rioja."

Nor have we scouted out a sleazy bar, drank too much Rioja, and shot pool. I know what she's doing. It's a game we used to play when we were younger, out on the town with friends, and we wanted to cut it short and go home and do the dirty. I consider a witty and novel retort, but I don't have one. It's been a long time since I've engaged in these sorts of shenanigans with my wife.

"Do you remember?" Ana peeks at me over the top of her glass.

The two Frenchmen are rapt with my wife's antics. They are all ears. As is René. He's oblivious to the growing line of guests who want drinks.

Ana thumps my chest. She inserts a manicured fingernail in between the buttons of my shirt, then beams.

I twitch like a windsock.

"What's the matter, Tony?" She whispers. "Did you forget how to play our little game?" She ups her seduction and unbuttons my shirt further.

The game becomes too much for René, and he turns his head and resumes his duties tending bar. The Frenchmen also move off and join other conversations, leaving Ana and I alone at the bar.

My cheeks warm. I don't confront her, but neither do I push her away. I sip my beer and hope it mitigates some of the unease now mounting in my chest. "I have not forgotten," I say.

My wife twirls. She presses her backside against my thighs and shimmies to the music with slow, jazzy movements. Her dress swings from side to side across her legs, then she hoists it up, just a little—just enough—and rocks her hips against mine.

I can't deny it; her behind feels soft against my legs, and I count in my head the number of hours it's been since I took my sex pill. Maybe we could get this right this time.

She turns to face me. "I don't need therapy," she says.

I purse my lips and look away. I refuse to resurrect our argument from this morning.

She stops dancing. She smooths the lines of her dress. "All that happened a long time ago—Chloe finding that letter. I see no reason to dredge up the past now."

I keep my mouth shut and slug down more beer. Didi's words resonate inside my head. She's right. I can't save my wife. I won't.

Ana scratches her arms. She folds them in front of her chest. "You always preferred Chloe," she says.

"And you always favored Evelyn." My wife connected with Evelyn as soon as the girl was out of the womb. Evelyn responded in kind, making it likely my middle daughter reacted to both my wife's affection as well as the continuous conflict that arose between her mother and our oldest. Whatever it was, it's a mutual admiration society between those two. Ana favors Evelyn, and Evelyn prefers my wife over me.

"Evelyn loves me," she says.

I weigh how much of this battle I want to have here with Ana. "They would all love you if you gave them half a chance," I say.

Ana looks at me. "It's hard."

"What's so difficult?" I ask. "They're your daughters."

"You wouldn't understand. You never had to parent a child of the same sex. No one talks about it, but a rivalry develops between the two of you. It's like looking at yourself in a fun house mirror. What stares back at you is ugly."

"What mother competes with her daughters?"

"It's not a competition," she says. "It's not like I *decided* to compete with Chloe. The contest was . . . there. Every time I looked at her, I saw her youth. I recognized the opportunities that were still available to her that I no longer had and that I *wouldn't* have because I was too old."

"Children are *supposed* to have more opportunities. That's how it is with the next generation."

"I know that." She looks over the growing crowd of guests. "It's just that . . . it's different when you see it, when you're faced with it in your own child, when she reminds you of your inadequacies."

I'm tongue-tied.

"Obviously, I want all of my daughters to have good lives," she says.

"We're not talking about all of your daughters. We're talking about Chloe."

Ana turns to me. She gives me the evil eye. "Things might've been different if you'd supported me once in a while."

I knew this moment of civility between us couldn't last. "Okay, I'm not going there with you right now." My voice mirrors my level of annoyance. "I've had more than enough of your craziness for one day."

"My *craziness*?"

"Whatever you want to call it."

"How about my *disorder*?"

"Right. Your *disorder*. A few short hours ago, you stabbed yourself in the neck with a knick-knack. But, sure, let's call it a *disorder*."

"Fuck off, Tony."

"You threatened to injure yourself. *Again*."

"I get over-emotional sometimes."

"Good God, Ana." I tap my fingers along the side of my beer bottle. I make like I'm keeping time to the music.

"And you like it. Remember that."

"All right, stop now."

"It's the reason you married me."

"Let's not do this here."

"I'm the most exciting, erotic woman you've ever met," she says.

I bite my tongue. I so desperately want to throw in Ana's face how I have a lover.

"I gave you a reason to stop brooding over your dead brother."

"What did you say?" My head explodes. I look at my wife in disbelief. "What about you?" I shout.

Several of the guests look over. Chace's secretary quickly turns away. She's never seen me this angry, but Ana lit a match under me, and I'm ready to rock and roll.

"What about what I provide for *you*?" I ask. "Like the pleasure of having someone at your beck and call twenty-four-seven? Or the guarantee of having your boy-toy nearby to catch you every time you fall? Maybe it's the ability to bask in the comfort that comes from knowing I'll save you whenever you decide to metaphorically throw yourself off a cliff?"

My wife can't look at me.

"There's something you've never understood, and it's the toll you take on the person who is expected to save you all the time. It gets old. I've spent a lot of years wrestling sharp objects out of your hands every time life doesn't go your way, and I'm exhausted."

"That's not how it is, and you know it."

"Right." I finish off the last of my beer. I break out in a sweat. More of the Buliers' guests have stopped to watch us. We're like a side-show.

"You don't think *I* get tired? Huh? How do you think this disorder feels for *me?*"

"I have no idea how you feel." I go to gulp down more beer, but remember the bottle is empty. I drop my hand by my side.

"Do you think I enjoy being this way?" Ana asks.

I don't want to argue anymore, and I attempt to walk back my last few comments. "I know you're tired, Ana."

"Who is fatigued?" Chace steps in between us. "The party is just getting started, yes?"

How is it this guy always seems to pop up where my wife is concerned?

He grins at me. It's more of a sneer. Then he nods in my direction as if to acknowledge Ana's inebriated state. "I would presume, my dear," he says to her, "that you are never too tired to enjoy a celebration."

It's definitely a sneer.

I take Ana by the arm. "It's time to go," I say. Right now, all I want to do is get out of here before we make bigger fools of ourselves than we already have.

But my wife releases herself and crosses the living room. She bangs her hand on the Buliers' provisional bar. "Barkeep!"

René smiles. He's charmed by her. He apparently finds this kind of abuse humorous.

Ana points to the bottle of Kir.

He places a high ball glass in front of her and fills it to the rim with vermouth.

Chace is right behind her, and I am on his heels. It is a procession of fools. "She is having a good time tonight, yes?" Chace asks.

"She certainly is." I don't bother to hide my annoyance.

"Let your wife have some fun," he says. "Or as we French like to say, *se détendre et se reposer.*" Then he whispers to me, "Let her relax."

Ana is past relaxed, however. She guzzles her drink and orders another. The u-shaped neckline of her dress droops off her shoulder, and a lacy strap peeks out. My wife is a sloppy drunk.

Chace leers at her. He puts an arm around her waist.

I slam my empty beer bottle on the bar.

My wife throws her head back and laughs. Her slinky dress hugs all the right curves.

Chase lowers his voice and compliments her. He's not discreet. He refers to her dress as "sensuous" and "delightful," and references the way it cleaves to her figure. Then he pulls her close.

It's like I'm invisible.

Ana giggles. It's exaggerated and designed to ensure I'm watching.

Oh, I'm watching.

Chace's hand slithers downward along Ana's spine. He fondles her backside. "I appreciate a woman in a thong," he says.

"At least somebody does." My wife drags her fingers through her hair. The recessed lighting in the living room rico-chets off the sapphires in her bracelet and blinds me. I'm ready to end this maelstrom when Chace steers her away from me.

"Médée is in the kitchen, *mon ami*," he calls back. "She would love to talk to you about your new project."

Loser would not even begin to describe how I feel right now.

13
ANA

"Come to me, my wild birdie." Chace closes the door behind us, and he's all hands.

I resist his advance and strut into the center of the room. I toss my bag on the bed and act as if coming upstairs with him to his bedroom is barely noteworthy. Which it is.

The only reason I did it was to make Tony jealous, to make him remember how much he loved me once.

How much he *still* loves me.

He *does* still love me, doesn't he?

Of course, he does.

Chace steers me over to the bed. He's drunk and nearly knocks us both to the floor, but it doesn't deter him. "*Embrassez moi.*" He slurs his words and presses himself against me. He gropes at my crotch. He's not a man who accepts rejection.

"Let's take it slow." I fumble with his hands. I keep them where I can see them.

"*Ah, oui.*" He accepts it as a challenge. "You would enjoy a bit more foreplay, yes?"

I look toward the door. Where is my husband? Why isn't he looking for me?

Chace undoes the buttons on his shirt. "I've waited a long time for you, my dear."

I'm all too clear about what he means. He's referring to a time when Tony and I lived closer to him and Médée, back in Belleville, when the four of us held *salons*, or gatherings, on the rooftop of our building. When we spent our evenings lounging on plastic lawn chairs and marveling at the way the sun melted below the hills. When we drank too much—all except Tony—and we nursed our personal issues and buried them as best we could in countless bottles of Merlot. When we gazed at the stars, and we dreamed and we bickered and we groused about our yet-to-be-determined lives.

It was then, during one of those drunken celebrations, that Chace suggested a four-way. He assumed that since we were all so close, it'd be fun. He didn't think anything would go wrong with a miniature orgy where none of the rules were negotiated ahead of time and nothing was off-limits. The more we discussed it, the hornier we all got, and the closer we came to doing it. If it wasn't for Tony, it would've happened.

Based on Chace's comment, it's been on his bucket list for some time.

I mumble something about needing air and sit up, but the room spins. *Shit.* I lie back down.

Chace continues to undress, and once he's naked, he straddles me. I try to wriggle free of him, but he shoves me back on the bed. He's a mean drunk. "You are a sensual woman," he says. "You should not have to tolerate Tony's nonsense."

Nonsense?

Images of Tony having sex with another woman blast through my brain.

Chace caresses my cheek. "Let me show you real pleasure," he says.

My skin tingles in response, but it's not nearly enough for me to stay and enjoy it. The notion that my husband could be with another woman, coupled with how he's yet to notice I've left the party, makes me livid. I maneuver myself away from Chace and count myself lucky he's too drunk to stop me. I hop off the bed, prepared to find Tony and put a stop to this bullshit, except I don't even know what this bullshit is.

"I am sorry if I've upset you," Chace says. "I will make it better, yes?" He eases himself off the bed and makes his way to the bathroom. He returns with a lit joint between his teeth—and Médée. He inhales and holds it out for his wife. She takes my hand, crosses the room, and seats us both on the bed. Her leg brushes against mine, and she leaves it there. It's a given we're having that threesome tonight.

"Naturally," Chace says. "This would not be a party without my beautiful wife." He retrieves the joint from his wife, pulls a few drags from it, then hands it to me. "I believe you could use a little of this tonight," he says.

I snatch it up so fast, I surprise myself. It's not that I forgot my promise to Tony; it's more that he's not here, nor has he shown any concern for my whereabouts. I bring it to my lips and take a good, long hit, then exhale. I draw again before I pass it to Médée.

"What happened to the good old days?" she asks. Vapor hemorrhages from her lips.

That's a good question. What *did* happen to the good old days? What happened to *us*? What happened to all those times past when she and Chace declared themselves to be our very best friends, and we did the same? When the four of us were confident nothing would ever be more important than who we were and what we had in that moment. When we were certain nothing would change us. Not our professions. Not where we lived. Not our accumulating wealth nor the diverse trajectories of our children. Nothing.

But we have changed, haven't we?

Everyone except me.

I take the weed from Médée and inhale like my life depends on it. It sears my throat, but I force it to stay in.

She plucks the joint from my fingers. "Chace tells me you have heard from your oldest daughter, Chloe?" She squints as she exhales. "How wonderful for you both. You must be so happy."

Médée has a knack for slicing out your heart and returning it to you on a crystal platter.

Anyone who understands my relationship with my oldest daughter should have the wherewithal *not* to frame it in this way, but Médée is too disconnected from others to understand the significance of her comment. What I once identified in her as a relaxed or carefree nature, is in reality a serious emotional gulf between her and everyone else in the world. There was a time when I would've done anything to be Médée's friend.

Chace removes the weed from his wife's hand. "What has it been, ten years since you last saw her?"

"Seven." My voice twists in my throat.

"Ah, seven." Chace again offers the joint to me. How is it my turn so soon? I draw in deep, then lie back on the bed. I take in the ceiling. The Rococo style molding is schmaltzy-looking. Grapevines and conch shells. I guess maybe it's pretty. It's so *them.* Is it the same pattern as the one in the living room? It must be. It looks like the same pattern. But *is* it? Would it be weird if both ceilings were the same? The same. The *same.* Both ceilings are the *same.* Wow. It's so crazy when two things are *exactly* the same. When they appear to be different, but they're really the *same*. I giggle, then look around the room. Tony's still not here.

Médée lies down beside me. Her eyes are slits. "I could never have endured such a tragic separation from any of my children," she says. She looks away; she also stares at the ceiling. "If even one of them had severed me from their life the way Chloe cut you and Tony out of hers . . ." She folds her arms across her chest in a dramatic display of sorrow. "I don't think I could have survived it," she says.

Chace practically crawls over me to get to her. He looks like an old fool stumbling through the bra section at La Perla.

I don't want to see what happens next, and I close my eyes. I feign sleep.

I could fall asleep right now. Right here. On this bed.

"What happened, do you think?" Médée tugs on my dress.

I open my eyes.

"What could have made your daughter leave in such a hostile manner?" she asks.

I brood over the ceiling.

"*Mon Dieu.*" Médée shakes me. "Do you think she discovered the real story? That she was . . . illegitimate?"

Once, in a moment of weakness, I confided in Médée about how I thought Chloe might not be Tony's biological daughter. It was a mistake. While another woman might have found this news upsetting, Médée decided to drive a Gap Stokke baby stroller right through the soul of our relationship. It was the kind of revelation a woman like Médée couldn't tolerate. It wreaked too much havoc on her perpetually cool and casual disposition.

I swallow my emotions. It'd be too easy to unleash them on her. While her dig feels like an attack, she's not my enemy.

With the three of us lying on the same bed together, in various stages of undress, Médée wants me to know Chace is loyal to her, which makes her no different from other women—she's no different from my mother. Or me. She needs Chace. He's critical to her survival. It's this necessity, more than anything, that continues to put women at odds with each other.

I recover my purse and dart into the bathroom. I dig through it until I find the vial of Prozac—my prescription meds —and I pop off the top. Green and white capsules bounce across the floor in all directions. "Crap." I crawl around on all fours, locate them, and force them all back in the bottle—all except two. I pop these in my mouth. Then I find my cell and speed scroll through Cool Babes. Jas sent me a tweet with a GIF. It's a woman. She breathes deeply, then relaxes as she exhales. Millie sent me another video clip of Sassy playing in the backyard. The dog looks so happy. Millie definitely under-stands that any form of media that features dogs will make me feel better. I reply with a beating red heart. I read the tweets from Adel next. She asks the same question in all of them. She wants to know if I'm all right. She demands that I call her. I send a text instead.

Had a rough afternoon! Doing better now.

I strive for upbeat and peppy, though I'm not sure she'll buy it. No sooner do I tap the Reply button, than my phone rings. It's Adel, but I let the call go to voice mail. I shuffle over to the sink, run the cold water, and splash some on my face. I let it dribble down my neck. I don't towel it off.

"A-a-a-a-n-n-a-a-a-a-a-a-a-a," Chace sings through the bathroom door. "We are w-a-a-a-i-i-i-i-i-ting for you-u-u-u-u-u-u-u."

I roll my eyes. My phone dings again, and my home screen lights up. It's Adel.

*Worried for you! Focus on the positives! What's your stress level
1-10?*

I'd say I'm a ten.

My phone dings again. It's Adel. Again.

*Review your life goals! Remind yourself of the good in your
world!*

I don't even finish reading the text when the phone dings
again.

*Your dogs are a sunny spot in your life! Go home and bury your
face in their fur!*

She got that one right.

I cross the bathroom and open a window. The air smells like
rain. While a haze hangs over Paris tonight, the lights of the Palais
du Luxembourg still dazzle. I can't see it from here, but the Medici
Fountain sits somewhere down there, on the same grounds. A
white marble sculpture, it depicts the love story between Acis, the
young shepherd boy, and Galatea, the beautiful sea nymph, and
how their love is in vain as the monstrous cyclops, Polyphemus,
lurks behind them. Sometimes borderline personality disorder
feels like this: like a demon that wreaks havoc on your life and cuts
you off from everyone you love. And you can't hide or outrun it.

Maybe I do need therapy.

It's a long shot, but I call Dr. Woodhouse. I'm certain he's
left the office for the day, but I can leave a message with his
answering service—say I'd like to do a phone consult with
him. Except when the service answers and the woman asks for
my name, I can't get the words out. I can't speak at all.

I press End.

I call Evelyn next.

"*Allo?* Uh. . . yes, *allo?*" She sounds sleepy.

"Hey, hon," I say. "It's Mom. Did I wake you?"

"What's wrong? Where are you?" she asks.

I know I shouldn't, but I count on Evelyn to steady me.

"I'm fine," I say. "I . . ."

"Are you drunk? You sound drunk."

"Honey, I'm fine. Really." I'm slurring my words. I can't hide it. Yet, before I consider the consequences of the following statement, it's out of my mouth. "Your father and I had a fight. I think he doesn't love me anymore."

Silence.

Her loss for words nearly breaks me. Tony may be an asshole of a husband, but he's still Evelyn's father and I splutter out an apology. Then I bawl into the phone. It lurches out of me in waves.

My daughter clears her throat. "*Christ*," she mumbles. "Look, Mom." There's real fear in her voice. "I don't know what happened between you and Dad, but you'll straighten it out. You've weathered a lot together. You just need to talk about it."

I'm an ass for alarming her like this, and I stop crying. "I know, honey." I blow my nose on one of the Buliers' nicer towels and pull myself together. I'm prepared to give her another apology and end the call when she whispers to someone.

She's not alone.

"You're right," I say. "Your father and I will figure this out. It's late. I shouldn't have called."

She whispers again in French. A voice whispers back. It's a woman's voice. Is there a woman in Evelyn's bedroom with her? At this late hour?

"I wanted to hear a kind voice," I say.

Is my daughter involved with a woman? Why did she think she couldn't share this with me? Doesn't she trust me?

"Are you sure?" Evelyn asks. "I could make some coffee and sit up with you. For a little while, at least."

She's so frightened she'll do the wrong thing, so nervous

she'll disappoint others—disappoint me. *I did this to her.* I yelled at her too much when she was growing up. I railed at them all. I was forever angry over one thing or another. It's why *none* of my daughters trust me. Children need to feel safe to want to talk to their parents, and it won't happen if all the parent does is criticize them. I clear my throat. I can barely swallow, the guilt is so thick.

"We had some good times when you and your sisters were growing up?" I ask. "Didn't we?"

"Why are you asking me this?"

"As a family," I say, "you never thought your home life was . . . traumatic? Or abusive? Did you?"

"Okay, Mom. You're scaring me. What's with the weird questions?"

"I want to know how much I loused things up for the three of you."

"You didn't mess anything up for us. My childhood was great. Meadow's childhood was great. Chloe was a pain in the ass, but—"

"Chloe wasn't a pain in the ass," I say. "I was, and I should've raised her better."

"Don't talk like that."

"I should've been a better mother to her, Evelyn."

"Mom, Chloe—"

"Chloe's a good girl. She could've been a better girl, but she didn't get what she needed from me, and that's on me."

"No, Mom."

"Look, honey. It's late. You're a wonderful daughter."

She speaks away from the phone, low and hushed.

"A mother couldn't ask for better. I love you, baby." I press End. I've bothered her enough with my petty problems.

I fumble through my purse for more Prozac. I pop two more before I tiptoe across the bathroom and open the door in time to see Chace coo at Médée. He flicks his tongue along her lips and murmurs to her in French. When he sees me in the doorway, he makes a production of thrusting his tongue in and out of Médée's mouth like some distorted version of a blow job. I slam the door, sink to the floor, and cross my legs in front of me.

Jesus, I fucked this night up, but good.

14

TONY

Someone knocks on the door.

"I'll be right out." For God's sake, will you look at me? I'm holed up in the Bulier's guest bathroom because I'm too uneasy and embarrassed to go out and look for my wife. I need to stop this—I need to stop *her* from doing whatever it is she plans to do with Chace.

What *does* she plan to do with Chace?

She can't *honestly* intend to have sex with him, can she?

If this is another one of her outrageous ploys to make me jealous, it won't work.

I clobber the door with my fist.

Blast it all.

I smack the door again.

I refuse to play into Ana's little game. I pace the floor. I run the hot water, then turn it off, then parade across the floor again. "Blast it, Ana." I box with the shower door, though not too hard. It closes and knocks a sponge off the ledge. I don't pick it up.

I won't fall for this.

Blast it all.

But she's my wife. If I don't look for her, everyone will think I'm the same old dumb-ass my father said I was, and who would blame them? It's not like I ever argued with him, or told him what I thought.

No one did.

We would've been seen as weak in his eyes, and nobody wanted that. Vincenzo DiSalvo, or Enzo as his buddies called him, was an angry, *angry* man. He'd chased my mother away much too early in their marriage, and he'd never stopped stewing over how she'd left him alone to raise five boys all while constructing a multimillion-dollar asphalt business. The last thing he expected from my four brothers or me was disobedience which made for a tricky undertaking when I refused his offer to run his business with him. I was eighteen. I had just graduated from high school. Laying asphalt for a living was the furthest thing from my mind.

"You're it, Antonio." He stood behind the silver bumper of his pride and joy: a Mack tank. He gave it a pat. "This is it, boy," he said. "The big enchilada."

I scrunched up my nose. My brother, Vinny, hadn't been in the ground even a year. Sweet, sensitive Vinny. He was the son who couldn't do anything right. The brother who broke the easiest, acquiesced the quickest, and held on to his grievances the longest, if he let them go at all. While Vinny never learned how to cope with my father's constant demands to perform, like the rest of us, he found a way out, and by nineteen, he was mainlining heroin on the streets of New Haven.

My father did his best to intervene. I'll give him that. He schlepped my brother from one luxurious rehab to the next in the hope that somebody would give Vinny a reason to live, but it never happened, and in the winter of 1985, my brother changed our lives forever. With all of us home that year to celebrate the holidays, my dad got drunk, again, and launched into a tirade about Vinny's drug abuse—a scene that never went well. That year, however, Vinny finished the argument—for good. He barricaded himself in the basement, balanced my father's Colt Mustang .380 between his teeth, and drove a bullet through his brain.

Merry fucking Christmas.

I was barely sixteen, but the significance of my brother's decision was not lost on me. It placed me next in line to fulfill my father's dream of handing down the business to one of his sons. By default, I'd become *the* chosen one. While I should've been ecstatic at the chance to be my father's favorite son, I'd wanted no part of it. What if what happened to my brother happened to me?

I was terrified. I couldn't chance it.

I moved out and never looked back. I moved to the city—New York City. I wanted to live someplace that afforded me the one thing I prized more than anything else in the world: control. So, when I was awarded a full scholarship to NYU, I took it. It was exactly what I needed to get me out from under my father's debilitating influence.

Damn it, I am *not* a dumb-ass.

I open the door and step out of the bathroom. There's an old man standing in the hallway, sucking on a Lucky Strike for all it's worth. "Take your time," he says. "When I finish my smoke, it is only to my wife's side I shall return."

I simper at him and make tracks through the living room. I sprint over to the staircase and brace myself against the railing. I place one foot on the bottom step. I place my other foot—nowhere. It melds to the carpet. I can't move. Blast it to hell. My wife is upstairs engaged in God knows what with my boss, and I'm standing here, at the foot of the staircase, paralyzed with anxiety.

Have I no guts at all?

I don't want to fight with Ana. It's a sure bet she'll blow her top and embarrass us both the minute I find her. I'd also wager that Chace will never forget this, and he's been known to hold a grudge against those who've provoked him.

But she's my wife. And she's upstairs, alone with him, in his bedroom.

I breathe in deep and analyze the staircase. I count fourteen steps. I do this a second time. Yes, there are fourteen. If I take them one at a time, incorporate a twelve-inch stride, and with a gait of, say, zero-point-zero-eight seconds, it'd take me four-point-two seconds to get up to the second floor. Let's say I recalculate this formula, however, and incorporate a more robust eighteen-inch stride, and a speed of, oh, I don't know, zero-point-one-two seconds. It's possible I could get to the second floor in two-point-two-zero—for crying out loud. Will you listen to me? My wife is upstairs knocking boots with my supervisor, and I'm down here calculating the variance between my assorted movements.

This is ridiculous. I'm ridiculous.

I dither around at the base of the stairs, but my inane jealousy and suspiciousness begin to outweigh my self-flagellation, and I try again. I plant my foot on the bottom step and lean into it. I hold the railing with one hand while I bury the other in my pocket.

Christ, now I look like the fucking Marlboro man.

I step away from the staircase and scan the room for another plate of tartlets when my father's voice explodes in my head.

You're a dumb-ass, boy.

That's it! I turn and charge the stairs. I take them two at a time and hit the second-floor landing with a jolt—big mistake as I'm too old for this. While I feel the slightest degree of a pinch in my lower back, I refuse to take it in. I sprint down the hall and head straight for the master bedroom where I position myself in front of the door and listen. But I can't hear a thing, so I lean in closer and flatten my ear against the wood. Noise emanates from the other side. I press myself further, and I can hear a man's voice. He's laughing, teasing; a woman's voice giggles in response.

Sweet Mother of God.

That's *Ana*!

15
ANA

I turn the corner.

Tony is standing outside of Chace and Médée's bedroom. He has his ear pressed to their door. "Ana?" he asks.

About an hour ago, I seized the opportunity to sneak out of their bathroom, tiptoe across the hall, and hide in their son's room, where I cried. Then I convinced myself Tony never bothered to look for me.

Yet he's here.

The fairy tale lives. The dream still holds true. Tony is my Knight in Shining Armor. He continues to desire me the way Francis Scott yearned for Zelda, or John Lennon cherished Yoko, or JFK Jr. required Carolyn Bessette. He remains the Heathcliff to my Catherine, the Rivera to my Kahlo, the Sid to my Nancy. His promise to love me unconditionally goes on.

But that's how it is in all the great love stories, isn't it? There's no point in living if someone doesn't want you. There's no reason to exist if there isn't at least one other person who'll stop dead in their tracks to touch your hand, or taste your kiss, or smell your skin. This planet is a wasteland if there isn't some other person in your cosmos who's ready to risk everything to get between your thighs, then go weak in the knees when you let them.

It's ecstasy; it's absolute symbiosis.

My husband swears under his breath. "Honestly, Ana. What the hell did you do *now?*"

Until it all falls apart and crushes you.

16

TONY

Rain peppers the windshield. I turn the key, and the Renault flinches with a low, sluggish whine. The passenger side door swings open, and Ana tumbles into the front seat. She fumbles with her seat belt. She provides neither an apology nor an explanation about what happened between Chace and her tonight. I shift into first, stomp on the gas, and the hatchback lurches into oncoming traffic.

Ana's head bumps backward against the seat.

Still, she says nothing.

I jam the vehicle into fifth and enter the circle at the Place Edmond Rostand at close to fifty miles an hour. I swerve around the Fontaine du Bassin Soufflot. I take the rotary much sharper than necessary.

Her cheek hits the passenger side window. She turns to me. Her expression is fierce.

"So." I grip the steering wheel. "Do you want to tell me what you and Chace were up to in his bedroom?"

"What are you, my father?" She fingers the hemline of her dress.

"No. I'm your husband, and I'd like to know why the two of you were alone together."

"I don't appreciate how that sounds."

"All right," I say. "How about this? Did you fuck Chace while we were at the party?"

"Why do you care?"

"If you plan to cheat on me again, and with my supervisor this time . . ."

"Do you think you will ever stop hurling my affair in my face?"

I guffaw and dribble saliva all over my chin. Her lack of humility infuriates me.

"That's funny?" Ana rakes some wayward hairs behind her ears.

"No, sweetheart, discussing your illicit affair is never humorous."

"It was twenty-three years ago."

"Not for me, sweetheart. For me, it's like it happened yesterday."

"You can stop with the 'sweethearts,' *sweetheart*."

"Hell, it was the defining act of our marriage."

Ana yells. She's so loud, the car vibrates.

I can't understand a word she's saying. I grit my teeth so hard my head hurts. Then I step on the gas and cut the corner too sharp onto Boulevard Saint-Martin. I change lanes without using my blinker, and I punch it. I can't get us home fast enough.

"Where were *you* during the party?" she asks. "What was so important that you couldn't save me from Chace's advances?"

I weigh the pros and cons of telling her how I found her, but couldn't bring myself to go inside Chace's bedroom. What does it matter? It's not relevant to this argument, and it doesn't excuse my wife's decision to . . . what *did* she do with Chace? And why does she smell like marijuana?

The rain comes down harder and pummels the roof of the car. It's an effort to see more than ten feet in front of me. The vehicle hydroplanes, and I clutch the wheel and make a mad dash around the Place de la République. The tourists left hours ago; the square is empty.

"You need to give up this baseless idea that we're going to somehow become the ideal family." Ana folds her arms across her chest and looks away.

I chafe at my wife's comment, but I hold my tongue. Ana has resurrected the one argument that means anything to me, and if we intend to get anywhere with it, one of us needs to stay levelheaded.

"Chloe destroyed everything good between us," she says.

I crank the wheel and careen toward the cemetery. Between the downpour and the continuous thump of the wipers, I can't even hear myself think. I turn onto Rue de la Réunion and hit the brake, hard. The front-end spasms. I aim straight for the parking garage, where I ram the car onto the sidewalk and head for the open door. I'm a raging firestorm, and with my foot still heavy on the gas, I spiral downward through the various levels of concrete. The tires screech at me, but I don't let up until we hit bottom, at which point I slice the vehicle into the last available space, jam it into first, and wrench the keys out of the ignition. The overheated engine ticks and pings.

I turn and look Ana straight in the eye. Thunder shreds the ground beneath us. It rattles everything: the garage, the car, me. I pray this is not a premonition about how the rest of this conversation will go. But if I ever want to see my daughter again . . . "I need you to think long and hard about what I'm about to say to you."

My wife glares at me.

"I want us to be together again as a family," I say. "*All* of us. Even Chloe."

"It's not possible," Ana says.

I bristle at her response. I'm teetering like Humpty Dumpty here, and if I don't find a stronghold soon, I'll fall and smash myself into a million pieces. I'm preparing my rebuttal, when I happen to glance in the rearview mirror. A pair of young lovers stroll hand in hand in our direction. As they pass, the woman angles her head, peers into our car, and whispers to her companion, who pulls her close and kisses her on the cheek. It's evident Ana and I are in the middle of a heated argument, and it's all I can do not to rocket out of this car and shake them both silly for their smugness. See, I know what they're thinking because Ana and I once thought it too—when we would never have believed our marriage would end up this way. When we, too, murmured, and whispered, and promised each other we'd never be *that* couple: the husband and wife who so easily came undone by their own unbearable rancor, unmet passions, and unrelenting spitefulness.

The point Ana and I are at tonight.

How easy it is to forget your promises to each other.

I turn to my wife. "You sound like you're unwilling to try," I say.

"I told you, Chloe's different. She's not like Evelyn. Or Meadow. She never loved me."

"Maybe if you hadn't made yourself so unlovable—"

"Chloe rejected me the moment she was born. She wouldn't make eye contact. She refused my nipple. She screamed all the time."

My wife's comments are outlandish. It's not the way I remember my oldest daughter at all. Chloe was a bright and joyful child, and definitely one who didn't deserve the mistreatment she received from my wife. "You punished her all the time," I say.

Ana looks off into the darkness.

"You were on her constantly and about the most insignificant things."

"They weren't insignificant."

"It was like you saw red whenever she was concerned."

"The girl needed discipline."

"Nonsense. There's discipline, then there's *discipline*. What you did to her—"

"You weren't there. You didn't see everything that went on."

"I didn't need to be there."

"You didn't see what she did to me."

"You liked to fight with her. You must have since you attacked her every chance you had."

"I told you, I *wanted* to love her," she says. "I didn't have it in me."

"That makes no sense."

"What are you saying? *I* make no sense?"

"I wish—"

"Why must you treat me like a mental patient?"

"Why must you *act* like a mental patient?"

"Jesus Christ, I can't believe you say this stuff to me, knowing it triggers me."

"For crying out loud, Ana. *Everything* triggers you." I roll my head from side to side. I wish I could beat it against the windshield until I'm anesthetized. "You're a therapist," I say. "You should know this stuff."

"Stop saying that. Just because I have a degree in psych, doesn't mean I can diagnose myself. No therapist can do that. My God, Tony. Fool for a lawyer."

I look away. I hate it when she's right.

"My childhood sucked."

"Lots of people had childhoods that sucked." I lower my voice. "You're not the only one."

Ana clutches her head in her hands. "It wasn't supposed to be this way," she says. "You were The One."

My forehead is throbbing. In the past twenty-four hours, I have not had a single conversation with my wife that didn't devolve into a grim recap of our past. "Good God, not this again," I say.

"You lied to me." Ana's unreasonableness returns with a vengeance. She kicks at the car door, and it flies open. She reaches for the door handle, but she misses it and falls out of the car. "Why couldn't you keep your promise?" She claws at the swinging door.

I leap out of the car and race around the front of it.

"I knew you'd break it." Ana rights herself. "I knew you couldn't keep it." She drags her palms across the hood, then hammers them down on top of it.

The explosion rips a hole through my head, and I, too, bang on the hood—all too aware I've plowed headfirst into the belly of my wife's madness.

"Nice, asshole," she says.

Blood pounds inside my cheeks. "Get out of my sight, Ana." I raise my fist and shake it like a two-year-old.

"Why couldn't you love me?"

The sound of my wife's heart turning into rubble does not go unnoticed, but it's too late. My rampage swings into high gear. "I swear to God, I don't know what I'll do if you don't—"

"You don't have the balls." Ana drapes herself across the front of the car like a show model. Spittle winks at me from the corners of her mouth.

I do an about-face. I aim for the stairwell when my wife verbally attacks me from behind.

"That's what your father said about you, isn't it?" she asks. Her voice eviscerates me into a jillion piddling pieces.

"That you don't have the guts," she says. "You're a pussy."

I grab on to the doorknob. The thing quivers in my hand.

"Do you hear me, Tony?" she shouts at me. "You're a loser."

I turn and face her. I trudge back across the garage until I'm inches from her face.

Ana stands straight. She looks me in the eye. "What? You want to hit me?"

My feet congeal to the cement floor. I can't move closer to her, and I can't turn away.

"I dare you." She usurps my personal space. She's like a gang member dying to rumble.

I ball my hands into sturdy fists.

"You won't do it," she says.

The sour smell of her breath makes me nauseous.

"You're a dumb-ass," she says.

She strikes at me with the worst disparagement she can find. It pummels my core, and my extremities go weak. In fact, my whole body becomes numb. The garage fades away, and my mind grows dark. "Livid" doesn't come close to defining how ticked off I am.

This isn't the way I wanted to tell Ana—or maybe it is. At this point, it hardly matters because it's how I do it.

"She's mine," I say.

"What?" My wife's face goes blank.

"Chloe," I say. "She's mine. She has my DNA." I release the tension in my hands.

"That's a lie," she says.

"Oh, but it's not, *darling*. Chloe is my biological daughter."

"She can't be."

"Maybe you forgot that while you were busy boning your famous artiste boyfriend you were also screwing me."

"No, it's . . . it's not possible."

The alarm in her voice angers me further. My wife has practically admitted to her desire to birth that man's child. The thought of it jars my nerves, and I cackle at her. "I purchased a blood test. The results are in, darling. Chloe is all mine."

My wife is mute.

"Chloe is *our* daughter. Yours and mine."

My wife is beside herself. She looks as if she's about to have kittens. I move closer and whisper in her ear. "Surprise." Then I turn on my heel, and once again, I march off in the direction of the stairs.

I have my hand on the doorknob when the clacking sound of my wife's heels mushrooms up behind me. I spin around to see Ana charging at me, brandishing a knife. The blade winks beneath the lights.

"Fucking fuck!" I lunge at the door handle, throw open the door, and hurtle myself through it. I slam it shut and propel the full weight of my body against it, hoping beyond hope it will hold.

The door bounces on its hinges. My wife releases a string of accusations and beats on the metal barrier with her fists.

I drive my shoulder into it even further.

Then, as fast as it started, the ambush ends. The garage is quiet.

I open the door and peer out.

My wife crosses the garage. Her legs buckle, and she disappears behind a row of parked cars.

"Shall I leave a light on?" I know full well she didn't hear me.

I don't repeat it.

I descend the stairs.

17
ANA

The door to the stairwell bristles as it slams shut.

I look down at the knife still in my hand. Oh, God. I drop it. I went after my husband with my knife. Jesus. I just tried to kill my own husband.

More thunder barrels through the garage, vibrating the ground, then it's quiet again.

What is happening?

Tony is Chloe's father—her biological father? How can this be true?

I sit up and rest my head against the guard rail. I stare into space, yet all I see in front of me are Chloe's eyes; a dark cobalt blue like the color of beach stones in Indonesia, or newly minted steel, or Venetian glassware. Eyes a cool Maya blue like the color of—

"The Mediterranean."

It *is* true. So, why do I feel so betrayed? It's what I've wanted, isn't it? To be connected to Tony like two pieces of silk sewn together with the same thread?

Or is it?

I holler out, but the garage is empty, and my voice only echoes off the walls. My eyes well up. Snot drips from my nose, and I wipe at it with the back of my hand, then I pick myself up and search through my purse for my cell. I dial Dr. Woodhouse again.

He answers this time. "Ana?" he asks. "Is this you? Are you all right?"

I want to respond. I want to tell him, no, I'm not okay. I'm sick from helping myself to too many glasses of sadness and dizzyingly large helpings of regret. I'd like him to know how I'd hoped I could be a good mother to Chloe and a better daughter to my mom. Only I didn't know how to do either one. I ache to ask him how a single human being can feel so ridiculously alone and unloved for so much of their life, but the question sounds too absurd.

"Ana, please talk to me," he says. "Let me help you with what you're going through."

His voice is kind, and his words are genuine, but I'm not ready, and I end the call.

As I dig back into my evening bag, hoping I've stashed a roach in a side pocket, a small bird dive-bombs me. I duck to avoid the strike, and the bird flies off, leaving me with goose-bumps but unharmed. From its markings, I can see it's a wood-warbler; the same species of bird that befriends Kooks each summer.

Why is it here, in this garage?

It beats its honey-speckled wings and orbits the ramp area, then it twists, loops, and pivots back in my direction. It zips past me a second time and aims straight for the canopy lighting where it flutters a bit before it settles along a strip of metal wiring only inches below the lights.

I weigh the bird's state again, the reason it's flying around this car-port, and in such an erratic manner, when it hits me.

It's the lights. Warblers use the moon to navigate, and the artificial lighting has flooded its internal radar. It's confused, and it can't find a way out.

This is bad.

What if it flies around in circles all night and exhausts itself?

What if it *dies*?

In my head, I see the warbler lying motionless on the cold concrete. Dear God, I can't let that happen.

The bird cries out from its perch. *Chip, chip, chip, chip, chip, chip, chip.*

I jog toward it, but it takes flight and zigzags across the garage again. It circles the area and comes to rest along the same stretch of wiring. It emits another staccato of toots. *Chip, chip, chip, chip, chip, chip, chip.*

I climb onto a nearby car and lunge at it, but I'm too slow.

The bird eludes me, flits about beneath the cement eaves, then lands again.

We eyeball each other from our respective posts. The warbler bobs its head; its posture droops.

Is it weeping?

It calls out another string of thin whistles. *Chip, chip, chip, chip, chip, chip.*

I have to save it, and I try to get closer, but it spooks and darts off. I squint into the lights, but I don't see it. I hop off the car's hood and comb the aisles, then search between the lanes of parked cars, but I can't find it anywhere when it shoots past me again. It releases another shrill staccato of cheeps.

It's here! The bird is still here. I clap my hands and skip along beneath it.

The warbler doesn't wait for me. It tours the area yet another time, only its wings are beginning to beat slower. It's tired and losing strength.

This can't be happening!

My childhood religious education rings in my ears, and I recite the Apostles' Creed, but all I can remember is the opening line. So, I attempt an Our Father instead, but I've forgotten the words to this devotion as well. That's when I chant the Hail Mary. Over and over I say it, singing out to the Blessed Mother with pure words, holy words, because only another woman would understand this ache.

The warbler whooshes through the garage one more time. It settles on another strip of wire. *Chip, chip, chip, chip, chip, chip.*

It sings the song of its soul.

It sings for a better life.

I will not let it die.

I look around and note where the bird is perched, how close it is to the stairwell, how it's adjacent to where the garage floor slopes upward and connects to the next level. What if I chase the warbler higher through the different floors until we get to the main level? Could I guide it out and return it to the sky where it belongs?

I don't know, but I have to try.

I approach the warbler and gingerly wave my arms.

It startles and hops deeper into the complex.

That won't work. Think, Ana. Think.

Then it hits me.

I run back to my purse and shake everything out of it. Cracker crumbs scatter across the cement. I sweep them into a pile, collect them in my hand, and choose one, then I sprint back to the warbler, lay it on the ground, and step back.

The bird scoops it up and returns to its wire. It swallows the crumb whole.

That's it! It's hungry. I zoom across the landing and drop a second piece, then back away again.

The warbler scrutinizes the area, then dives at the crumb. It eats this one in a frenzy as well. Yes! This will work. We repeat this process several more times, and each time, the warbler follows me through a new and higher level of the car park. When we get to the final platform, I stop and collect myself.

The yellow-breasted warbler takes a post opposite me. It eyes me, then tilts its head. *Chip, chip, chip, chip.*

"C'mon, Ana," I say out loud. "You can do this."

I wave the last bit of wafer at the bird. If it follows me this final time, it'll clear this place, regain its sense of direction, and be on its way. So, with one eye on the warbler, I inch back toward the open doorway, where I stop, place the crumb on the ground, and sprint out of the garage.

Outside on the sidewalk, I look up. The sky is clear, the rain has ended, and the moon is a white ball of glowing light. I turn back toward the garage and look for the warbler, to see if there's any more I can do for it, but the bird with the steely wings and the devout heart has been reborn. It whooshes past me. Up, up, up, it soars as it races toward its destiny.

Free.

18

TONY

Holy hell, my wife just tried to *murder* me.

I kick off my shoes, shuffle down the hall, and crumble at the kitchen table. I press my forehead to the wood and work to calm myself down, but my heart is pounding so hard it feels like I'm going into cardiac arrest. Could I be going into cardiac arrest? Sweet Mother of Jesus, my wife almost *executed* me a few minutes ago. I'm lucky I'm *not* having a coronary infarction.

When my breathing slows to a steadier pace, I lift my head. A note card sits propped against our salt shaker. Three miniature kittens in tutus pirouette across the front. I don't need to see anymore. The card is from Janot Lever, our friend and neighbor who lives below us. She watches our dogs whenever Ana and I go out, and she writes a few words about the night before she leaves. Tonight, she says everything went fine, so she left early when Meadow got home.

Meadow's home? She was supposed to be away for the weekend. Did her boyfriend cancel their plans? Someone, please tell me my daughter did not have a fight with Aurelien.

He's such a fine young man; he's an economist like myself. He's smart. He's upstanding—for crying out loud, can anyone do *anything* right around here?

I get up and cross the kitchen. I take out my BlackBerry and call Didi.

She answers pronto, but I can tell I've woken her.

"I can't talk," I say. "I needed to hear your voice, that's all." It's late, and I should explain myself, but I'm as hot as a cattle prod and nowhere near ready to discuss tonight's commotion. "Ana's in the car," I say. "Or she's lying face down behind the car. I have no idea. We had another argument, but it's late, and you don't need all the details."

Didi says it's okay because she's awake now, and she asks what happened.

"The evening was a calamity." I peruse the cabinets for a snack. "I really called to say you were accurate, about what you said about my marriage. It's a sham."

Didi probes me about the party, but I don't want to discuss my wife anymore.

"Hey," I say. "Good luck with your visit this weekend. With your girls. It'll be great, really great. I know it will because you're great, Didi. You're so wonderful, and I don't deserve you."

She continues to pepper me with questions. She wants to know about Ana's mental state and its effect on our family. She says she's concerned about my wife's competency to provide for our daughters.

This topic is too intense for me, however, and I zone out and opt for a change of scenery. I scuff down the hall, traverse the living room, and throw open the French doors. I step onto the balcony, careful not to disturb any of Ana's greenery, and I check the street below. I note how the bar next door is still open, and I half expect to see my wife stumble through their front door on her way inside, but there's no sign of her.

I'm still half listening when I catch Didi's last remark. It sounds like she thinks I'm to blame for the fight, and I puff up my chest. "I didn't start it," I say. "Having a DNA test done was the best decision I ever made. I didn't want to tell her like that, but I had to defend myself." Didi quickly rattles off a cluster of legal terms like "summons" and "petitions" and says her primary concern is for our future. Then she tosses around some more legal gobbledygook, and even though I don't understand any of it, it reassures me she's on my side, and I shut up and relax.

I search the length of the street again, but there's still no sign of Ana.

With my adrenaline now reasonably decelerated, I tell Didi I'll call her in the morning, and we can finish this conversation then. Honestly, I'd rather not finish it at all except I don't want to upset her. I've had enough conflict for one night. I don't think I could handle any more.

I pad back into the kitchen, set my cell on the table, and open the refrigerator door. I debate making a sandwich, but I'm too tired. I should just end this night and go to bed. So, I stretch out my back and head back down the hall to our bedroom.

I'm passing Meadow's bedroom, when I see her door is ajar. I stop short in front of it. Is she really home? I tap it and peek inside. Her duffel bag is open and clothing is scattered around the room. A human shape fills the bed. She *is* home. My chest loosens knowing she's safe, and I quietly close her door and continue on to Chloe's old room. I give her door a light rap as well, and my eyes turn glossy. Can I really go in there again? It's like I'm stuck in time—like someone hit the replay button in my head and my last memory of her is on repeat.

I force myself to enter, and I sit on her bed. Images of our last winter together race through my head. It snowed so much that year, it disrupted all our schedules. Schools closed, businesses shuttered their doors, and the city refused to plow the streets. It was hard to get anything done. We couldn't even run the most mundane of errands, and it would be days before any of us could get out of the house, for anything. We were confined together behind these same four walls.

I roamed the apartment, who knows how many times. I'm sure I was debating how I could get organized when I passed Chloe's room and looked inside. She was sitting cross-legged on her bed, strumming her guitar. She looked up, caught me in the doorway, and stopped playing, but she laughed. It was dynamic and hardy, and it filled the room with her fiery spirit. Chloe's happiness was like that; it had a way of consuming you. She was similar to her mother in that respect: their mirth is infectious.

"Pretty sneaky," she said. "What's this, your third day *trapped* in the house?" It was a gentle rebuke of my Type A personality.

I sat on her bed. "Wow," I said. "Whatever it was you were playing, it sounded nice from the hallway."

She toyed with the bedspread.

Her reaction threw me. I'd never known her to be shy, so I prodded her to play some more. "Know any songs by Journey?" I asked.

She made some snarky comment about my age and strummed a few classic chord progressions, then stopped playing again. She wouldn't look at me.

When had my firebrand of a daughter become so self-conscious and insecure? I plowed ahead. I sang the first verse of one of their more popular songs, stopping intermittently to joke about how my voice was lousy but how I also didn't care because the song was for her. When I tackled the next verse, or as much of it as I could remember, Chloe joined me. Once we reached the chorus, she took the harmony, and I stayed with the melody. It was a beautiful effort on both our parts, and when we finished, we sat in silence together and shared the moment.

I don't remember what happened next. Undoubtedly, I spent the rest of the week writing another useless research paper or developing another absurd grant I thought might further my career. What I do recall is Chloe and I never sang together like that again.

Again and again, I talk about how much I've wanted us to be a family, yet I've wasted the opportunity every time it's been presented and all because of my vindictive attitude and my overblown ego. Chace is right. There is no more reliable statement about me than this: all I know is academia. The part he neglected to mention was the reason. It's because I lack the courage to tackle anything in the emotional realm. I'm afraid to take the risk, even in love.

Especially in love.

Maybe I should've shown Ana more tenderness when we arrived in Europe. Perhaps I could've listened more closely when she said she was lonely, and she needed me to be more attentive. Instead, I refused to let her stand in the way of my career. I committed myself to becoming a junior faculty member at a preeminent university, and I left her on her own. I was so hard on her. What was I supposed to do, though? She wanted to have a baby. A baby! We were scarcely getting by as it was, we were so dependent on her father's money, and all she could think about was having a baby.

I never thought she'd break our marriage vows.

Now I have Didi, and it's like I'm twenty-eight again. I'm as excited as when I first fell in love with Ana. I loved my wife once. I did, but I let it wither away, and it's too late now to save it.

So, I guess that's that.

I turn out the light in the bathroom, cross the bedroom, and drape my jacket over the back of Ana's chaise. The blouse Ana wore earlier today continues to hang there, and I'm careful not to let the two garments touch. I strip to my boxers and nosedive into bed, but I'm sweltering, and I can't sleep. So, I throw off the covers, but I'm still hot. I force my eyes to shut, but I'm wide awake.

My groin stirs.

Should I? Masturbation will definitely help me sleep. I'm a little self-conscious, but I edge my hand under the waistband of my boxers anyway and evoke sexy images of Didi like how she stands before me wearing her best lacy undergarments. They're red hot, and she toys with one of the bra straps and lets it drop from her shoulder, then she unhooks it and removes it. She looks at me. She wants me. She wants me bad. She asks me to give it to her good, and, oh boy, that's exactly what I'm going to do. I'm going to give it to her so good—

I stop. Nothing is going on down there.

I change position. This time, I visualize her sitting in a chair. She's in a peek-a-boo-bra and matching panties. She touches herself and beckons me to come closer. She shows me what she wants me to do to her . . .

I stop again. Nope. *Still* nothing.

What about a different fantasy? Maybe another position would help, except it's late and I'm getting tired, so I yawn and close my eyes, but I keep my hand on my privates. You never know, it could still happen.

∾

I wake from a dead sleep and pat Ana's side of the bed. It's empty. I sit up and look over. She's not here. The muscles in my lower back pull like a tightrope across Niagara Falls. I check the clock. It's 4:36 a.m. This is all my fault. I should never have told her about the paternity test. Should I search for her? Should I call around to the hospitals? Should I alert the police?

I bury my face in my pillow. I don't want do this again. I want to go back to sleep. Ana is a big girl. She'll find her own way home. I am *not* her savior. I don't want to be her Prince Charming anymore.

"Blast it all." I leap out of bed. The apartment is dark. What if something bad happened? Why did I have to argue with her? Why did I have to tell her I had a paternity test done? I will rue this night for the rest of my life. Good God, would you listen to me? Do I have to make everything about me? I accelerate my gait until I reach the living room. I swing around the corner and stop. I hear breathing. It's hampered and irregular, but it's definitely coming from the living room.

My wife is here.

Thank goodness she's home.

What if she cut herself again? I flail my hands in the air. I let out a litany of swears without uttering a sound. It's been a long time since I've washed and bandaged her wounds. What if she hit a vein? Dear God, what if she's bleeding out? No, no, no, no, no! The fluttery sensation in my stomach escalates, and I latch on to the arm of the couch and peer into the dark. I can almost make out a body there on the floor.

Why did I do it? Why did I have to tell her about Chloe?

Dear God, please don't die on me now.

19
ANA

The sun rises, and the Prussian blue skyline erupts in a spray of rose and lavender. In the foreground, starlings line my neighbors' cable wires, reflecting the new light off their iridescent backs. Without warning, they upswell in a poetic display of murmuration, each one rolls as its neighbor rolls, loops as its neighbor loops, all connected by an invisible thread so mystical, so sensual, it's beyond our comprehension.

I'm like the starling: when Tony reasons, I understand; when he succeeds, I blossom; and when he dreams, I see our future.

It's a deficiency I've yet to overcome.

I sit up and massage the cramp in the center of my knee. Kooks's soot-stained eyes scrutinize me as he tries to make sense of what happened here last night. I attempt to scratch the fur between his brows, but he shifts position and sniffs my oncoming hand. He wants to know if the worst is over. I embrace his frosty muzzle and give it a scratch. He's still a little unsure, but he accepts my offer of peace and lumbers off. He sinks to the floor and extends his hind legs. He wakes Dharma who lifts her head and looks at me. She thumps her tail. She's happy I'm here and awake, content the house is calm again. What would I do without these two? Dogs teach us about real love, so we can know it and demonstrate it for others.

A lesson I'd do well to remember.

Last night, I found Tony's BlackBerry on the kitchen table, and I rifled through his call log. There was one entry I didn't recognize. It was marked "No Caller ID." He's called it on a frequent basis. A very continual basis. Including last night. The son of a bitch phoned someone minutes after he left me bawling in the parking garage.

Is this it? Is this the "nonsense" Chace referred to at the party? Is my husband contacting another woman?

Is he *cheating* on me?

I had to sit down. I couldn't see straight and was afraid I might black out, right there on the kitchen floor. Images of Tony and a strange woman flooded my mind. Images of them in bed together. In *our* bed together. Naked. Tony's face jammed between her thighs.

Jesus.

My head feels buoyant, and I lie back down on the rug. I unwind the towel around my arm, but the fibers tug at the raw incisions, so I leave it alone and pull my knees in tight and hug my chest. I cut myself again last night. I couldn't help it. My guts were spilling out all over the floor, and I didn't know how to make it stop.

I didn't grow up in a family surrounded by real love. While it might've looked like I had it all, that wasn't my whole story. My father thought if he bought us everything we wanted, we'd be happy, and it'd be enough. Except the truth is more complicated than that. We weren't, and it wasn't. Wealth isn't love, and if you don't have love, you don't have anything. Like me. I grew up believing no one wanted me, so I spent the rest of my life trying to prove how lovable I was.

This is the real message I took from my parents.

You're an evil child.

My mother disliked children. Then she had me. Her unhappiness sent me some pretty mixed-up messages.

No one else will love you the way I do.

No, they wouldn't. Neither would they hurt me the way she did.

You're lucky to have me for a mother.

They also wouldn't expect lifelong gratitude for everything, *everything*, they'd ever done for me, no matter how trivial. Then berate me when they didn't get it. Or, at least, the way they wanted it.

My mother's life was and still is steeped in rage. She was raised during a time when women weren't allowed to govern their own lives. Women weren't men. Girls weren't boys. Boys were allowed to leave the nest, explore their world, and develop a sense of independence. Girls were taught to conform, acquiesce, and obey. Rather than break new ground, girls were taught to place the needs of others ahead of their own. Girls learned to nurture and care for others—to nurture and care for boys. Instead of being given the tools to go forth into the world and challenge convention, girls were taught to stay home and rely on others for their self-worth.

It's a shitty message. It forces women into a state of dependency and demands they assume a subservient role; a role Simone de Beauvoir called the object to the man's subject. The compliant to the assertive. The server to the receiver.

White feminists believe that a lifetime of such sexist indoctrination manifests itself in women in ways the psychiatric world classifies as hysteria, depression, or a personality disorder such as BPD, when in reality, acts of cruelty, self-harm, and masochism are the normal results of oppression turned inward. Worse, any woman who rejects her predetermined role risks being labeled bad, mad, or psychotic; gambles with the possibility of being deemed unbalanced, disturbed, or deranged; and braves the likelihood she'll be christened a jezebel, shrew, or hysteric. She might even hazard further consequences such as abuse or rape by those who see themselves as having authority over her just to ensure she stays in her place. All this taken together is reason enough for a woman's lifelong silence.

Multiply this presumed education by one, five, or a hundred—a hundred thousand—and you get a better understanding of the magnitude of the crisis. You get a better idea of the self-abasement mothers unknowingly pass on to their daughters. Generation to generation. It's like an outdated family heirloom nobody wants. As Kurt Vonnegut once said, so it goes.

Kooks continues to monitor me. His breathing slows; it's more comfortable, even though his soulful eyes still look worried. I give him a pet, then I stagger into the kitchen and rummage through the drawer near the stove. I find the shears and remove them.

Why do I cut?

I cut to bleed. I cut so someone will see how much I hurt, so they'll see *me*. I cut because if I don't, I'll cry, and I'm afraid if I start, I won't stop. I cut because I couldn't save her—my mother—and because of it I would never be good enough in her eyes, and I can't forgive myself for not being good enough. That's when I cut to articulate my pain.

Pain proves I'm alive.

It gives me a voice.

What if I don't want to be this Ana anymore?

I stand in front of the sink, my belly braced against the

basin. I hold the scissors with my right hand and collect a lock of hair with my left. Then I snip it off and toss it in the sink. I shear off another. And another. Again, and again, I lop off fistfuls of hair. They pile up at the bottom of the basin. I keep clipping until bangs no longer sweep across my forehead and waves don't brush along my shoulders. I stay at it until the full outline of my ear becomes visible, and I've cropped my hair so close to my head I can barely run my fingers through it. In less than five minutes, I've removed thirty years' worth of heating, styling, and coloring. I place the scissors in the sink and return to the living room.

Leo Buscaglia once said the person who risks nothing, does nothing, has nothing, is nothing, and becomes nothing. He may avoid suffering and sorrow, but he cannot learn, or feel, or change, or grow, or love.

I don't want to be nothing.

I don't want to be an amoeba.

I don't want to be a protozoan, hugging my environment, willing to change my shape at a moment's notice, possessing no unique and definitive form of my own.

"Ana?" My husband's voice ruptures the veiled light. He tiptoes into the living room, circles the couch, and sits on the floor beside me. He twists his legs into a relaxed yoga position and covers his knees with his hands. His face looks distressed, but I can't tell who he thinks is the injured party, him or me.

I turn and face the wall.

Tony once asked me, what do women want?

It's simple. We want to live.

20

TONY

"It's okay, Ana," I whisper so as not to startle her.

"No," she says. "It's not."

"Can I see what you did?" I rub my head. What *did* she do? She's a mess. Her dress is filthy—and what on God's green earth did she do to her hair? I should comfort her, maybe hold her hand, but I'm too shook up to do anything productive.

Ana continues to lie motionless.

I note the trajectory of blood splattered along the carpet and the second trail below the window. She promised. She swore she wouldn't do this again. A torrent of defiance clouds my judgment. I look over at her.

"Why didn't you tell me?" she asks. "As soon as you knew Chloe had your DNA. Why didn't you tell me?"

I shouldn't have told her about the paternity test. Not tonight. "I'm sorry," I say.

"Bite me."

I look down at the floor.

"All these years," she says, "you've made me out to be the

ogre in this marriage. You've never let me live down how I broke your trust. When it turns out, you're no better than me."

"How do you figure?" I gawk at her.

"You betrayed me," she says.

"I *betrayed* you?" I sit back on my heels. "You slept with another man weeks after we were married, then spent years believing you delivered his child—when it was false. Then you shared this information with me only—*only*—when you were up against a wall. Now you want *me* to understand that I betrayed *you*? Are you *joking*?"

My wife rolls over and faces me. Her posture is rigid. She pants in small clips as she vents. "This situation is about you, and you know it. The most important thing to you is controlling other people. The only time you're happy is when you're in the driver's seat, and I gave you that with my affair. It gave you the ammunition you needed to dig in your heels and immortalize yourself as the perpetually aggrieved husband."

I look away and duck her scrutiny. I don't need Ana to comment on the reasons I crave power over others. I appreciate it better than anyone.

"You accuse me of needing to be the center of everyone's world," she says, "but you've consistently used my unfaithfulness to make yourself the epicenter of this marriage."

"What the—you're saying *I* do that?" I fume and flail my hands. "That *I* make myself the focal point of this marriage?" Whatever amount of guilt I've harbored concerning Ana's past duplicity evaporates, and my ego fills the vacuum.

"You're the prototypical narcissist," she says.

"Wait. Now *I'm* the narcissist?"

"A textbook example, my friend."

"Then how do you explain it was just yesterday you told me Chloe wasn't my biological daughter? Huh? How do you excuse *that*? How do you explain that you've *never* told me what happened the night she left? The night *our* daughter ran away from home?"

Ana closes her eyes. She knits her eyebrows together. "All right," she says. "I had that one coming to me."

I wait for her to do it—to tell me what happened between her and Chloe that night—but she doesn't say anything. I eject myself off the floor and stomp across the living room. I can't get away from her fast enough.

"What about *you*?" She asks.

My legs wobble. I turn around.

Ana shakes her finger at me. "Whose phone number is listed as "No Caller ID" on your cell?"

My body starts to quiver. Can she tell? Can she read the tension on my face?

"Is *she* the 'nonsense' Chace referred to tonight?"

What the hell did Chace tell her? How much does my wife know?

No, I will not capitulate. I will not show Ana any mercy. I don't care what Chace said, or what she thinks I'm doing, this is my pity party, damn it, and I'm going to enjoy it.

"The reason we're in this position is because of *your* sexual indiscretion," I say.

"I'm bleeding." Ana collapses onto the rug.

I punch the door with my fist.

"Damn you, Tony!" she shouts. "This is not my fault."

I storm back over to her. I crouch in front of her. "No? Whose fault is it, then?"

Ana unwinds the towel from her arm. She pelts me with it.

"Sweet Mother of God." I fall on my behind.

The commotion awakens Kooks. He lifts his head and growls. It's low and from the gut, and it's his way of saying he has his eye on me.

How is it Ana and I end every argument the same way—ready to throttle each other?

"Did you ever love me?" My wife stares at the floor. Her voice shakes with exhaustion. "Did you?" she asks.

I look away. Ana is not wrong about me. I have no balls. I rant and rave and carry on about life's most trivial issues, but when it comes down to it, I'm all talk and no action. Thus, I respond to my wife the same way I answered my father.

I exit the living room.

Meadow meets me in the hall. She's dazed but awake enough to know what's transpired between Ana and me was serious. I consider concocting a story, but quite frankly, it's nothing she hasn't witnessed before.

"We're fine," I mumble. "Go back to bed."

I give Ana a departing look, and for a split second, I want to sprint back to her and relieve her sadness, but I have nothing left for her or this marriage. I promised her a fairytale. It was wrong. Dull-eyed, I continue to observe my wife. "There's no such thing as unconditional love," I say.

21

ANA

Tuesday, August 7, 2018
Four days before Chloe's rescue

I send Adel a text. It's a snippet of dribble about blue skies, lowering my stress, and how I loved on my dogs like she told me to—a follow up to the advice she gave me Sunday night when I was hiding in the Buliers' bathroom. I don't tell her I cut myself when I got home that night, or that I'm standing outside my husband's office at his university because I found an unknown number on his call list. Or how I'm betting it belongs to a woman. Or that I stayed awake all night ruminating about how he might be cheating on me . . . or how I still want him, and I refuse to let him go.

I inspect the hall, but there's no one here. I couldn't have planned this any better. It's lunchtime, and Tony takes his meal outside so he can lollygag around the campus while he eats. What makes this even more ideal is that his assistant, Mme de la Folle, is also away from her workspace, and Tony's door is wide open.

So, I stroll into his office, close the door behind me, and lock it before I sprint over to his desk and give it a once-over. What a mess. There's so much junk on it, I can't find the surface. It's a shame since this piece of furniture is a work of art. It was constructed out of restored rosewood and has a polished exterior and bronze highlights. You wouldn't know it, though. Mounds of paperwork hide its beauty.

I shuffle around his stuff and hunt for anything that might be incriminating, but most of what's here is the usual professorial smattering of administrative transcripts and announcements, old newspapers, outdated periodicals, and stacks of student blue books. So, I dig deeper. A rumpled, yellow legal pad calls my name, and I look through it, but it's mostly filled with formulas and equations. I drop it and set my sights on a stack of Tony's interdepartmental memos instead. I speed-read through as much of it as I can stand, but it's futile. It's all gibberish. Everything here is innocent. What I need is a sticky note with a cutesy saying or a carelessly handwritten note in a margin that reveals more than a friendship.

I need a smoking gun.

I need something that will expose an intimate moment because when two people are sexually involved, they can't hide it. It doesn't matter what they do, they leave behind clues to their familiarity. It's in the personal jokes they share with each other that only they understand; it's in how they sign their name when they think no one else will see it.

I dig further into the mess, and that's when I find it. Tony's weekly planner. This *has* to be my smoking gun. I swipe it from the desk. There's no way my husband hasn't scribbled notes about a private meeting or a secret date, yet as I skim through it, there's nothing here. No appointments. No meetings. No luncheons. Zip. Is he kidding? The man can't remember to pick up my dry cleaning, but he knows when and where to meet this supposed other woman without writing anything down? I can't believe it, and I surf through the rest of his datebook for more material when a printed document falls out and lands on the floor.

It's a manuscript—a work in progress. *Regulating Monopolies in the Presence of Asymmetric Information.* I pick it up and flip it over. Bits of crusty cheese fall off the back page and scatter across Tony's desk. I ignore them and glance through the list of authors, but the only name I recognize is my husband's. I trace my fingers over it, leaf through the first few pages, then read through the comments in the margins. *Be cautious with your spelling. Remember there vs. their. Please include my most recent citations.* Blah, blah, blah, this is useless, and I toss it on his desk with the planner.

I sit in his chair and spin around in it. A wall of oak-veneer book shelves rise up behind Tony's desk. They span the length of the room, and every shelf is full. It's an impressive collection and not surprising, given how much my husband loves books. And he does *love* books. It's because he understands them. Books are dependable. Human relationships are not. Human relationships are muddy, and they sometimes leave you with more questions than answers, and Tony doesn't like questions. Questions make him anxious.

What if I'm wrong?

What if he's not having sex with another woman? What if I'm wasting my time here?

I pull myself to my feet and stroll alongside the mountain of shelves. Most of these books are mundane and not unusual for a professor of economics. Tony has all the traditional textbooks. Micro and macroeconomics, behavioral and environmental economics. There're a few on the European Bank, and one or two about the Euro Zone. He has several about data collection methods, and there's a big, fat one tailored to the specifics of European trade. This one here is about finance and the European Commission, and here's one about . . . wait a minute . . . what's this book?

I remove it and turn it over in my hand. It looks different. I investigate the rows of shelves again. These books are old. Their bindings are worn and damaged. They've been used and reused. I look at the book in my hand; it's new, and it's slim— too slim to be a course book—and its cover is a flaming hot, lipstick red.

La Poésie de l'Amour. It's a book of love poems.

It's a book of *love* poems?

I open the cover and read the inscription.

There are times in our lives when hanging on only leads to more upset, and we need to let go.

Someone has told my husband to let go? Let go of *what*? Let go of—

ME?

I need to throw up.

My eyes shoot straight to the last line.

Je t'aime, dd

I love you, dd?

WHO IS DD?

Two letters, both in lower case, but they mock me like they're a tome.

I return to his desk. I pounce on the manuscript and speed-read through the pages. There they are again. The same two initials. DD. DD scribbled alongside comments about poor grammar. DD scrawled next to citations about statistical vari-ance. I return to the list of authors. She's there, too. Didine Fidéline. She's the DD. She's the "No Caller ID" Tony phoned Sunday night.

It's my husband's . . . it's *her*.

I slam the poetry book on the desk. "DD?" I rip out a

handful of pages and fire them across his office. "DD!" I take hold of another set and pitch these on the floor. Sweat beads across my forehead and drips down my temples, but I can't stop. Batch after batch, I wrench out the pages and hurl them everywhere.

Heavy footsteps race down the corridor.

I stop mid-raze.

They head toward Tony's office; they quicken as they get closer.

It's my husband. It has to be. He's spotted my car in the parking lot and knows I'm here.

The clattering gets louder.

I look down at the mound of debris that covers his desk. I scoop up the shredded pages and stuff them back in the book, but they no longer fit.

The commotion stops on the other side of the door.

I pound on the book and force it to close, but it's impossible.

Keys jiggle in the lock. The knob turns.

Screw it, and I pitch the whole lot of it into his wastebasket. Then I cover it up with today's edition of the *Times*.

Tony's door swings wide open. My husband stands there like a sentry. He gets a load of his desk and the scattered pages of what's left of his dumb poetry book. His face explains it all; he's been caught with his pants down. "Let me explain," he says.

"*Mother.*" I launch his date book at him.

Tony bobs. The book misses him and hits a chair. "Ana, stop," he says.

Seriously, did he just ask me to stop? I *can't* stop. I *won't* stop. Nothing matters right now. I'll keep going until I destroy everyone and everything—him and me included. Stop? Hell, no. Not until I draw blood and leave bruises. Not until I *crush* him . . . except I love him, and I want him to love me. Why doesn't he love me? Why can't he honor his commitment? Maybe it sounds juvenile, but I want it, and I want him to beg for forgiveness because he broke it. I want him to tell me he's sorry and all this was a huge mistake. I want him to say he didn't intend for it to happen, that she means nothing to him, and that he'll tell her good-bye. Because I'm the only woman he wants.

Only, I'm *not* the one woman he wants.

My husband's been with another woman.

My head goes eerily silent. Every structure I've come to rely on to preserve order—my home, my family, my daughters, this marriage—implodes right in front of me. I don't recognize any of it.

I don't recognize him.

Who *is* this man?

Tony was supposed to be the honorable one in this marriage, the one who wouldn't cheat, the one who wouldn't be unfaithful. It wasn't his style. Not Tony. Not *my* husband. He's too responsible, too steadfast, too self-righteous. A little naïve, even. He's a constant, and those sorts of people don't have affairs.

"Who is she?" Like a fool, I expect an answer. Does it even matter whether he gives me one? I've floated too far from the shore. I'm barely treading water as it is.

"Ana, please. I can straighten this out."

Maybe he only did it once. Like I did. I could handle that. While it was mean and thoughtless, it was a lapse in judgment. A mistake. It was two colleagues working late one night. They were tired and hungry and huddled over a book. Or a manuscript. Sharing a computer screen. They didn't mean for it to happen, but the evening got carried away. Nobody was supposed to get hurt.

He watches me. He looks repentant.

"How long have you been—?"

He looks down at the floor.

My eyes water. This was no one-night stand.

"Why, Tony?" The words are out of my mouth before I'm even sure I want the answer.

My husband stutters. "I . . ."

This is the best he can do? Spit all over himself? I don't even get an apology for what he's done—for what he's doing? "You cheated on me," I say.

"You cheated on me first," he shouts.

"Is that what this is about? Payback?"

"Call it what you want," he said. "Payback, retribution, damages—"

"*Damages*. Damages? Why would you do this to us?"

"Us, Ana?" His voice trails off. He looks away.

Is this what he's doing? Is my husband paying me back for an anguish I caused him decades ago?

"I don't believe it," I say. "You've been holding a grudge for twenty-three years." The agony I've been feeling for this situation, for me, dissolves.

Tony' face hardens. "We wouldn't be in this position if it wasn't for *your* indiscretion," he says. "I'm simply getting my due."

"Getting you're *due*?" Why do I keep repeating his comments? "You mean you're getting *even* with me?"

But my husband has lost interest. It's suddenly registered on him that all the meticulously stacked piles of clutter on his desk are out of place.

I take pride in my handi work.

The blue in Tony's eyes darkens, and the peaceful sea I once found in them turns menacing. Manically, he goes about reordering and reorganizing it all until he's returned the surface of his desk to its original state. He looks up at me. His stare is icy.

I inspect my nails.

He gives his desk a second appraisal, then looks at his waste-basket.

I take a seat in a shoddy desk chair near the window.

Tony lunges at the basket and turns it upside down. The ratty pages of his stupid poetry book cascade to the floor like a teeny tiny ticker-tape parade.

I pick a bit of lint off my shirt.

My husband has a hissy fit. As if in a trance, he recoups the trampled pages of his deranged love poems, spreads them out across his desk, and tucks each one into his husk of a book in some half-baked attempt to secure them into their proper order. He holds it up and shakes it.

"Looks like I discovered your tart," I say.

The veins in his temples protrude. His mouth opens and closes like a grouper, but no words come out.

I twirl a strand of hair.

"Who do you think you are?" he asks.

It takes me all of a second to spring up, run over, and seize hold of his idiotic book. But Tony refuses to let go of it, and we end up in a tug of war until it flies out of our hands. Pages scatter across the floor. Tony grabs me, but I repel him, and we knock around his office like two bums in a drunken bar fight. It's childish, but all I care about this second is knocking my husband to the ground in a victorious finish, and I jab my heel into his ankle.

"Owwww." He winces.

It's the tip of the ice berg of what I'd *like* to do to him. "Cheater!" I shout.

"Pick up my book, Ana."

"Does she idolize you?" I ask. "You know how much you need to have women worship you."

"Pick it up." He pushes me toward the mess.

I stumble into his desk. A stack of journals plummets to the floor.

Mme de la Folle calls through the door. "Dr. DiSalvo? *Est-ce que tout va bien?*" Is everything all right, she asks.

"Yes, uh, we're fine," Tony says. "A book fell, and I, um, I hit my head on the desk when I picked it up. You know how clumsy I am." He laughs. It sounds too weak to be believable.

Tony's assistant doesn't question him, though. "Dr. Bulier has contacted you about the departmental meeting and—"

"Yes. Yes, I remember about the meeting." My husband turns to me and growls. "I want you out of here."

I neaten my shirt and tuck it back into my shorts.

He seizes my purse and heaves it at me. "Now!" Then he crosses the room and throws open his office door.

I march out with my husband right behind me. I smile politely at Mme de la Folle, but I'm far from done. I mumble something about forgetting my datebook, race back into his office, and slam the door behind me. Then I lock it. There's no way I'm going to let him get away with this. I will find this woman's phone number, and I will eliminate her.

Tony pounds on the door.

I rush over to his computer.

He punches the door with his fist. "*Ana.*" The wood stifles his aggravation.

I tap the return key; his screen refreshes. It's blue. A bleak, dismal blue. He has no photos, no slideshows, no hovering words. There's nothing on his screen but a sea of stupefying blue.

Tony grumbles something else. He waits, then he strikes the door a second time and races off to his meeting.

I return to his computer; now it wants a password. Crap. I didn't expect this, and I enter all the usual suspects—all the essential figures in our lives like his birth date, mine, the girls. I even enter the birth dates of our dogs. Nada. I try our anniversary. Nope. I enter the date Evelyn went to university, Meadow's first day of kindergarten, even the day Chloe left. Goose egg.

Then I consider the source. This is my husband we're talking about. I type in the word *password*, and the screen revives. Next, I double-click through the different icons on his desktop, but the list isn't here. I delve into his documents file, but I come up flat there, too. Think. Think. Think like Tony. My husband would never keep anything personal on this computer. It's too much of a risk. So, I switch over to his USB port, steamroll through his thumb drive, and—*violà*, there it is. Tony's "List of Secret Contacts." I click on it, scroll down to the D's, and—there she is.

Didine Fidéline.

AKA DD.

AKA Tony's *mistress*.

I scribble her number on the inside of my palm.

Once outside in the parking lot, I rustle through my purse, find my cell, and hold it out like a beacon in the dark. I need to end this. I need to stop whatever is happening between my husband and this woman, this *witch*, and bring him back to me. I grit my teeth and enter her number on the keypad, but my fingers begin to shake, and it comes out wrong.

I delete it and breathe in deep. Slow it down, Ana. Let's take this one digit at a time. Tap. There's the first one, and it's correct. Tap, tap. Good. Tap, tap, tap. Great, all the numbers are correct so far, but a wall of heat surges through me, and I whack the delete key until I've again cleared the number from the screen.

What am I doing?

Tony will be furious with me if he finds out I've contacted this woman.

Why do I care?

My husband is sleeping with another woman—my husband is sleeping with *this* woman—and I'm all wound up about whether I should call her ass and find out why.

Screw this.

I drum out the number again. I hold my finger over the Call button . . . I hold it there. Over the Call button. But I don't press it.

My eyes well up.

Get it together, Ana. Press the button. Do it. Tap Call. Press the button—

I press Call.

There's a moment of silence. Then a phone rings on the other end.

Shit. Fuck! It's ringing. Her phone is ringing.

What have I done? Tony's going to kill me.

Hit End. HIT END!

"*Allo?*" A woman's voice answers the phone. Silence. "*Allo?*" she asks again.

It's her. Is it her? It's *her*. It's DD.

"*Al-lo,*" she says.

I tap the speaker button.

"*Il ya quelqu'un?*" The woman asks whether someone is on the other end.

Over the course of my marriage, I've lost count of the number of women I've called and denounced for taking too much of my husband's time. Women I battered with word chains filled with vulgarities and obscenities. Women I regarded as both enemies and competitors for my husband's affection. Yet, as I stand here and listen to this woman speak, I'm tongue tied. There's something different about her, about her voice. It's elegant and refined; it's educated. And it startles me. What would someone with such a cultured voice want with my husband?

I press End. My stomach is queasy as the adrenalin continues to speed pump through my head.

I don't want to believe it, but it's true. My husband is having an affair.

Now, what am I supposed to do?

22

TONY

Friday, August 10, 2018
One day before Chloe's rescue

"What are you doing in my pocketbook?" Ana stands in the kitchen's entryway.

I'm taken by surprise, and I drop her bag. It crashes to the floor as does another misspent opportunity to read Chloe's text message. Any second, I expect to be scolded about how I shouldn't meddle in other people's personal belongings.

My wife doesn't say a word. She enters the kitchen and tosses today's edition of *Le Monde* on the table. She retrieves her bag and sets it beside the paper, then she pulls out a chair and sits. Her hair looks better today. It's at least presentable.

"I don't know," I say. "I . . . uh, might've gotten some stuff on your purse." I swish at a spot of milk on the counter. I peek over to see if she's watching me.

She's not, she's too busy leafing through the newspaper.

I skulk over to the cupboards under the stove and

rummage around for a sauté pan. Kooks approaches me from behind and sniffs my ear. Next, he smells the contents of the cupboard. Finding nothing of interest lodged between our pots and pans, he lumbers over to the window, lowers himself to the floor, and somehow fits his hulking frame into a slender strip of sun.

I proceed to the refrigerator, where I remove the ingredients for my famous crème brûlée French Toast. It's one of Chloe's favorite dishes, and this morning, rather than go into the office, I decided to make it. It's a signal to my wife that I would like for Chloe to return home. There's no doubt the plan could blow up in my face.

Ana eyes my wares. "Wasn't that Chloe's favorite breakfast?"

"It was."

My wife drops the paper, stands, and meanders over to the freezer. She removes the coffee beans, pours several scoops into the grinder, and pummels them into a fine mocha silt. She dumps it in the French press and plugs in the electric tea kettle.

"I want to see if I still have the magic touch." I continue to wait for the explosion. The waistband of my pajamas dampens with perspiration.

"That's nice of you."

I grin at her. It's not friendly.

"No, really," she says. "It's a nice gesture on your part." Ana leaves the sack of coffee on the counter and retrieves a mixing bowl from the cabinet. "Want help?" She sets the bowl on the counter beside the eggs, cracks a few, adds milk, then whips it into a dairy smoothie. She adds a pinch of cinnamon and gives the bowl a final stir. The kitchen smells like a German *Schneckennudeln*. "I'll let you do the honors," she says, and she places the fork on the counter. Then she rips off a small hunk of bread from the end of the loaf and bites into it. She smiles at me as she retreats to the table, where she continues to peruse her newspaper.

I slice the bread and lay several pieces on the counter. The delightfully sweet smell of the egg mixture charms Dharma, who lifts her nose. She gives it a good sniff before she hobbles across the room and lies on Ana's slippers. Kooks lifts his head to see if he's missing out on anything, but he doesn't get up. He monitors them, however, in the event the circumstances could change.

I fire up the front burner on our gas stove. The flame jolts to life.

"Do you love her?" Ana places a hand on Dharma's back and stops the dog from licking her paws. Dharma lowers her head. She rests her chin on the tiles.

Ana and I watch the old girl long after Dharma has ceased slobbering on herself.

It's easier than acknowledging the elephant in the room.

I turn and face the counter. I know what my wife is asking, but I don't have a response. I'm walking a tightrope between these two women, and it takes all my concentration to maintain my balance.

Moments pass, and the division becomes palpable. I can't bear it, and I begin the cooking process, taking the bread, dunking it in the eggs, and placing it in the hot pan. The bread hisses as it connects with the cast iron.

Ana returns to her paper.

I focus on the toast. I slip the spatula underneath each one and check their progress.

Ana continues to read the newspaper.

The silence is comfortable again, and I have to force myself to remember how things got so out of hand between Ana and me. Honestly, there was a time, not too long ago, when I thought everything in my life had come together. I had a good job, a lovely home, and three beautiful daughters, and while my marriage was nowhere near idyllic, I was as happy as a man could be at my age.

Then my oldest daughter disappeared.

That was the icing on the cake.

The kettle whistles.

Ana remains buried in her paper.

Steam explodes all over the counter.

"Do you intend to get that or what?" My frustration flares along with the hot spray.

"Crap." Ana vaults across the room and yanks the plug out of the wall. The whistling abruptly ends.

"Where'd you go?" I sound like an interrogator. "You were a million miles away."

"Hey, what if I also made one of Chloe's favorite dishes?" She fills the French Press with the hot water. "I could bake that macaroni and cheese dish we all like. The one with the farmed sea scallops and all that gooey Comté cheese. Chloe used to love that dish. We could invite Evelyn, and Meadow, and Meadow could ask Aurelien if he'd like to join us. I'll see if Evelyn wants to bring someone—I think she's seeing someone, but I'm not sure. She hasn't *told* me. Anyway, it seems as if we could all use a celebration around here. What do you think?"

"All right." I set the spatula on the counter. "What's this all about?"

"You don't want mac and cheese?"

"I'm not referring to the menu. I'm talking about right now. You. Me. Us. Cooking together. The concept of planning a dinner party around Chloe's favorite meals. What's going on?"

Her smile fades, and she wanders back to her seat. "You said you wanted to reconnect with Chloe."

"I did, but—"

"I want you to know I heard you."

"Your behavior is still a bit over the top," I say. "Even for you."

"I heard what you said about me," she says. "About my childhood problems."

I want to trust my wife, I do, but she's burned me on too many occasions with her lies and manipulations.

Ana holds my gaze. "Tony—"

"I remember what I said the other night."

"I think—"

"What I don't understand is—"

"Tony, your—" My wife cringes.

Impatiently, I wait for her to finish. I gawk at her like a doofus.

"Your French toast is burning?"

I turn toward the stove. "For the love of—" It's engulfed in a mountain of smoke. I hurtle myself at the pan and pitch it onto a cold burner, then I dart across the room, throw open a window, and race back to the stove, where I snag a dishtowel from the rack beside it and fan at the smoke. It's too late. My crème brûlée French toast is nothing more than two carbonized pieces of bread. I heave the entire mess into the sink. The cast iron buzzes inside the basin.

Kooks lifts himself off the floor and patrols the area around the stove. Dharma aims straight for the stove.

With my hand to my forehead, I frown at the disaster.

"Don't act so surprised," Ana laughs. "I do listen to you sometimes."

I observe the charred vestiges of my breakfast and scratch at the pan with the spatula, but it's useless. It's ruined. I dump the food turner into the sink along with everything else.

"You don't believe me?" she asks.

"Let's say I'm suspicious."

"Wow, I can't do anything right where you're concerned."

"It's a rapid rethink, that's all."

"I'm trying, Tony. It's the best I can do."

I sponge up some of the splattered bits of egg that outline the stove.

"It's not easy for me to look at myself," Ana says.

I scrutinize her face. I want to dispute her, but I can't. She's right, and there's no way to cushion it. I should say a kind word, maybe give her some encouragement about how she should continue this new trend. I could even provide some advice that would inspire her to try harder, but I don't do any of these things. Instead, I callously seize the opportunity for myself. "If you're so intent on changing your ways," I say, "then you won't mind if I read Chloe's text?"

Ana reaches for her purse. She searches through it, takes out her phone, and scrolls around on it. She crosses the kitchen and hands it to me.

Like a boy with a new comic book, I seize it from her. I don't have to read too much to realize I was right all along.

Chloe wants to come home.

My daughter reached out to her mother to ask if she could move back in with us. There is still the very real possibility that my entire family will be reunited again. When I get to the section about her travel plans, I look at my wife. "She's arriving by train?" I ask. "This afternoon?"

"I thought I'd be the one to pick her up, but you can do the honors if you like."

The words burst out of me. "Yes," I say. "Yes, I'll do it. I'll go get her."

Ana returns to her seat. "I never intended to cause this family so much harm," she says.

The kitchen falls silent except for Kooks, who is in front of the stove, licking up what bits of egg splashed across the tiles. I toss the sponge in the sink.

"You were a good father to Chloe." Ana neatens up the paper. "She couldn't ask for a better one."

I turn and face the counter again. I'm embarrassed by her compliment. It's untrue and undeserved, even I know that. I place another pan on the stove, get a clean fork, and whip the eggs.

"Chloe loves you very much," she says.

I toss two fresh pieces of bread in the bowl.

"More than she ever loved me, that's for sure."

I slop the bread around in the eggs, then I toss it in the pan. I hone in on Kooks. He continues to wash the floor with his tongue.

"I didn't do much to warrant it, though . . . so . . . there's that, I guess."

"Chloe loved you." My sense of guilt gets the better of me, and I blurt out the words.

My wife looks at me.

"More than anything else, she wanted you to love her," I say.

Ana turns her head, but not before I catch a glimpse of the redness in her eyes.

"She might have gone about it all wrong—"

"We should take her out to eat," Ana says. "I mean, we should let her rest a few nights, then we should live it up—go out on the town." My wife gets up from the table and crouches in front of Kooks. She pets his cheeks, then scratches behind his ears. The dog wilts in her hands. "We could meet at the Café de Belle Nourriture," she says. "I guarantee Chloe misses their bouillabaisse."

I like her suggestion, and I appreciate how she's attempting to give this some thought, to plan out some events for everyone to welcome Chloe home. It would be nice if Chloe could return to a semi-happy household, or at least one that's not so unhinged. I want to tell Ana how much her gesture means to me, but it feels too much like a concession. So, I futz with my toast instead.

"Are you still planning to grocery shop this morning?" she asks.

"I am."

"Can I give you a list?"

"Of course." I relax my stance.

She pulls a crumpled piece of paper out of her front pocket and lays it on the counter.

Still holding the spatula, I pick it up and glance through it. "Is this everything?" I ask. "I don't want to have to go out again once Chloe gets here." My tone comes off snootier than I'd intended. If Ana is willing to show me a little more respect, then I should be expected to do the same.

"I wouldn't ask you to go out twice," she says.

"Don't act like you've never forgotten anything." Old ways are hard to change, and I revert to my default which is to take jabs at her.

"I didn't mean to insult you." My wife disregards my tone. "I'm just saying, I get it. When Chloe gets here, you'll want to spend time with her." She gives Kooks another scratch and heads out. Kooks raises himself off the floor and barks at her as if to say come back, come back. Dharma scrambles to her feet as well and catches up with my wife in the hallway. Kooks joins them, and all three of them disappear around the corner.

"I'm sorry," I say, but my words go unheard. It's apropos, I guess. Like everything I've given my wife, it's too little too late.

23
ANA

"Would a café and some cookies help to cheer you?" Naitee stands in the doorway.

I stop texting and look up. This afternoon, she's wearing a lemonade pink T-shirt with a white skirt that ends mid-calf and looks as if someone made it by stitching together multiple pieces of ragged tulle. She looks like a fairy princess. "Pretty," I say.

She dangles a white paper bag in front of me, then places two small Styrofoam cups on my desk. Liquid leaks out from under the lid of one of them, and a thin stream of coffee drips down the side. "They were sold out of the madeleines you enjoy," she says. "So today, I bought for you some macaroons." She tosses the bag of cookies on my desk and takes a sip of the coffee with the non-leaky lid. She sits in the metal folding chair that's still in front of my desk.

I'm not entirely sure why I'm here this morning, except it's better than being home. There, I'll only sit and count the hours until Tony returns with Chloe, and I have to face the aftermath of my former actions.

I pop the top off my coffee. The thin stream turns into a channel and forms a tiny puddle in the middle of my desk. I brush at it with my sleeve. I despise macaroons, but I dig into the bag and take one hoping a cookie, any cookie, will improve my attitude. "I don't know what I was thinking," I say.

Nait pulls out a palmier and nibbles at it. Bits of flaky crust and confectioners' sugar scatter in her lap and around the legs of her chair. She doesn't notice; she's engrossed in her cookie.

"I guess I wanted to have it all."

Naitee eyes me.

"The other day?" I explore her face for a hint of recognition. "Our conversation?"

"Everyone wants to have it all." She dusts white powder from her lips. "Do you not think this is true?"

"No matter what the cost?"

"I guess it depends on what we want," she says. "What we are willing to sacrifice for it."

Wise words from the mouth of such a young woman, but it's no surprise. Naitee's eyes reveal a deep-rooted wound that's not yet healed.

She's right, of course. The question is about desire, and what we'll do to have it, why we'll push ourselves beyond our limits to sustain it. It's the reason some of us can't live without homemade chocolate donuts dripping with mocha icing, or having that perfect latte, rich and creamy, first thing in the morning, or clinging to our app-filled smartphones, counting and recounting the number of likes we received for our latest tweet. It's Buddhism 101, and it's all about how we *need* those things in our lives because they stimulate us and make us feel important, appreciated, and loved.

It's also why we're miserable when we don't get them. Desire is the purest definition of *want*—I want, you want, we are wanting. It's that ever present and murky aspect of being human we just can't shake. Yet it's also what we're expected to relinquish if we want to achieve true happiness. Seriously? Who among us is willing to give up their lusts and cravings if they're all that satisfy our barren soul? If having them is the only way we can tolerate the insignificance of our existence? For some of us, our desires are what give our lives meaning. Not all of us are on a direct path to Nirvana.

"What if," I ask, "when you made your decision, you had no idea what you had to sacrifice?" I talk with my mouth full.

Nait pulls a second palmier out of the bag. She nibbles all around its circumference. "Oh," she says. "I suspect somewhere in the back of each of our minds, we have a sense of what we have to surrender when we choose one thing over another."

Right again. Nothing in life is free. Every action demands a reaction. It's the way the universe stays in balance. Call it karma, fate, destiny, what have you. What a person puts into this world is what they'll get out of it. Fuck with the rules and —well, you had it coming to you. I get it. I do, but I can't seem to stop myself from wanting my cake and wishing to devour it all in one sitting. I have two settings: stop and run as fast as you can. There's nothing in between. I'm numb without constant stimulation. I've never had an experience I didn't take straight from want to greed.

"What were you searching for?" Nait asks. She holds up the paper bag and signals for me to take another cookie. When she sees I'm not interested, she drops the bag on my desk. She licks the sugar from her fingers.

"I'm not sure." I pop the last bit of macaroon in my mouth. I wish I had a better answer for her, but it's not that easy.

"You said you did not love him," she says, "but do you think there must have been a deeper purpose for why you slept with him?" She finishes her cookie and uses her skirt as a napkin.

I dig through my purse for what's left of an old joint, and I light it up. I take a few hits, pass it to her, then play with my phone. I scroll through Cool Babes and consider tweeting out Nait's question—how do we search for meaning in our lives? But I'm not sure I want to have this talk yet, with Nait or anyone else. So, I tweet out a cheesier version of it. "Is there anything better than Buddhism?"

Nait hands back the joint, stands, stretches, and in a swoosh of tulle and lace, exits my office. She's like a child with her frilly clothes, wearing her innocence for all the world to see. It's an aspect of her personality that brings out my maternal side, a stance I couldn't seem to express while I was raising Chloe. I inhale again, then stub it out in an ashtray I keep in the bottom drawer of my desk.

Why *did* I do it—have sex with him? What *was* it that drew me to him?

Was it the sex?

Yes, well, yes and no. It wasn't only the sex, but this was no relationship, and it definitely wasn't about love.

The only thing I know for sure was that it *was* about risk, the risk that comes with having sex in the moment. The danger that goes along with making love to a stranger, someone you don't know, who lets you completely be yourself. Who encourages you to remove your shield and to which you, in turn, allow to penetrate your senses.

I don't know. Maybe.

It haunts me to this day, and I've never gotten over it, nor have I ever resolved it with Tony.

His name was Géraud Barrett, and we met by accident, at a charity luncheon I attended with Médée not long after Tony and I had settled into Belleville. It was hosted by the French philanthropist Claude Boucher, proprietor of an 18th Century farmhouse, in the Perche region of Normandie, an area known especially for its countless little villages, pea-green pastures, and free roaming milking cows. A place where the summers are long, and the smell of manure is dense. No locale could be lusher, and it was an idyllic setting for an affair.

Médée and I weren't there long before I lost interest. Spending the afternoon with the aristocracy of the art world was Médée's thing. I was always more of a wall art kind of girl. So, after a few cocktails, maybe more, I stole away from the group and explored the grounds. When I discovered someone had left the door open to Monsieur Boucher's private art collection, I let myself in and had a look around. Magic arose from every direction: oil paintings covered the walls, and sculptures filled the corners. I wandered about for a bit before I stopped to admire what appeared to be an early pencil sketch by Matisse. I'm not an art critic, but I found his work highly sensual, and this piece was no exception.

A man's voice addressed me from behind. "I believe Claude purchased that particular lithograph last summer while at an auction." His voice was sensual, provocative. "Although," he said, "philanthropy was not the primary reason for its purchase."

I didn't turn around. I was caught—and not by anyone, but by someone who was familiar with our host. "It's beautiful," I said.

"It should be," the voice laughed. "He paid a handsome price for it."

"He must be fond of it then."

"It was a gift for his wife."

"How nice to be so loved." Some women were born to have it all, and I wasn't one of them.

"No," the voice said. "I am quite certain he does not love

her at all. He only wishes to keep her happy so she will not leave him and take all of his money."

Did I hear him correctly? Who was this man who held such little regard for his spouse? I had to know, and I turned around. It was him.

Géraud Barrett.

It was the French artist who, at the still youthful age of twenty-nine, had pierced the contemporary art world with his neo-expressionist use of the human body flanked by global shapes to bring our attention to the destruction of the planet —to how we're dismantling everything here. Except us. His work was ugly. It was meant to be. Following in the footsteps of Jean-Michel Basquiat, he took Basquiat's furious energy and love of color and poured it into a one-man crusade to save us. It worked. The French paid him handsomely for it.

While few loved him, millions respected him. He was hard to ignore; he was a warrior, a wolf in wolf's clothing. He was an alpha male's male, although as I was about to learn that summer, he was also at a low point in his life. Géraud had conquered so much in such a short time, he believed he'd achieved everything there was to have in the art world. He'd fallen into a slump. He felt his best years were behind him, and there was nothing left for him to gain.

I fiddled with my sleeves. "How sad," I said.

Géraud sat forward. He plunged a hand into a full head of mahogany hair, then let it fall strategically around his face. Handsome didn't come close to describing his looks. "Sad?" he asked. "How can such a beautiful gift bring such condemnation?"

"His wife is trapped in a passionless marriage," I said. "She's with a man who uses material things as a substitute for love." Something I understood only too well.

"*Mon Dieu.*" He swung his arm over the back of the couch.

His T-shirt stretched across his chest. He scratched himself below his arm. "I would think this to be quite a delicious situation for his wife. What is better than to have such an irresistible position over one's spouse?"

His comment took me by surprise. "Power doesn't belong in relationships," I said.

"Ah, yet power is the most noteworthy characteristic of every relationship, *n'est-ce pas?*"

No. *Ce n'est pas ça.* Power was what men used against women.

"Power is about man's fight for dominance," he said. "It is the reason we get up in the morning. It's why we take in oxygen."

"Power corrupts," I said. "It poisons love."

"Love," he laughed. "Love is fleeting. It is an experience best had during one's youth." He spoke like a man much older than his years. He crossed his legs in the other direction. His eyes fell to the third open button on my blouse.

I dug my hands in my pockets. I toyed with my wedding band. I knew I shouldn't be here, alone in this room with this man, having this conversation, but there was something exciting about being with an artist, about the possibility of being his newest muse—about being one of his chosen few.

"Please," he said. "Call me Géraud."

His politeness felt overblown, but I was flattered by the invitation to be more intimate, and I responded in kind.

He flashed a generous smile; it was the smile of a winner. Men like him, like my father, didn't waste time getting what they wanted from women, and they only wanted one thing. Submission. I was appalled at what I was about to do, but his attention was intoxicating.

Looking back, I should've run. I should've thanked Géraud for his time and his conversation, cut my losses, and bolted, but I didn't. I wanted it to continue—there in his friend's study, then later at his estate in Honfluer, then even later as we lied between his sheets, naked. God forgive me, I knew it was wrong, but I didn't care. Géraud made the blackness light, and for a moment, someone saw me.

"You want more out of life than the average person," he said afterward. "You want to be adored, and you will not stop until you have it. No matter what it takes or who it hurts."

I averted my eyes.

He kissed my forehead.

A ball of heat formed in my chest, and my body stiffened. He sensed it.

"Please do not play coy with me," he said. "It's in your eyes. It's as if I am observing myself in a mirror, only a few short years earlier. It is how we are built. It is the anger inside of us that drives us. This fire in our bellies is what motivates us to demand more."

How could I fight it? He was right.

"You will get nowhere, my dear Ana, until you embrace it." He rolled on top of me and pressed himself between my thighs. "It is who we are."

Why did I do it? Because Géraud was the only person in my life who ripped through my defenses and uncovered the driving need that had plagued me since I was a child. He removed my mask and exposed the malevolent side of my personality, yet he still desired me.

Is there a stronger aphrodisiac than this?

"One and the same," he said. "You and I, my dear Ana. We are one and the same."

I pop the last piece of macaroon in my mouth.

Are we, though?

What I did was wrong, and no amount of self-pity will refute it.

Everything I do can't begin and end with my emptiness.

Psychiatrist Aaron Lazare said one of the greatest human interactions is the offering and accepting of an apology. It can heal a humiliation, resolve a grudge, and even yield forgiveness for the receiver. It can also relieve guilt and shame for the offender.

I resent that my husband's having an affair, for turning to someone else instead of me, but I ruptured this marriage a long time ago when I betrayed him, and I've never taken an ounce of responsibility for it.

While I can't undo what I did, I can apologize for it. Maybe it'll heal some of Tony's pain.

Maybe it'll make him reconsider his affair with this woman.

Maybe he'll even stop seeing her.

I can only hope.

It's worth a try, at least.

24

TONY

I push through the front doors of the Gare du Nord and stop inside the main hall. People bustle at me from all directions. The entire station is humming, and I want to take it in—the amplified sense of anticipation everyone has that wonderful things are about to happen for them. It makes me want to believe that wonderful things are about to happen for me, too, because after seven long years, my daughter is coming home.

So, with a skip in my step, I follow the aroma of fresh gourmet patisseries and newly brewed coffee, and it leads me to Chez Bouffe. It's a lovely brasserie, but it has an enormous queue, and my temper flares at the sight of it. Stop, Tony. Count to ten. Everyone is hungry. Everyone wants to have lunch. You can't blow your daughter's homecoming because you're impatient and insensitive. Then, I count to ten again, suck it up, and stand at the end of the line.

Eventually, it's my turn at the counter, and I order, claim my breakfast, and look for someplace to sit—except there isn't one. The station is in chaos. Every seat in the food court is taken. I count to ten again. It's okay. I will not have a fit over this, and I brace myself against a cement column, unwrap my toasty, and have a good-sized bite. A trio of flavors: warm bread, maple flavored ham, and Dijon mustard melt in my mouth. It's delicious.

My stomach roils.

I spit the morsel back in the bag. What's wrong with my sandwich? What's wrong with *me*? Am I sick? I don't feel sick. What if I'm coming down with something? What if I'm getting sick with a late summer cold? Christ, there's nothing worse than an end-of-season head cold, and I check my forehead, but I'm not warm. I snuffle air into my nose, but my sinuses are clear.

Was it something in the sandwich? I bite into it again, but, no, the flavors are all wrong, and I cough up this mouthful as well. My temper soars. I close my eyes. What's that thing Ana is always telling me to do to calm down—imagine you're on a beach or something? I chuckle to myself and open my eyes. I don't know why I'm wasting my time with any of this, and I discard the whole thing in a waste bin and head for the platforms. I came here with the intention of waiting for my daughter, and I search out an available seat and plant myself in it. I open my tablet.

Soon, someone takes the seat next to me. He positions his briefcase in his lap, then he takes out a hoagie. It's packed with bean sprouts and hummus. I can't look at it. I've been repulsed by bean sprouts ever since Ana put them in our scrambled eggs one morning and neglected to tell me. Then the guy boots up one of those new netbooks. He connects to the station's WiFi and skims the BBC's news site.

I consider connecting my device, but I worry about using personal tech gadgetry in public spaces—between downloading viruses and the possibility of hackers accessing my

computer, I can't see the logic in it. Instead, I take my Black-
Berry out of my pocket, and I call Ana.

"What's wrong?" she asks.

"Did Chloe call?"

"You're two hours early."

I note the time on hoagie boy's laptop. She knows me well.
"I wondered if maybe—"

"She's fine," Ana says. "I'm sure she's on her way."

"She could've missed the train. She always packs too
much." A trait she inherited from my wife, no doubt.

"Did you check the arrival boards?"

"Damn it all." I feel like an idiot, and without so much as a
good-bye, I press End and dart back through the pedestrian
passageway. But rather than check the boards, I have a better
idea, and I race over to the ticket counter instead. If anyone has
the most up-to-date news concerning this afternoon's train
schedules, it's the staff behind the information counter.

I approach the counter, and for a change, I'm first in line.
The young woman behind the desk can't be more than nineteen, and like so many of my students, I notice her blouse—
how can I not? It's cut too low. So, in an attempt not to embarrass either her or myself, I focus on the travel poster behind her
head, then I ask whether the trains from Le Raincy-Villemonble-Montfermeil are running on time this afternoon.

The young woman doesn't even look up. She taps away at
her keyboard and gives me some offhanded response about
how the trains are indeed running on time and that it's not her
job to oversee the arrival boards. That's why they're posted all
over the station, she tells me. Then she deliberately looks past
me and calls to the next person in line.

I feel small, like a bug that needs to be disposed of, and I
want to rebut this woman, perhaps say a thing or two about
respect, but I can't allow myself to get mad, not today. Today,

my precious eldest daughter returns home, so I redirect myself and step away from the counter.

I revisit the platform area, but I pace this time rather than sit. While I understand pacing in and of itself won't mollify me, it's possible it could calm me down, maybe even loosen the muscles in my lower back. It could even help me shed some of the weight I gained over the summer. Boy, that would be a big plus. It would make sex with Didi easier, and I eagerly begin to record my laps around the esplanade.

I gather a total of two laps when I stop in my tracks.

Hell. I'm not fooling anyone. No way I'm going to manage my impatience by traipsing up and down this walkway. Neither will I shed an ounce of fat, and rather than torture myself any further, I find a kiosk and buy a copy of today's *Times*. As I hand the merchant the euros, I can't help but notice the row of cheerfully packaged homemade cookies that are stacked up behind him. I move in closer—he has so *many* different kinds of cookies. There are chocolate chip, meringue, French sables, and—madeleines! My heart soars. Chloe *loves* madeleines. I fling another handful of euros at the man and point to them.

It's genius. I'll present these to her as soon as she steps off the train. It's the consummate welcome home gift, and I secure the cookies and skip away from the hut when it dawns on me. It's been nearly a decade since I saw my daughter last. She was sixteen then. Do I really expect to know what kind of cookie she likes *now*?

Good Lord, I'm no genius. I'm just an old fool. Not only do I not know what my daughter prefers in cookies, but at this point in her life, I couldn't tell you a thing about her. I couldn't tell you the color of her hair, or her height, or what she weighs. I couldn't tell you what she does in her spare time any more than I could say what she does for a living. Does she still shun anything made with animal products and run weekend errands in her track shoes?

Will I even recognize her when she steps off the train?

What if she can't recognize *me*?

She's my flesh and blood . . . and it's all I can do not to drop to my knees right here.

I pinch my eyelids together, blink back the tears, and plod over to the nearest trash bin and ditch the cookies.

I look for a seat, but, as the station become busier, there are none, so I heave myself onto the floor. I peruse the first few pages of the newspaper, but the cement is too hard, and I'm uncomfortable. I shift to the left, then realign my butt to the right, then flatten myself against the wall, but nothing helps. I go to reposition myself one more time when the overhead loudspeaker snaps to life with the latest arrival times. I stop and listen, and—yes! Chloe's train is among them!

I jump up and race back through the underground passageway, then I run over to the platform area and hurdle the turnstiles. I arrive at Platform Five with no time to spare. Chloe's train is pulling into the station. I can't believe my luck, and I jog alongside it until it stops. I position myself so I'll be in full view of the passengers when they disembark. I'll be damned if my daughter steps off this train and misses me.

Chloe will *not* pass me by as if I'm a total stranger.

In a single motion, the train's compartment doors slide open, and chaos reigns. The passengers exit the train, and they bump, bang, and pummel me. I'm undeterred, however, and I comb the platform for my daughter. I search over their heads and in between their shoulders. I look past their luggage. Is that Chloe over there? Is this her here? The commuters continue to disembark, and I continue to trundle up and down the platform. They locate and embrace loved ones, but I still don't see my daughter.

Soon, the flood of exiting riders slows to a trickle.

The last few passengers step off the train.

Yet Chloe is not here.

There must be some mistake.

She must be inside—in one of the passenger cars.

So, I poke my head into several of the open doorways. I'll bet she's struggling with her luggage. Or she's having difficulties rolling her suitcase down the aisle. What if she's still in the lavatory? Or fallen asleep in her seat unaware the train is even in the station? Holy smokes. I have to wake her, and I hop onto the nearest car and search through the rows of seats. I sprint into the next car, and the next, but I don't see her. She's not in any of them. I hunt through several more cars, but it's hopeless.

All the passengers have disembarked.

The platform is deserted.

My daughter isn't here.

I take out my BlackBerry and text her on the number Ana gave me. Then I wait, but there's no response. I take a seat and watch the screen some more, but still, there's nothing. I drop my cell in my pocket and bolt through the passageway. I leap over the turnstiles again. What if she got past me? What if I missed her with all my racing around the station like a crazy man?

But my heartbeat slows to a crawl, and I can't make the obvious go away. There is no one else here. Anywhere. There is no one else on board this train, or standing on the dais, or roaming about the platform. While I don't want to admit it, the facts are clear. There is no one else here waiting to meet their loved one.

There is no one else here waiting to meet their dad.

My bottom lip quivers, and I skulk back over to the information desk. It's the same young woman behind the counter.

She notices me and lowers her eyes.

I massage the back of my neck and approach her, and before she has a chance to say anything, I launch into my account about how there's been a terrible mistake. I say I've waited hours for the Le Raincy-Villemonble-Montfermeil train to arrive, and that I expected my daughter to be on it, but she was not. Then I watch her face and gauge her tolerance for my plight before I disclose our entire history—the fight between my wife and daughter, how my eldest stormed out of our lives, the way she's recently contacted us again. And I don't even stop there. Something comes over me, and I carry on about how I've waited so long for this day, and how much it means to me. I babble indiscriminately about the way I imagine it will feel to have my daughter home, hell, to have my entire family back together again after seven long lonely years. Finally, when I can think of nothing more to say that will convince this woman to look at her damn screen, I bite my tongue, thank her for listening to my story, and I ask her, and with utmost respect, if she'd please check her computer to see if the RER E train from Le Raincy-Villemonble-Montfermeil has arrived at the station yet. Then I add one more "please" for good measure, and I wait for the quarrel to ensue.

But the woman doesn't argue with me. She doesn't say a word, in fact. She types and scrolls, types and scrolls, and as I wait for her to give me some information—any information—on the whereabouts of this train, I glance across her desk. I don't know why I didn't notice it before. It's a framed photograph of a boy. It sits adjacent to her computer screen. The child in the picture is maybe six, and he has on a pair of miniature denim overalls. He pouts at the camera and holds the hand of a much older woman. It's not the woman who sits before me.

The attendant stops typing, and her expression relaxes.

The skin around her eyes softens. She looks up from her screen and apologizes and says the train from Le Raincy-Villemonble-Montfermeil arrived a few minutes ago. Then she asks if I'd give her my daughter's name she could—

I don't need to hear any more. I drag myself away and glom onto the nearest wall and call Ana. "Chloe didn't get off the train," I say.

"What?"

"She didn't get off the train. Chloe's not here."

"And you were at Platform Five?" Judging by her tone, I'd say she's as surprised as I am.

"Did you try calling or texting her?" Ana asks. "To see if something is wrong?"

"Yes, yes, I waited at the right platform. I texted her after the train emptied out. I did everything right. Chloe didn't get off the train. I even spoke to someone at the information desk who double-checked the schedule." I fight to keep from crying. "I had everything exact for once. Chloe's not here . . . she's . . . not here," I say. "She's not here." I stop talking and wait for Ana to gloat. I wait for her to tell me how I'm a fool and to provide me with some version of, "I told you so."

She doesn't. She tells me instead how me she made the macaroni and cheese dish we like, and she thinks we should still have it for dinner tonight. Even if it's just the two of us. She says we did our best, and we should reward ourselves.

A celebration is the last thing on my mind, and I stammer out a pointless lie about how I need to swing by PSE and finish some long-overdue student assignments.

Ana interjects and tells me to come home. "There's a bottle of chilled wine in the refrigerator," she says. "It has our name on it."

What if my wife was right about Chloe all along? What if Chloe's true intention was to have us send her money whenever she needed it—and that was it? What if our daughter never wanted anything more to do with us than that? All of a sudden, I feel more connected to Ana than I have in years. Maybe I should give her the box of madeleines. If I recall, my wife also loves madeleines. I'll present them as a peace offering, as my way of strengthening our relationship and showing her that I want to work on our marriage.

What am I thinking? I can't give Ana a box of cookies I threw away. I'll buy a new box.

But they're so expensive.

Would I be able to locate the same bin?

I make a u-turn in the middle of the terminal, then another one, then I stop. I scuffle over to the nearest kiosk and point to the macaroons.

It's no wonder Chloe doesn't want to come home.

Ana's wrong. I'm not a good father; I'm an ass.

25
ANA

Tony buries his head in his tablet. "If you don't mind," he says, "I'd like to relax a little before we eat." He tosses a box of cookies at me and trudges into the living room.

Macaroons? I shrug my shoulders and set the cookies on the counter beside the still steaming dish of mac and cheese. I pride myself on my timing. It couldn't be better. I'll give Tony a few minutes to unwind, then we can eat, and I grab two wine glasses and a bottle of Locations French red and follow him into the living room.

"If you have it in mind to say 'I warned you'," he says, "don't bother."

I pour a glass of wine and offer it to him.

He doesn't refuse it.

I fill the other glass, place the bottle on the coffee table, and sit beside him. I clink my glass against his. "We could both use some of this tonight."

Tony salutes me and takes a sip of his wine. He sets his glass on the table, reaches for the remote, and turns on the television. He switches channels until he finds FR3, France's news channel.

"It's been a long time since we lazed around the house and drank cheap wine," I say.

He nods as he mulls over the news broadcast.

"Or should I say, *guzzled* cheap wine."

No smile from Tony. No light in his eyes.

"We certainly had our share of crazy nights, didn't we?"

My husband nods again.

"I experimented with so many new recipes," I laugh. "I forced you to taste them all." I look over at him. "You wanted to murder me, but you tried them. Every single one."

No response.

"Remember how I'd pair them with some cheap wine I found in that liquor store down on Spring Street?" I sip from my glass. "Some nights all we did was drink and eat until we couldn't, then we'd go to bed. We didn't even have sex."

Tony places the remote between us. He covers it with his hand and continues to watch the telecast.

I polish off the rest of my glass and refill it.

"Why did you do it?" he asks.

My stomach twitches. Tony's question is not about the amount of alcohol we drank in SoHo. I face forward and keep my eyes on the television. Scenes of the severe flooding occurring all across France flash across the screen. "It's complicated," I say.

"You had an affair, what's so baffling about it?"

Droplets of sweat crop up along my upper lip. I dab them with my sleeve, then sit back. I glean what comfort I can from the cotton batting in the couch. I really don't want to have another argument tonight. "Maybe I was too young to get married," I say.

"I don't believe your age was a factor."

He's right, it wasn't.

My husband finishes his wine.

I check how much is left in the bottle, then fiddle with the neckline of my shirt. "You're not going to make this easy for me, are you?" I ask.

"No, I'm not." He keys in on the flooding. Yesterday, an elderly German man was swept away as he helped a group of children break free of the rushing currents. It's sad, but no one is safe when water rages.

I drain my glass, sit forward, and place it on the coffee table. "I'm sorry." I turn and look at him. "I am. I'm sorry for all the terrible things I've done to you: the affair, the lies, Géraud's foolish letter. All of it. You didn't deserve any of it."

Tony sets his glass down beside mine, then sits back. He surfs through the channels again. We continue like this, side by side, not a word between us, as an unbroken flow of game, porn, and reality shows rolls across the screen.

"I don't know why I did it." I recline into the couch again. "I don't have an answer, not a good one," I say. "I knew it was wrong, but I wanted so much more than what you were willing to give me."

More silence. My husband studies the screen. He drops the remote in his lap. "It wasn't that I was *unwilling* to give it to you," he says.

I roll my thumbs and cross my legs in the other direction.

"I tried." He jiggles his knee. "In my own lowly way."

"I know."

"I wasn't opposed to starting a family, but I was working eighty hours a week. I couldn't simply—"

"I know, Tony." I place my hand on his knee. "It's not easy to be with me. I demand a lot, and I don't give much back. I'm not making excuses . . . I don't know. Maybe I am."

Tony points the channel changer at the television again.

"What I'm saying is it's hard to describe how it feels to turn yourself inside out to discover there's nothing good there. It fills you with so much contempt for yourself . . . so much hopelessness, that you lash out at everyone around you, especially the people who love you the most." I futz with my shirt again, then gently rub my arms. "I won't say I don't know the difference between right and wrong. It's more like I convince myself it's okay to hurt other people because I hurt, and because all that matters in the heat of that moment is stopping the thoughts that tell me I'm a worthless piece of shit."

Tony resumes his quest for the perfect news broadcast. *Click, click, click.* Finally, he stops and looks at the remote. He turns it over in his hand.

I comb my fingers through my hair, let the loose strands dance across my face. "I've spent the majority of my life gobbling up other women's personalities like a piranha. I've sucked the life out of everyone who's ever gotten close to me. I've stolen their dreams and pilfered their desires and all so I could mold myself into an exact replica of them and show the world I wasn't repulsive. I wasn't bad or evil. Then I begged— no, I pleaded for God to turn me into a person somebody else could love. Somebody you could love." I look over at my husband, watch his face for any testiness, but the lines along his forehead are soft; his expression is kind.

"You were the best thing to happen to me," I say. "You were so smart, and driven, and accomplished. Men like you don't look at women like me. All I wanted was for you to love me."

Tony tosses the remote. He places his hand on mine.

"I hate myself." I dab at my cheeks.

He touches my shoulder. He lets his hand rest there for a second. "Thank you," he says. "This is the first time you've apologized to me."

Our eyes meet, and we unite in a way that's more honest

and intimate than at any other point in our marriage, and it frightens me. "Wow." I get up from the couch. "It's after ten, and we haven't had dinner yet."

"I'm not really hungry," he says.

This is definitely one thing Tony and I can agree on tonight. My stomach is so topsy-turvy right now, I couldn't eat a thing. "Me, neither," I say. "If you take out the dogs, I'll put the food away, and we can all go to bed early and get a good night's sleep. It's been a long day."

When Tony leaves with the dogs, I finish up in the kitchen, then retreat to the bedroom where I brush my teeth and fall into bed. The portable air conditioning unit has been running all afternoon, and I eagerly nestle under the comforter. The dogs are quick tonight, and twenty minutes later, Dharma and Kooks hobble across the room and flop onto their own beds. My husband is so tired, he doesn't even bother to brush his teeth. He undresses, climbs into bed beside me, and rolls onto his back. He folds an arm across his forehead.

I take in the fragrance of his skin. It's unwashed and honest, and I want to reach across the mattress and touch him. Or ask him to touch me. I want to hold him like we did when we were young and before I gutted everything.

What if I rest my hand on his back, or his shoulder, or the nape of his neck?

Would he let me?

Would it heal all the wrongs? Or soften our past offenses?

I inch my hand across the sheet and touch him. I cup my fingers around his knuckles, and we lie like this for a while until my skin feels like it's on fire, and I have to let go. I turn and face away from him.

Now Tony shifts position. The sheets swoosh as he moves closer; he snuggles his front against my back and molds himself to the curve of my body. He stretches his legs and explores my feet with his toes.

I rotate back in his direction, and we face each other. Our noses touch, and I take in his breath. I angle my head and peck lightly at his lips. He responds right off, and we kiss. Once, twice. They're tentative but sincere, and I cup his face with my hands. Soon, our mouths are moving slower, and our kisses are becoming wetter, and our bond begins to feel like it did at the start of our relationship: thrilling and generous. But it's not enough for me. I want more. I always want more, and I strip off my nightshirt.

Tony doesn't hesitate. He moves his mouth lower, along the curves of my body; he kisses my throat, my neck, my chest. He tickles my belly button, then covers me with his heft, and there are no more words. No more thoughts. No more judgment or blame, and we turn back the clock to an earlier time, a more erotic time—before Tony had a lover, or our relationship stagnated, or I had an affair. We revisit a chapter of our lives that was written before Paris and before we had children, when the most incredible thing we experienced was the sensation of each other's skin on our own and the way it linked our bodies and left no room for misunderstanding. Or insecurity. Or disillusionment. As our excitement heightens and our actions become less restrained, we allow ourselves to lose all control, and I hold on tight as my husband slips inside me and pushes pushes pushes us into what's yet to come.

Eventually, we exhaust ourselves, but we don't separate. We lie next to each other, with our limbs entwined, until Tony drifts off. As his sleep becomes heavier, so does his array of exhalations, and the more audibly he emits them. If I didn't know better, I'd think his airway is obstructed. Years of pent-up tension will do that to a person: stifle their breath.

Conversely, the dogs sleep and unleash breaths that are

long and opulent and waltz around the room. Deep in the night, their paws jerk, and their bodies twitch, and they run free in their dreams. Why shouldn't they? Good dogs with pure hearts, they're unencumbered by rage or vengeance or pride. They sleep free of worry.

Then there's my own breath, and I touch my hand to my chest and search out the familiar tightness, but it's not there tonight. Tonight, I'm at peace. Tonight, as I lie surrounded by my family and connected by the invisible bonds of our love, I feel closer to heaven than I've ever been, and I'm convinced there's a God and that we're not alone in this universe. Nor are we the result of some long string of random evolutionary accidents. No, tonight, I have no misgivings, and I rest assured that tour existence, our whole reason for being, is so much more than this.

Then the phone rings.

26

TONY

It intrudes on my dream like a fire alarm, and I bolt upright in bed. The landline is ringing—it's ringing off the hook. Who would be calling us at this hour?

Chloe. It has to be Chloe.

I grope at the nightstand, but I can't find the receiver, then my hand hits it. It crashes to the floor. "*Allo?*" I scrabble around on the rug. "*Allo?*" I locate the cord and yank it. I shout into the receiver. "*Allo?*"

"Dad?"

"Chloe?"

"Is Mom there? Please put Mom on the phone, okay? Please?"

Did my daughter just ask for Ana? "You want to—"

My wife swipes the receiver from my hand.

"Chloe," she says. "Where are you? What's going on?"

I hoist myself back into bed. "What time is it?"

Ana shushes me. "I can't understand you," she says. "Are you high? You sound like you're high. It's okay if you are. I'll come and get you."

My hands are numb, and I open and close my fingers, but it's not enough to bring the feeling back. So, I flex them against my legs, but I push too hard and leave big white marks on my skin.

"I said it was okay. We'll come get you." Ana threads the sheet through her fingers. She winds the material so tight, it looks like she's holding on for dear life. "Where *are* you?" she asks.

I don't like the way this conversation sounds, and I take in more air, but it only adheres to the inside of my lungs. You don't need to be a rocket scientist to know my daughter is in some sort of danger. I zero in on the telephone cord, which is snarled around the base of the lamp. Someone was too lazy to untangle it the last time they used the phone. I unwind it, and an old water stain reveals itself.

"Wait." Ana pokes around in the top drawer of the night-stand. She pulls out a pencil. Someone's chewed the eraser off the end of it. Can we have anything nice in this house?

"Chloe, tell me where you are." Ana pats my hand.

I trace my finger over the stain. I outline its circumference. How did that *get* there?

"I understand, but, where are you?" Ana asks.

For the life of me, I cannot remember how that damn mark *got* there.

"I'm not judging you," she says. "All you need is one thing to go wrong, and it feels like your whole world is falling apart."

I arrange the phone cord so the water mark sits in the center of the cord's loop.

"Don't apologize." Ana presses her fingers against the bridge of her nose. "I'm the one who should be asking for *your* forgiveness," she whispers. "How about we get you home first, then we can discuss it all you want, all right?" She fumbles inside the drawer of the nightstand again. She removes an old Christmas card and jots something on the back. She stops writing. She looks over at me. "Baby?" she asks.

"What the—?"

"Who had—? When did you?" Ana asks. "I didn't realize—"

"A *baby*? Who had a baby?"

"It *is* good news. It's great news."

"What the devil is going on?"

"Wow, I . . . I can't believe there's a new baby in the family," Ana says. "Oh, honey, she's the whole reason you're hanging on."

"*Chloe* had a *baby*?"

"What's her name?" my wife asks. "*A*-sia?" She repeats it, placing the accent on the first syllable.

"What's the name?" I ask.

"AA-*see*-ya." Ana repeats the word again. This time she underscores the second syllable. She scribbles on the back of the card again.

I flick at the cord. It sails across the nightstand and over the edge, but it does no damage, certainly not enough to mitigate the alarm that is now spreading through my chest.

"Yes, it's a *wonderful* name for a girl," my wife says.

I snap my fingers. "Hello? Can someone please explain to me what this is all about?"

"We're wide awake," she says to my daughter. "We could be there in an hour."

Goddamn it. I sweep at the cord, and it flies off the nightstand. It all but takes the base of the phone with it.

"Fine," Ana says. "We'll get you first thing in the morning, but I don't like it . . . I *am* working with you, Chloe . . . all right. I said all right . . . I just want you to be safe. Dad and I love you. Very much. You know that, right?" She pauses before she returns the receiver to its cradle, then she falls back on the bed. She clutches her forehead.

"What in God's name is happening with our daughter?" I ask.

My wife continues to lie flat.

My face is hot and becoming hotter. My daughter is experiencing a crisis, and I'm being kept in the dark. If I don't do something, I'm going to lose it. I stand and stagger into the hallway. I wait for Ana to say something, then I brace myself against the sheetrock and move along the wall until I reach the kitchen, where I switch on the light beneath the stove, then slump into a chair. Slow and determined footsteps follow me, and I look to see Dharma, the perennial worrywart of our flawed pack, plod across the kitchen in my direction. Her weary form stops at my feet. She lowers herself to the floor and places her nose between her paws. Her eyebrows quiz me.

I give her a head scratch, hoping this will suffice, when Ana enters the kitchen right behind her. My wife flips on the overhead light and fractures the quiet like the Bellagio in Las Vegas.

"This is all your fault." I'm wide awake now.

Ana stops short. "You heard me tell her we'd come get her tonight," she says. "She refused."

A nerve pinches behind my eye.

My wife moves to the sink. She avoids my eye contact. "I tried, Tony. What else did you want me to do?"

I clench and unclench my fists. I embrace the energy now building in my muscles. This is not the answer that I want. I want a definitive response. I want every piece of information—extraneous or otherwise—that Chloe shared with her, including everything she knows about this child, which is evidently my daughter's child. "And why weren't we aware our daughter had a baby?" I ask

"How would I know she had a baby?" Ana briefly meets my gaze again, then looks away.

"This is exactly my point, Ana."

She whirls around to face me. "You heard me on the phone. She *refused* to let me get her tonight. What more did you want me to say?"

"We shouldn't be in this position."

"We shouldn't be doing a lot of things." My wife returns her attention to the counter. She pulls an old map out of one of the junk drawers.

The compression in my forehead intensifies. It feels like someone jammed a stick of dynamite in my brain, then lit the fuse. I need to make it stop, and I rise from my chair and stumble over to the counter. I seize the French press. I raise it over my head.

Ana catches sight of me out of the corner of her eye. She screams and faces me.

The pinch thumps, the fuse shortens, and the carafe quakes in my hands. I clench my teeth.

"Tony, don't!"

With both eyes trained on my wife, I discharge the damn thing. A grotesque symphony of glass shatters across the kitchen floor.

Footsteps jerk in our neighbors' apartment upstairs.

Dharma leaps to her feet, but her hind end collapses, and she howls as she labors to flee the sight.

Ana leaps at the dog. She secures her arms under Dharma's belly and lifts her, then she takes the old girl by her collar and weaves a path through the crushed glass for them to escape. When they reach the hall, Dharma runs off. My wife follows.

I bolt into the hall after them. I point my finger in Ana's face. "I told you, this is all your fault."

Ana waves me away. She returns to the kitchen.

In my peripheral vision, I take note of Meadow standing at the far end of the hall. My youngest glowers at me. She shouldn't see this, but I'm on a roll. "You did this to her." I follow my wife. I hover inside the archway.

"You make it sound like I—"

"Like you what? Like you wrecked our oldest daughter's life?"

"Don't say that."

"Say what? That you drove her away? That you pushed her out of our lives?"

"Don't you dare pin this on me. I told you Chloe had a drug problem."

"Oh, that's rich coming from you." I laugh, but it's contrived. "So, what, that makes you a hero now?"

"You didn't want to hear it. Never in your wildest imagination did you think such a thing could happen to one of *your* daughters, certainly not to the daughter of such an important university professor like yourself."

I curl my lip. Foul can't even begin to explain my depreciating disposition. "I know what you did that night," I say. "You banished Chloe from our home."

"That's ridiculous."

"I'm not blind. I saw what went on in this house. Of all our daughters, you treated her the worst."

Ana steps into the hallway again. If she thinks she can escape my ire, she has another thing coming. I vault in front of her. "You treated Chloe like she was a disgrace," I say. "Hell, the way you regarded her, it was almost like you resented her for being born."

"Stop it, Tony."

"Wait a minute." I suck in my breath. I can't believe I haven't thought of this before now. "All these years, and I'm finally getting a handle on it." I look hard at my wife. "That's it, though, isn't it? That's what this is all about. That's what it's *always* been about. As far as you were concerned, she *was* a disgrace."

"You don't know what you're talking about." Ana deflects me with her shoulder.

"Holy cow," I say. "I can't believe I didn't see it sooner, but I finally understand."

"Don't do this," she says.

"You thought Chloe was illegitimate."

"Don't go there with this."

"Sweet Mother of God." I scratch my head. "I had no idea."

"Don't take us back there, Tony. Not after everything we've weathered."

"You thought she belonged to *him*. You thought our daughter was *his* biological child. Do I have this right?"

"Tony. Please." Ana returns to the kitchen. She slumps against the counter.

I'm right behind her. "Each communication, every interaction you had with her, reminded you of *him*."

"Do we have to do this?"

"But that *is* it. Chloe was a constant reminder of what you'd done, and you couldn't avoid it. So, you had to avoid her."

"I am so sorry," Ana says. "Last night, when I apologized, I meant it." She presses the hems of her shirt sleeves against her eyes. "I can't erase the past," she says.

"No," I say. "What you can't erase is the lifetime of misery you caused our daughter."

"Don't you think I regret how I treated Chloe?" She shouts at me, then makes a production of rubbing her eyes.

Her performance doesn't fool me. This is a display of faux humility. I've listened to Ana's lies and schemes for over two decades, and I recognize when I'm being bamboozled.

"What about you?" she asks. "What did you do to search for our daughter after she left? I don't remember seeing you combing the neighborhood for her, or badgering her teachers, or calling all her friends for some word, any word, as to her whereabouts. Did you even try to reconnect with any of her old boyfriends? Or beg them for any crumb of information they could provide about the last time they saw her? Did you drive with me down to the Petite Ceinture and follow the train tracks, trying to identify whether she was there somewhere, strung out with the other heroin addicts."

"This isn't about me."

"Of course, it's not about you because you didn't do any of those things," she says. "How could you? You were too busy closing your eyes to it all. Just like you ignored all the syringes we unearthed under the floorboards in her bedroom, and all the empty heroin bags we found in her coat pockets. Just like all the times you never said a word when she came home from school and fell asleep at the dinner table. You didn't have to. You let me do it."

Every muscle in my body hardens. I shake my finger at her again, but nothing comes out of my mouth.

My wife presses on. "Or the mornings we went in her room to wake her up for school, but she was so zoned out we thought she was dead?"

The word *dead* kicks me in the teeth, and adrenaline fires through my veins. "I swear, Ana. If you say one more word."

My wife returns to the morass of broken glass strewn across the floor. She plucks at the larger pieces and drops them into the waste basket. She continues to shout at me for my lack of concern for our daughter's situation.

I watch her lips move, but I can't hear a word she's saying. Everything goes higgledy-piggledy in my head, and it's as if all the things I've used to determine what's real in my life were incorrect. Was I *not* a good father to my oldest daughter? Was it the same for my other daughters? Did I treat them poorly, too? Am I truly as self-centered as Ana says I am? Maybe if she stopped talking, I could understand her. If she would only stop talking, just for a minute, but she keeps talking and talking and talking . . . if she would just stop—

I reach out and grab a fistful of Ana's hair.

She staggers into me and shouts, but her voice is muffled. She digs her fingernails into my skin.

"Good *God*." I let go of her and slap her. Hard.

She grunts at the impact. The strength of the blow throws her off balance, and her body slams against the tiles. She doesn't get up.

"NO!" Meadow leaps in front of me. She wails and claws at my face.

I shove my youngest out of the way and holler at my wife again. "Get up." My arms, my legs, my entire body trembles with the force of my vindictiveness. This is the first time I've hit my wife out of anger, but she made me feel small.

Ana remains face down on the kitchen floor.

"You're exactly like your mother." Ana's told me stories about how her father abused her mother. I'm a dick for throwing it in her face, but we've moved way beyond pleasantries. "Your father threw her against walls, and she begged him not to leave her."

Ana allows Meadow to pull her upright. "You'll never understand women," she says.

My wife's comment is a blow to my ego, and it triggers the nerve in my head again. This time, nothing short of total obliteration will silence it. "You're right about that," I say. "But I understand *you*. And I know how much you crave sex, and I have to say, it's worked for me. In fact, it's the reason I'm still with you. It's the intense pleasure I get sexing you."

"Shut up, Tony."

"Whether it's in your pussy, your ass, your mouth—I love it all. Every position, every fantasy, every kinky-ass game we've acted out on each other. You're a whore, my love. You're an exquisite opportunist, and banging you has been the greatest triumph of my life."

"Stop that." Her eyes are thick with tears.

"Marrying you was the best thing I ever did. It transformed me. It took me from being a morose and mistreated child to the babe I am today. I never thought I'd say this, honey, but I'm a catch. Women gravitate to me, and it's all because of you."

"SHUT UP!" Ana curses at me.

"If it weren't for our daughters . . . Hell, I would've left you a long time ago."

"You haven't transformed into anything," she says. Her voice is low. The words retch from her lips. "You're a fraud. You're nothing. Zip. Zilch. Zero. You're a *dumb-ass*, and you'll never be anything more than a bore with a dead brother. *I'm* the one who shines a light on you. I'm the one who *transforms* you. Without me, you're *nobody*."

The feeling of wrapping my fingers around my wife's neck almost becomes too real, and I give her a last menacing look before I lumber out of the kitchen. I head in the direction of our bedroom, but the thought of going inside nauseates me. So, I do an about-face and aim for Chloe's old room, where I enter and fight hard to hold back the tears. Seven years. It's been seven long wasted years since I've seen my daughter smile, or heard her laugh, or sat with her while she cried. I perch at the edge of her bed and run my hand across the mattress. I unearth her pillows and bury my head in them. Then I lie back, roll onto my side, and draw my knees to my chest.

This is all my wife's fault, and I will never forgive her for it.

27
ANA

Saturday, August 11, 2018
Only hours before Chloe's rescue

"I'm leaving." There's a sharp pang in my neck. It's a reminder of last night.

Tony sits at the kitchen table. He clasps his hands around a partially filled coffee cup. A tea bag string hangs over the side. A stream of snot soils the front of his shirt.

I want to talk about what happened between us, but I don't know where to begin. Last night was ugly. *Tony* was ugly—and in front of Meadow. What must our youngest think of her father?

What must she think of *me*?

Another woman would've called the police. Or at least walked out with her dignity intact.

"The dog's meals are in the fridge," I say. "I packed up a separate container for each of them. I also sorted their meds and marked the packets with the times they need to take them." I'm blathering, but I don't know what else to do. I can only hope this act of altruism on my part, of bringing our daughter home, will translate into an act of forgiveness on Tony's part. "I shouldn't be long."

My husband lifts the cup to his mouth and swallows what's left in it. "How does a mother develop such an aversion to her own daughter?" he asks.

My fingers are tacky, and I push on my cuticles. "I don't dislike Chloe."

"Did you give her Géraud's letter?" Tony stares at his cup. "Chloe. Did you give her the letter?"

"No," I say. "She found it. I assumed she was looking for the reason we weren't close."

"So, why did she leave?" My husband glances over at me.

I look around for Dharma and Kooks.

Tony's eyes erupt in anger, but the emotion fades just as fast, and he replaces it with gut level disappointment.

He knows I'm lying.

Why can't I just tell him the truth, for once?

I eye him defiantly, instead. I hold his stare to ridicule him, to force him to believe my version of events, but a fever of shame sweeps through me, and I wrap my arms around my middle, cross the kitchen, and gaze out the window. I watch the early morning urbanites as they wind their way through the town's tight, crooked streets, all of them intent on affecting their lives with purpose. Rich with their morning lattes, they go forward into the new day with the same unyielding passion I use to remain idle in mine.

When is enough, enough?

Nothing good will happen for me unless I free myself from the past.

It's time, Ana. Make the leap.

I turn to my husband. "I got scared," I say. "Chloe had the letter in her hand. She threatened to tell you about it."

Tony looks away. "What did you do?" His voice softens.

My husband was half-right last night when he said Chloe was a reminder of what I had done. She was also a reminder of what had been done to me. While my oldest daughter was the greatest memento I had of Géraud, she also represented the coldblooded way he'd discarded me when he was done with our affair. You could say I had a love-hate relationship with my eldest daughter. As long as I had Chloe, I had him, but I paid dearly for it.

"I threw her out," I say. "I couldn't take the chance you would leave me."

The kitchen is quiet. Someone flushes a toilet upstairs, then treks cautiously across the floor.

"I destroyed this family," I say. "But I'm doing my best to repair it."

"So, you think you can snap your fingers and make it all better?"

I cross the kitchen and drop into the chair opposite him.

"When Chloe needed a mother, she didn't get one," he says. "Face it: you ruined her life. You ruined all our lives."

"I did a horrendous thing, Tony, I get it, but I can do better. If Chloe will give me another chance, I'll work my ass off this time around."

"Chloe no longer needs a mother."

"Chloe needs a mother now more than ever." I massage my arms, neaten up my sleeves. "So does her little girl. I can be that for both of them, but I need you to work with me."

"Please don't bullshit me with some half-assed speech about solidarity." My husband stands and drifts to the other side of the kitchen. He pauses in front of the same window. "You're the last person on this planet to talk about unity."

"You want to reunite with your daughter," I say. "If we do this together, we can make it happen."

"There is no *together* here." His voice alters. It sounds like no musical instrument I've ever known.

A wave of chills ripples through me. "Baby, please. I'm doing this for us," I say. "We've been given an opportunity to make amends for all the lousy things we've done to each other —okay, I've been given an opportunity to make amends, and I want to do that, for us. I want to make up for all the cruel things I've done to you. I want to redeem myself, but I can't unless you let me." I fiddle with my sleeves. "Can you do that, Tony? Can you give me a chance to prove myself, to prove I can learn from my mistakes? I don't have all the answers yet, but I can make this marriage work again. I know I can. I always do."

I can see my husband doesn't buy any of it, though, and I don't know what else to say.

Tony returns to the table, picks up his cup, and carries it to the sink. He turns toward the door.

"I need you, Tony. Let me fix this." I stuff my hands in my pockets and wait for him to turn around, to make eye contact with me, or at least finish our conversation.

He plods out of the kitchen.

I want to run after him. I want to bury my fingers in his skin and make him listen to me. I want to convince him that if he can trust me again, this one last time, I won't let him down, but chasing him will only prove I'm the same old Ana. So, I sling my purse over my shoulder instead, and I head for the front door.

Dharma and Kooks block my path. I'm going on an adventure, and they want to be included. I take out my cellphone and snap their picture, then I post it in a tweet. "Who better to teach us about love! Wish we could keep them forever!" I kneel between them and scratch up both of their woolly necks. Dharma nudges closer and rubs the top of her head against my chest while Kooks stands at his post and monopolizes the doorway with his body mass.

"You have a flake for a mother," I say. "But things are going to change around here and for the better." Then, in my finest baby talk, I add, "I see you two soon, okay?"

28

TONY

"God, you are so amazing." Within minutes of Ana's departure, I asked Meadow to run an errand, then I popped a Viagra, called Didi, and investigated whether she'd like to come over. We're now prone across the living room floor, engaged in some pretty rough sex. Didi and I have gotten wild in the past, but it was nowhere near what we've been into this morning.

Yet it is small change compared to what I'm ready for today, and I need to know if she's willing to go further. I need to take it to the extreme today. I need to immerse myself so deep in this woman's body that I lose all sense of reality. Between my wife's deceit and the loss of my oldest daughter, my life has imploded before my eyes, and I don't know how else to free myself from the grief except through hardcore sex.

I pinch Didi's backside. Hard.

"Tony—"

I love it when she calls out my name, her voice all low and husky. I lean into her and start giving it to her good.

She buries her nails in my back. They're like razor blades.

This jacks up even more, and I twist her nipples.

She pulls my hair.

Wowzah. I can't believe she's totally digging this. "Who's been a bad girl?"

She elbows me in the face. "What is wrong with you?" she shouts.

"What the hell?" I scramble off her and sit back on my heels. I raise my hands like a pickpocket caught red handed on the Champs-Élysées.

"Did you not hear me say *enough*?" Didi sits up, and in a snap, she stands and locates her bra.

"I thought you were enjoying it?" I pat at the perspiration along the top of my hairline. For the life of me, I can't fathom what I did that was so wrong. "You like it . . . rough. We both do."

"What you were into a minute ago was not *rough*." She furls her eyebrows.

Her words smart, and I retreat into my usual air of superiority. "If you didn't like it, then you should've said so."

"I *did* say so." She combs the living room for the rest of her attire; she retrieves her blouse from behind the couch. "I won't be your stand-in while you excise yourself of your wife."

"I wouldn't do that to you."

She extricates her underpants from between the cushions.

"What are you doing?" I ask.

"What does it appear I am doing?"

"It looks as if you are done with me today." I plunk my butt on the carpet.

Didi pulls on her shorts and sits on the sofa. She slides her feet into a pair of beaded sandals.

"Why are you leaving?" I clamber onto my knees again. I'm certain she expects a proper apology from me, but I have no plan to give one.

"Is this how you act whenever you don't get your way?" she asks. "Or are you normally an asshole, and I haven't paid attention until now?"

"Well." I galvanize my arrogance. "The answer to your first question is yes, this is how I act when I'm not in a position of authority, and as for your second question, the answer is again, yes, I can be quite the asshole. Obviously, you haven't paid much attention to me at all." I jut out my chin and scan the rug for the remote. I point the thing at the television and wait for what should be a significant lecture about my behavior.

"You don't believe you owe me an apology?"

I flip through the channels. "I don't feel I engaged in anything that requires an apology."

"*Really?*"

"Really."

Didi sucks in air through her teeth.

"How was I to know the sex would be too risqué for you today? I can't read your mind, you know." Honestly, I don't have the patience today to cope with this woman's emotional drama today. My plate is plenty full of my own hubris.

Didi places her purse in her lap and looks at me. "Are you not concerned at all about offending me?"

"I warned you I was an asshole."

Her eyes tunnel into me. Didi is a smart woman and doesn't need this garbage from me. I look away. "My daughter rejected me," I say.

"Excuse me?"

"Chloe called last night, but she didn't ask for me. She asked for her mother. Can you believe it? She wanted to speak to Ana." I can't look her in the eye. I only pray she swallows this drivel, because I have nothing else. "Chloe can't stand Ana," I say. "My oldest can't stand her mother. Yet there they were, together on the phone, like two cozy peas in a pod. Why is Ana given the opportunity to save our daughter while I'm the one who is kicked to the curb?" I glance over at her, try and gauge her expression.

"You can't be serious."

She doesn't sound sympathetic. I need to recast this so she will feel sorry for me, at least.

"This is what you are so angry about?" she asks.

"It's selfish, I know."

"Do you?" She clutches her purse. "You sound like a child wallowing in self-pity."

"Oh, I'm indulging in a lot more than self-pity," I say. "This here is one big dose of unadulterated self-disgust. My daughter's been in constant crisis since she was sixteen-years-old. She was heavy into drugs then, and she's similarly hooked on them now. She was high while she was on the phone with Ana last night."

Didi's face eases. Her forehead softens.

"Yet I ignored it," I continue on with my display of self-debasement. "I ignored it the same way I ignored it when she was a teen." I lower my voice. "I pretended it was normal adolescent behavior."

She adjusts a crease in her shorts.

"I didn't protect her," I say. "I'm her father, and I didn't keep her safe. That was the one job I had, and I didn't do it. I failed her." There. I've said it. It's out there, and I can't take it back. My jaw relaxes, and a small portion of the venom I've clung to these last seven years drains out.

"This is foolish," she says.

"My daughter has been in serious trouble for years, and I've excused it. I'm *still* excusing it."

"In order to protect her, you have to find her."

"I know where she is." I face Didi now.

Didi's eyes grow large. She's taken aback by my comment.

My eyes blink uncontrollably. My words come out faster. "Chloe lives here," I say. "On the outskirts of Paris. She's holed up in some deserted dwelling like a squatter."

"There's no need to cast aspersions—"

"My oldest daughter is a ward of the state, a recipient of the many features of our generous social security system."

"Then, it would seem you should be thanking the Lord for their services."

"She shouldn't be out there, is my point. She shouldn't be living on the streets."

"But she is," Didi says. "And it is not so unusual. Women make up nearly half the homeless population in France."

"She's not *homeless*," I shout. "She has a home."

"At this moment, she does not."

"No child of mine should be surviving like a vagrant." I twist my head in both directions, but it does nothing to ease the tension in my neck.

"Family dysfunction is a major key cause why so many young adults sleep rough these days."

"My family is *not* dysfunctional," I bark at Didi. "Nor is my daughter defective. She doesn't deserve to be out there with . . . those people."

"*Those people?*" Didi asks. "I was not aware you were so narrow-minded, Tony. Particularly since you are so eager to pass yourself off as someone who has evolved past such societal bigotry."

Her reaction catches me off guard.

"What happened to Tony DiSalvo, the tolerant and free-thinking scholar?"

"I am neither of those things." I stumble over my words. "Unlike you, I'm a true academic. I'm an observer of life, not a participant."

Didi fidgets with the buttons on her blouse, fastens another, and conceals more skin.

She knows I'm an imposter, a spineless jellyfish. While I'm the first to point the finger at someone else, when it comes to my mistakes, I've never had the gumption to face them, and I don't plan to start now. I shift gears and appeal to her sense of compassion. "It's like I'm reliving my brother's suicide all over again. I've failed my daughter the same way I failed him. I could've prevented Vinny from taking his life. I *knew* he had my father's pistol. I *knew* he was holed up in the basement." I rub my eyes. They're bone-dry. "Sweet, sensitive Vinny. I should've told someone. Yet I did nothing."

Didi crosses her legs in the other direction.

"And it was all because I didn't want my father to be angry with me."

"You are not responsible for your brother's suicide."

"Then I let history repeat itself when Chloe ran away."

"You are being unreasonable—"

"Chloe called me after she left."

She looks at me. She's quiet.

"My daughter left a message on my cell." I wait for my lover to respond, to tell me it's all right, but she doesn't. The anxiety nips at my heels. "I knew something had happened between her and Ana, and that was why she moved out, but I couldn't return her call. Even years later when she emailed and asked for money, I never questioned her about where she was. I just sent her the cash. I was so worried that Ana would find out and have a fit."

Didi remains silent.

The portable air conditioning unit kicks on. It's a welcomed distraction.

I drop my chin. "Then I blamed everything on my wife."

"I do not know what to say," she says.

"Ana still thinks the whole predicament was her fault."

"Dear *Lord*."

This is bad. I've shared too much. I need to reverse this ASAP and show her a chastened Tony, or at least a Tony who feels remorse for his actions. "I did a horrible thing to my wife and daughter." I cover my face with my hands. I peek at Didi through my fingers. "I behaved dreadfully toward my family."

"Yes, you did, and you need to resolve it." She gives me a stern look. The skin along her forehead puckers like a rotting jack-o-lantern.

I suddenly become cognizant of my nakedness, but I can't find my shirt. I crawl over to my chair and hoist myself into it. Air escapes my lungs as if from a child's deflated balloon. "I'm a hypocrite," I say. "I'm aware of that. I complain about Ana all day long, but I've never resolved any of my own childhood troubles." I check Didi's expression again. Is she softening at all?

She digs her car keys out of her purse. "If you are so distraught over your daughter," she says, "then why is Ana the one searching for her while you are here, waiting at home, whining and sputtering all over yourself?"

My chest breaks out in a sweat. I can't focus on anything other than those metal shanks in her hand. There must be *something* I can say to make her stay. "There's also a child."

Didi stops monkeying with her keys.

"My daughter has a child. She's eighteen months. I was made aware of this last night." I expect her to commiserate with me now, especially as she grasps how emotional this situation is for me.

Instead, she groans. Honestly, it's more of an incensed grumble.

This is not the response I expected.

"I cannot believe what I am hearing," she says.

I fill my cheeks with air and blow it out. I look akin to Old Man Winter. I'm afraid to say any more.

"Tony, please listen to me," she says. "I am sorry about your brother's death, I truly am, and although I may not know how you feel, what I do know is all this so-called inconsolable grief is about you more than it is about anyone else. While you have been busy mourning all your losses, you've neglected to consider what's most important in this situation, and it is Chloe's daughter, the bright and shining star who, due to circumstances beyond her control, has had the incredible misfortune of landing square in the center of this family's domestic disaster."

Didi gets angrier with every word.

I press random buttons on the remote.

"Above and beyond everything that has transpired between you and your wife," she says, "that little girl needs a mother, and her fate should be the single most concern that pulls this family together to take action. She is the mainspring of this family's story now. Are you at *all* conscious of the gravity of this situation? Do you have any idea the *danger* they face living on the street? Homeless women fall victim to violence more than any other group."

I continue to keep my mouth shut.

"You are this child's grandfather. You need to resolve this crisis. *Now.*"

I've never seen Didi this irate.

"There is no question your wife has done a great deal of harm to this family." She swings her keys. The noise crushes my eardrums. "In this particular situation, however, you are the jackass."

I squeeze the remote. Never in my wildest imagination would I have envisioned Ana and my lover on the same side of an argument, any argument, let alone one concerning my family.

I look over at her.

She's ready to go.

Dread overtakes me. "Please don't leave me," I say.

29
ANA

CHLOE'S RESCUE

I hoist myself through the open window. A radio blares somewhere in the house, but the acoustics in here are so awful, I can't tell where it's coming from. I tiptoe across the room and quietly step into the hallway. This place is a dump—the floorboards are cracked or split in half, and most the wallpaper has been peeled off. Yet the hall is littered with piles of blankets and open sleeping bags. People actually live here?

A young man swings around the corner and nearly bumps into me. He startles at my presence, and we size each other up. He's maybe nineteen or twenty and tall with long stringy hair. It's evident he hasn't eaten in days. He tries to dodge me and runs into an empty room, but I race over and grab the doorknob before he can close it. I shove my foot in the entryway.

He kicks at it.

I hang on tighter. He thinks I'm the police, but I can't let go of the door. If Chloe's here, he's my one chance to find her.

"*Je suis ici pour voir Chloé DiSalvo,*" I shout.

He pulls on the handle. He's strong, but so am I.

"*Je suis sa mère.*" I'm her mother. "*Je veux la voir.*" I want to see her.

He releases the door. He steps past me and into the hall, then he hurries off.

I chase after him, alarmed at everything I see along the way. Cockroaches run straight up the walls, discarded containers and food wrappers line the window sills, and hash pipes, papers, and scales monopolize the floors. Someone's stood a twin-sized mattress on its end and leaned it against the wall. The thing is old and soiled and partially blocks the doorway of what was once a bedroom. Two toddlers play beneath it like it's normal, or proper, or safe.

As we continue along, the music gets louder, and we enter a room that might have once passed for a living room. An open laptop sits on top of a stack of cardboard boxes and live streams a game show. A young woman, half-asleep, watches from where she slouches in a ratty armchair. A one-year-old dozes in her lap. An older man sits on a sofa nearby. The couch is missing most of its cushions, but he slumps across it anyway and stares off into space.

The room is a mix of ethnicities—honest to God, the whole place is a multicultural study on how not to raise a child. If I could take a match to it, I'd set it on fire.

I look around for Chloe, but I don't see her. A light-skinned child, maybe four years old, runs into the room. She aims straight for the couch. Her precious little body is tucked into flannel pajama bottoms and an adult-sized T-shirt that says "LES BLEUS." She holds a Barbie by its arm—a white-skinned model with blonde hair, though most of the doll's mop is gone. The child scales the furniture, but her legs get tangled in the T-shirt, and she tumbles to the floor. Undeterred, she throws the doll and launches herself at the couch again. She climbs into the lap of the man who is lying there. She sits the doll on his chest. He doesn't stir.

A second child, darker in complexion and closer to eighteen months, races into the room after her. The younger girl has on a diaper and nothing else. Her long, carbon black hair flows wildly along her back. Judging by the circles under her eyes, she hasn't had a decent nap in weeks.

Shit. Every muscle, every tissue of my being constricts.

Chloe said her daughter is eighteen-months.

Could this be? Is this . . . Aasia?

The younger girl runs for the same couch but stops short of it. She hops onto her tippy toes and delivers an ear-splitting scream.

No one notices.

My eyes fill with water. Where is my daughter?

The older girl now taunts the smaller child with Forlorn Barbie, but the eighteen-month-old is fast, and she snatches the doll away and chucks it. The figure lands on the ground inches in front of her. She belts out another high-pitched shriek.

Still, nobody hears her.

I search for my companion, but he's disappeared. A young Black man, probably the same age, lounges a few feet from me in an old La-Z-Boy. His hair is clipped short and dyed orange. A bright carrot orange. It's a bad dye job, to say the least. A stack of medical books sits on the floor beside him. They're old, and the bindings are held together with blue duct tape. An open notebook lays there, too. I step closer and realize it's filled with handwritten notes on the history of microbiology. Seeing as he's the one person here who's awake, I approach him for answers.

"*Où est Chloe?*" I ask.

He lights up a cigarette. "Your daughter is not here," he says. His voice is hoarse. It's no more than a whisper.

I want to explain how this can't be true, how Chloe called me last night and said she wanted to come home, but before I can get the words out, I'm distracted again by the eighteen-month-old. She throws herself at my feet and swivels around on her stomach, then rolls onto her back and sings to herself. She flies the doll above her head like it's an airplane. What a handful; she's tiny mass of pure energy, and I can't take my eyes off her. I mutter at the man, "I'm here to take her and her daughter home."

He takes a drag of his cigarette. He keeps his focus on the community laptop, which now hosts a European version of another exploitative home shopping channel. "She is out," he says.

"*Out?*" I finger my turtleneck. It's so tight I can't swallow.

The child on the floor finishes her song, sits up, and hammers the doll headfirst into the marred hardwood. Not satisfied with this, she reverses it and pounds it into the floor until its legs snap off. Giddy with excitement, she springs to her feet and nearly stumbles into me. She doesn't even *see* me. She's not even two, and she's completely detached from the rest of the world. She's a baby, and she already carries the dulled expression of the walking dead.

"You speak to me like I am a piece of dirt," he says.

I pretend I don't hear him. I check the room again. Maybe he's wrong. Maybe Chloe is here, and I didn't see her.

"Being homeless does not make me worthless."

While I understand his feelings more than most, the realization my daughter is in this position and I'm the one who put her here, strikes a nerve. I fall back on my training. "I hear your anger," I say.

"Is that so, Snow White?"

I cross my arms in front of me. "I suppose you're the one who . . . got her pregnant." I struggle with the words.

He laughs and puffs on his cigarette. The smoke lingers on his lips. "No, I am not," he says.

"So, who is he?" I look around. "Who's the father?"

"You are as I thought you would be."

"What's that supposed to mean?" I fidget with my bracelet. The sapphires are as cold as dry ice.

"You do not see outside of your high-class world."

"How dare you?" I want to project indignation, but instead I whine like an adolescent. I want to explain myself, say all the right things that will make me forgivable in his eyes, or at least show sympathy for me and tell me where my daughter is, when the eighteen-month-old whizzes by me again. She flings herself at the couch, squirms across the cushions, and pinches the older girl. The four-year-old slaps her hand away, then kicks at her. The little one yells again, and it sets ablaze all my humiliation at being such a shit lousy mother who had to cling to love at any cost that I turned everybody's world upside down to make sure I got it.

I never thought things would go this far.

I replace my anguish with a white-hot inferno of rage. It blasts out of me like a lethal gas. "What about this child's parents?" I ask. "For someone who sees my cash rich depravity as having screwed up my daughter's life, I don't see you doing any better. Why has nobody dressed this child, or brushed her hair, or washed the juice stains off her face?"

The man grins at me. "You are certain you want to know the story of this child's family?" he asks.

I give him a hard look and wait for his answer.

He positions the cigarette between his teeth and inhales again, then lets the smoke unfurl with the unhurried nature of a man who knows he has the upper hand. "This girl's mother," he meets my glare, "is your daughter, and at this moment, she is out buying drugs."

"Oh *God*." Tony's right. I destroyed Chloe's life, and I dig a fingernail under the cuff of my sleeve. I gouge at one of the unhealed lesions, but it does no good. This grief goes too deep, and no amount of scratching will relieve it. "Okay," I say. "Okay."

"I understand Chloe better now," he says. "I understand why she is a junky."

"Don't say that, damn you. Don't you say that about her. I had problems, terrible problems while I was raising my daughter."

"So I have been told," he says.

"I don't know what my daughter said to you—"

"Your daughter suffers very much. She needs someone to love her."

Someone to love her.

The words reverberate in my head. It was the one thing my daughter wanted. It was also the one thing I couldn't give her.

I force myself to stay cool, lighten up. I still have to get Chloe, and I still need this man to work with me. "What's your name?" I ask.

He draws lightly on the cigarette, then goes back to watching the computer screen. "Jibreel," he says.

"Well, Jibreel." I force a smile. It's sheepish. "When does my daughter come back when . . . she goes out like this?"

"When she runs out of money." The muscles in his jaw stiffen, and he grinds his teeth. "That is when she will come home."

"This is not her home!" My eyes burn.

Jibreel couldn't care less: he's done with me. He stubs out his cigarette and settles further into his chair. The four-year-old scampers over to him, and he repositions himself so she can climb into his lap. She rests her head on his chest and points at the nice lady on the screen who is now hawking overpriced stainless-steel food dehydrators.

A flurry of single syllables flashes through my frontal lobe. Hide. Fight. Cry. Run.

What about Chloe's daughter?

She's not my concern.

Crap. I can't leave her here.

I can't take her with me, either. I'm too old to parent another toddler.

At the very least, I can find her something to wear, and I approach her.

The child is sprawled across the couch. Her inner motor is idle at the moment.

I remove my sweater and drape it across her shoulders.

She looks up at me, and our eyes meet.

We *connect.* She *sees* me.

Aasia hops off the couch and pokes her twig-like arms through the sleeves, then she tries to run from me. I snag her by her armpits, hoist her up, and balance her on my hip. "How about we find you a cute outfit to go with your new sweater?" I lower her to the ground, let her find her footing, then hold out my hand. She takes it and pulls me in the direction of her room. Her heels pound the floor, and she drags me down the dirty hallway and into what she believes is an actual bedroom, but the space is empty except for a pile of sheets heaped in the middle of the floor.

I want to scream.

I search around for anything that resembles children's clothing, when I find a rumpled T-shirt beside the bedclothes. It's black. The words "Car Doctor" are written in big, white letters across the front. I haul it out, and the girl raises her arms so I can dress her in it. It looks ridiculous, but it'll have to

do. She looks at me and twinkles, and I marvel at her innocence. I run my fingers through her ratty hair and fantasize
about braiding it into a crown.

Maybe I *can* take her with me. I could buy her something
nice to wear and make her a plate of butter noodles—every
kid's dream. I'll return for Chloe tomorrow when my daughter
is sober and reasonable, and we can see where things stand
between us. I turn to Aasia, "I know where we can find a whole
new outfit for you to wear." My voice bubbles with delight.

Her eyes grow large; they glisten.

"Do you want to come with me?"

She nods so vigorously, I worry she'll hurt herself. I hold
out my arms, and she climbs into them and squeezes her legs
around my waist. Her bony heel stabs me in the back, but I
don't scold her, and I don't stop her because I can't remember
the last time I held a child this tight and so close to my heart.
Then we creep down the hall toward the front door. As we
close in on it, I notice it's deadbolted from the inside.

This ordeal isn't over yet.

I reach for the lock and manipulate it. A bottle falls in a
room nearby. It rolls across the broken tiles.

I look at Aasia, and she meets my gaze. She has no idea
how much danger we're in.

Now someone swears at the bottle and picks it up.

Aasia pays no attention. She toys with a strand of my hair,
then flings it in the air.

I size up the entryway, search out a place for us to hide, but
there's nothing here to conceal us.

Jibreel steps into the hall. His back is to me.

Aasia swings her foot, and I'm pretty sure it connects with
my kidney. I make an ouchy face, then place my finger to her
lips.

Jibreel stoops and removes a bottle from the cooler on the

floor. He twists off the cap and flicks it, sending the metal top skidding across the parquet. Then he sidles further into the hallway, then he stops, then he turns in my direction.

We lock eyes.

I hold my breath as the universe stands still and a lifetime of excuses march before me.

Jibreel looks at the girl.

I keep my focus on him and pull her close.

He waits, then lowers his and moves off to another room.

Does he plan to return? Will he stop me from taking Aasia? I need to relax, but I can't. So, we wait. We wait and see if anyone becomes suspicious because they don't see Aasia's knotted head roaring up and down the hallway. We wait and see if someone becomes alarmed because the wild girl's doll is in pieces across the hardwood, but she's nowhere to be found. We wait and see if at least one other person becomes concerned because the only sound in the room is some ridiculous gameshow, and the child who can stop a crowd hasn't let one loose for a while, but no one does any of these things.

It's all right.

I give Aasia a peck on the cheek, and she wraps her skinny arms around my neck. Then I finish with the lock, turn the knob, and we slip out. I close the door behind us.

30
TONY

I lie back and fold my arm across my eyes. Didi has quit me and for good reason. She's correct when she says my need to continuously rescue my wife bolsters my fractured ego. I get enormous pleasure in being the one man in Ana's world who can save her.

Oh, God. What have I done?

I sit up and bury my head in my hands. I press on my eyelids, but I can't shake the fact that it's Ana's face I see—the girl I knew in SoHo, the woman who dropped everything to follow me to Paris, the relentless lover whose single requirement was to be with me. The woman who convinced me we were soulmates.

What if I'm still in love with her?

Good Lord.

I pry myself off the couch.

I don't believe in soulmates. I'm an economist, a man of science. I respect numbers, data, facts. These are what are important in this world—not love. Fairy tales are for dreamers, as is the belief there is a God or an afterlife. There is no second act. There is no tender deity busily preparing a spot for us for when we reach our end of days. It's all supernatural natter. There's nothing else beyond this world. We leave nothing behind when we die other than a mound of clay. A lump of dirt. This is the summation of our entire life; the representation of everything we've ever done, believed, experienced, invented, and achieved on this witless, niggling, and insignificant planet.

Which means I get one shot at this.

It also means I might have blown it.

Is it possible? Could I have just lost the only woman who's ever loved *me*?

Damn it. I grab my shirt and keys, and I race out of the apartment. I charge the stairwell and fly down it. When I reach the basement, I barrel through the parking garage, throw myself behind the wheel of the Renault, and burn up the streets of Ménilmontant.

Within minutes, I arrive at Didi's building and drag myself out of the car. I slump across the courtyard, except when I reach the front door, I don't go inside. Instead, I take a seat at the base of the stairs. The energy and excitement have come to an end. The weight of the world has pressed down on me and made me see reason. I'm a fool for coming here. "I'm the last person she wants to see."

"And why would that be true?"

I spin around and look up.

Didi is standing on the terrace above the door. She looks relaxed in a pair of jean shorts and a gray T-shirt. Her hair is loose around her shoulders.

"How long have you been there?" I feel my cheeks bloom.

"Wait," she says. "I'll be right down." She disappears, and I hear footsteps move about the building. She steps through the front door and sits beside me.

"I'm not very good at this," I say.

She smiles. Didi is a wise woman. Maybe even a little shrewd. "It's okay," she says. "Take as much time as you need."

We sit like this for a bit, in silence. An orange tabby strolls over and nudges her hand, and she obliges. She tends to it the way a mother might soothe her young. It's quite charitable and puts me at ease.

"You were right," I say. "I was wrong." I spit out the words before I have time to change my mind.

"I know," she says.

"I was so worried about my needs, I didn't consider what anyone else might require." I try to assess her forehead and determine whether my apology is enough for her to forgive me. I wait for her to respond, for her to say she wants to stay with me.

Didi remains quiet.

The alarm I felt earlier returns, and I belch out more. "I *do* have a savior complex. It *is* the reason I've stayed with Ana as long as I have, but I can rectify it. I can make everything right." I watch her face. She has to know Ana is not the *only* one who made a decent and responsible decision today. She has to see that I can also be a good parent—and I can be that, I know it.

Well, I can try, at least.

Didi weaves a free arm under my elbow and laces her fingers through mine. She bumps me with her shoulder.

"I'm such an asshole." I bow my head.

"So," she says, "you will repair this situation and cooperate with your wife to figure out the best way to care for your granddaughter?"

The word "granddaughter" sends shivers down my spine. I didn't do such a hot job raising my own children. How am I supposed to grandparent a child I've never met? "Yes," I say. It's a bold-faced lie. "I will do whatever Ana needs me to do to create a good life for the child."

"You must also mend your relationship with Chloe."

"I will." I twist my neck to loosen the muscles. I'm convinced I can't meet this expectation either. I've never been good at denying my firstborn daughter anything, and all the while she was growing up, she played me like a fiddle. She knew exactly how to get what she wanted from me, no matter what line I held. Ana called her to task, and it was at great cost to their relationship. Will I reveal to Chloe how I shut my eyes to her drug use, how this makes me a terrible father, and risk losing her respect? I highly doubt it.

"You have done some low-down things to the people in your life you claimed to love," Didi says. "Self-assured adults do not behave this way."

We exchange looks.

"I understand." I am a desperate man. I will say whatever I need to say to stop Didi from breaking up with me. I take her hand and kiss her fingers. Then I kiss her fingers some more. Then some more before I move up her arm. I will do whatever is required of me to keep her happy.

We spend the rest of the afternoon in bed. We wrap ourselves in each other's arms, and we talk. It's the most romantic we've ever been without having sex, and although Didi is enjoying this time together, it doesn't do much to release my feelings of inadequacy. This is not the kind of closeness I look forward to when I am with *ma maîtresse*. I cast my eyes around the room. Where are all her naughty underthings? Certainly, she must have something dirty lying around.

"When will you speak to Ana?" Didi nestles her body closer to mine. She drapes her leg across my thigh. I can smell her sex, and for the first time this afternoon, I realize I've cheated on her—with my wife. The notion that I should confess this to her rips through my mind, but I know better. Boy, do I know better.

Didi lazily strokes my chest. "We need to discuss our living situation."

"I'm not sure I understand." I look into her eyes.

"I would like to make more permanent plans for us."

I can't break her gaze. I must look like the unfortunate ruminant mammal that's been caught in the proverbial headlights. I let too much time pass without a reply. The moment becomes awkward.

She taps me. "I am asking if you would like to move in with me," she says.

My stomach does a twisty loop. This is not the request I expected to hear from the mouth of my lover today.

She drums her fingers on my chest.

My blood pressure spikes, and I'm afraid I might pass out. You don't let a woman like Didi dangle for long without giving her an answer. So, what's stopping me? My life is a disaster. All of my dreams of a family reunion have gone straight into the toilet. Didi is offering me everything I've wanted in a long-term relationship, a woman who doesn't define herself by her emotional needs and who will love me for who I am.

What more could a man want out of life?

The answer is nothing.

So, why can't I respond? Because it's only a matter of time before she discovers the real me and drop kicks me like a rotten potato.

Why does anything have to change between us?

What's so bad about living with Ana and meeting Didi on the side?

No one knows; no one gets hurt.

I climb on top of her. I plant an elbow on either side of her face, and I frame her cheeks with my hands. "Yes," I say. "Yes, I want to talk about moving in with you." Then I kiss her, confident she took no heed of the key words *talk about*. I will, of course, discuss the topic with her. I'm also certain I can prolong any changes to our situation as I weigh things down with numerous concerns about any potential apartment's location, price, condition, etc. Then I move my lips along her neck, and I kiss her in all the places that should encourage her to forget about this exchange and join me in a quick round of X-rated sex.

She moans and makes her body more available. "Do you plan to keep the dogs?" she asks.

"Holy hell," I shout. "The dogs." I roll off her and jump up. I search the room for my shorts.

"You don't want the dogs?" Didi sits up.

The sight of her naked breasts gives me pause. Maybe I could stay a bit longer, maybe I could—God, I'm an ass. "I forgot all about them," I say. "They need to go out. They have to be fed. I was supposed to give them their meds." I crawl across the bed and give her a kiss on the forehead, then I climb off again and head for the door. "I'll call you later," I say. "Or tomorrow."

Didi flops back down on the pillows.

I take one last look at her, then scurry back to the bed. I kiss her, long and slow, and I plant one on each of her nipples. "It'll be great," I say. "I promise."

If those aren't the most famous last words that were ever said to anyone.

I'm still the same old Tony.

31
ANA

God, I hope I'm doing the right thing. I wrap the seatbelt around Aasia as best I can to secure her in the backseat, then I ring Tony's cell. It goes straight to voicemail. I call a second time. Same thing. I call a third and fourth time, and still it goes to voicemail. I hang up and call again.

He picks up. "What, Ana?"

"I have Aasia," I say. "Chloe wasn't there, but I took the girl."

"Mm-hmm."

"It isn't good, Tony. She's living with a bunch of people in this filthy, old house. Everybody's high. She's into it again. Heroin. It's just like before."

"Okay."

"Did you hear what I said? Our daughter's doing heroin again, and I have her little girl with me."

"Why are you calling?"

"Jesus, what a question. Is it that easy for you to turn your back on your daughter?"

"You did it."

"You son of a bitch."

"Good answer."

"I apologized," I say. "I accepted responsibility for my actions, and it's all in the past now."

"Well, there you have it, folks. The world is a better place now that my wife has embraced the fine art of accountability."

"Suck it, Tony."

"Nice."

"Can we please not do this to each other? Not today."

"I don't know what you want from me."

"Are you listening to me at all? I have Aasia in the car with me."

"I *heard* you."

"Why are you yelling?" My skin pricks with sweat. I can't believe he's still mad at me. "I did this for us, Tony."

"You did this for you."

"You said you want to be a family again. This girl is our new beginning—"

"Damn it, Ana. Please tell me you are not manipulating me with this child. This is a new low, even for you."

He's right. I'm despicable, but I can't let him give up on me now. "I'll go back to therapy, I promise." My words are fast, breathy. "You're not actually planning to leave me . . . are you?"

Tony doesn't answer. He stutters on about something, but he makes no sense.

"You don't even know this woman," I say.

"For God's sake."

"This is our chance to start over."

"Stop it."

"How could you *do* this to us?"

"Enough."

"You promised." My voice shakes. "You said you'd love me forever."

"Not this again."

"We made love last night. We opened ourselves to each other."

"We had sex."

"I'll call Dr. Woodhouse."

"I'm not having this conversation with you."

"Baby, please." My mother's voice pounds in my ears as she pleads with my father not to leave her. I despise myself for begging, but it's what we Sutton women do.

The line goes dead.

"Tony? Tony!" I pitch my cell. It bounces off the dashboard and lands on the seat. The commotion upsets Aasia, and she strains against the seatbelt. She kicks at the back of my chair.

Fuck.

I need to ground myself. I close my eyes and concentrate on what I'm wearing, but Aasia's yelling so loud, I can't remember what I put on this morning. All I know is my pants are too tight, and I'm sweating so much my shirt is stuck to my chest. I finger it. What is it? Cotton? Polyester?

FUCK.

Aasia cries out, and it echoes off the walls. The interior of the car throbs.

What the hell have I done? I can't raise another child.

I check Cool Babes, but the list is quiet. There are no tweets, no likes, no replies.

The silence guts me.

Aasia lets out another deafening war cry.

I gaze out at the mostly empty street. A group of kids kick around a football.

Aasia hollers again. It's louder this time.

I cringe and cover my ears.

Now, what did you do?

My head aches.

How dare you embarrass me like this.

I'm so tired.

Sometimes, I wish you were never born.

I turn my purse upside down, and the knife falls out. I hold the stone handle in my hand and rub my thumb across its glassy surface. The back of my neck shivers, and dry heaves stab at my throat.

I don't need to do this.

What else do I have?

Nothing.

I scrunch up my sleeves and look at my forearms. They're scarred and pockmarked, and the sight of them repulses me. I'm so sick and tired of being sick and tired.

I look out on the street again.

My life is one big pool of regret for the person I've become, for the person I should've been.

I'll never learn.

Now I'm responsible for a little girl who's miserable and confused, and who misses her mother. What was I thinking? Cold rolls over me like a deluge, and I shiver and wrap my arms around my middle. A deathlike stillness descends on the car.

It's so quiet.

It's *too* quiet.

Wait—why is it so quiet in here all of a sudden?

Shit. I drop the knife and turn around.

The girl's eyes have rolled into the back of her head, and she's breathing fast like she can't catch her breath.

I reach over the seat and touch her arm.

Jesus Christ. Her skin is on fire!

I jam the key in the ignition, crank the engine, and blast the air conditioning. Then I scramble into the backseat with her and unhook her seatbelt. I drag her into my lap where I make her sit up and take in big gulps of cold air. Within seconds, she lets out an earth-trembling howl, then cries. It's intense.

"Oh, my goodness." I don't know when a toddler's scream has ever sounded so sweet.

Soon, her breathing becomes more regular, and she stops wailing and looks at me. She studies my face.

I reach down and gather together a handful of Burger and Fils napkins from the floor, then I dab at her cheeks and wipe the snot from under her nose. I remove the oversized T-shirt she has on and use it to soak up the moisture on her back, along her neck, and down her tiny arms. The car fills with the sweet blend of toddler sweat and baby powder.

Aasia's mood softens, and she notices my bracelet. She makes a game of capturing the sapphires, so I unhook it and offer it to her. She takes the gemstones in her fist and shakes them, and the stones refract the light. The car comes alive with beams of lavender, white, and indigo blue. They bounce off the windshield, shoot over the dashboard, and dance between the seats as they enclose us in their fire.

How is it I never noticed their brilliance before now?

The girl giggles, and I'm in heaven.

While it's true that I've spent the majority of my life honing the brash and unscrupulous behaviors that for the most part, have helped me get my way, in the last twenty-four hours these same behaviors have also caused me to lose everything and fail everyone: Tony. Chloe. Me. I can't dive any deeper. Yet here I sit, prepared to bring Chloe's daughter home and care for her. This has got to be one of the most compassionate things I've ever done for another human being. No, this *is* the most compassionate thing I've ever done for someone else. Period.

Maybe my mother was wrong.

Maybe I *am* a good person.

I rest my shoulder against the seat. Imagine that? Me, Ana Storm, compassionate and kind. My whole life I've wanted someone to believe in me, to believe I was worthy of love.

I never thought that someone would be me.

Aasia throws the bracelet. It strikes the back of the seat and lands at my feet. I pick it up and stuff it in my pocket. Then I rewrap her in the seatbelt and climb back behind the wheel. I'm about to shift the car into gear when someone taps the driver's side window.

It's Jibreel. His expression is kind. It's a significant change from the way he looked at me in the apartment.

I roll down the window.

"Someone wants to join you." He nods toward the house.

I follow his line of sight to see Chloe walking toward the car. She's holding a trash bag. She's coming home the same way she left: with her entire world stuffed into a garbage bag. I jump out and run to her. She looks the same, only tired, more so than I remember. Yet she's still my Clover; she's still my baby girl. I take the bag from her and pull her toward me. She lets me wrap my arms around her. She drapes her hand at my waist.

I whisper in her ear, "Your father . . . he *is* your father." Maybe this isn't the right time, but I have to get this off my chest. Now. I've waited too many years for her to forgive me, and I don't want anything to stand in the way.

Her head jerks back. Her eyes shred me into pieces.

I hold her tighter. "Please, *please* forgive me," I say. "Let me make it up to you. Give me the chance to prove I can be a better mother than I was the first time around."

My daughter hesitates, then her face breaks and her body shudders as she cries in silence and releases twenty-three years of repressed heartbreak. All of it because of me—because

I'm weak and self-serving. The most I can hope for now is that our mother-daughter bond is more resilient than what our history dictates.

"I *will* make it up to you," I say.

When my daughter regains her composure, I escort her around the car to the passenger side, but she resists me. She wants to sit in the back with Aasia. So, I wait for Jibreel to hand her daughter back to her and for both of them to settle in the back seat, then I get behind the wheel again. Jibreel closes the door for me and gives it a light tap. Then he steps back, and we pull into the street. I wave to him, but he doesn't repay the gesture. He turns and heads back to the house—this is the last image I have of the man who returned my daughter to me.

I follow the road to the end, make a right, and take the highway.

We're going home.

32
TONY

I enter the apartment and stumble over my wife's sandals. She stands in the foyer. She's bouncing a child on her hip. The girl can't yet be two.

It's her; it's my granddaughter.

"I fed the dogs," Ana says. "Dharma pooped in the apartment again. It was right in front of the door. She would've made it out if—"

"I know. I'm a dope."

"I cleaned it up, then I called Evelyn. She came right over and helped me." Ana transfers the child to her other hip. "Where were you?" she asks.

"Busy." I kick off my shoes and skirt the dogs, who are positioned beside my wife. Their eyes are glued to the child—Chloe's daughter. I'm dumbstruck. Why can't I rally a single emotion? I point my chin away from my wife and skulk off.

Ana shadows me into the living room. Now, she has dogs in tow. It's a parade, and I'm the lead clown.

"This is Aasia." She lowers the child to the floor. The girl scrabbles at my wife's knees and hides her face. Kooks plods over and pokes at her with his muzzle, then he sinks into a lopsided sit. He's all but on top of her. If I didn't know better, I'd swear he was grinning. The child points at him and roars with glee. It's loud enough to wake the dead. The noise excites Dharma, and she barks and thwacks her tail on the floor.

I snub them all and scan the rug for the channel changer. I circle the room with my arms outstretched like I'm dowsing for water. I make more of a production of it than is necessary. "Does Chloe know you stole her child?"

"I didn't steal her," Ana says. "She's our granddaughter. I'm lending a hand." Ana fixes the girl's shirt, but the toddler is too enamored with the dogs to stand still. She pats Kooks on the head, then emits another ear-piercing squeal.

"For God's sake." I flail my arms, lumber over to my favorite poly-leather chair, and catapult myself into it.

"You can't believe how the homeless live," Ana says. "The conditions are wretched."

I slump into the seat.

My wife steers the girl over to the couch. She makes a face and sits on the cushion farthest from the patch of blemished carpet. The fibers there are trampled and flattened. It's the spot where Didi and I had sex this morning. She looks at me with disgust. "*Christ*, Tony. Is this the reason you didn't answer the phone when I called back?"

I drop my eyes. I don't respond.

Ana picks up the child and pulls her onto her lap. She works to detangle a mass of knots in her hair. My wife's hands move at a frantic pace, and the girl hollers. Ana stops and takes a deep breath. She whispers in the tyke's ear, and the small fry laughs, then she turns to me. "Having seen it first hand," she says, "I now have a better understanding of the drug epidemic in this country."

"For the love of Pete." I stand and stretch out the muscles

in my lower back. I peer over at the girl again. I may be an old fool, but I swear this child has my cheekbone structure. I cross the room and step out onto the balcony. I continue to make like I'm angry at Ana and that I plan to leave her for another woman. I expect soon enough she'll beg me not to go and make quite a production of it. She'll work on me until she softens my prolonged belligerent mood, then she'll pester me to tell her what she did that was so wrong, and all of it will continue until I relent, recommit to the marriage, and promise to love her again, unconditionally.

Which I *will* do.

I may talk a good game, but I know where my bread is buttered. I can't live without Ana. Who else would tolerate me?

Not Didi.

Not anyone.

Maybe it's true. Maybe we *are* soulmates.

For my wife's part, however, she's not doing any of these things. With the girl asleep in her lap, she eases the child onto the couch, then follows me, but only as far as the French doors. She leans against the jamb. She doesn't take her eyes off the child.

My entire body tenses up, and there's a sensation in my middle I can't explain. It feels like being a yoyo right before the throw. It's out of character for Ana not to badger me, or to pepper me with questions, or to show her desperation at the very notion of being abandoned and having to live her life without me.

"Anyway," she says, "None of it involves our daughter any longer."

I turn around and gawk at her.

"Chloe's home," she says. "She's sound asleep in her old room. She was out like a light before her head even hit the pillow." She laughs. It's genial.

I look in the direction of my eldest daughter's old room, yet Ana's reference to my daughter doesn't register. Chloe is home? My family has reunited? How can it be my wife and daughters have done the very thing I've dreamed about for the past seven years? Without me? Who in this world would be so stupid as to squash their own dreams?

Me, that's who.

"I plan to get her into an outpatient drug treatment program," Ana says. "She swears she won't fight me this time."

I continue to stare into the empty hallway.

"She agreed to go if I promised to restart *my* therapy." Ana pauses. She takes a deep breath. "I said yes, of course."

I'm tongue-tied. My wife wouldn't go back to therapy for me, but she'll do it for Chloe.

"This way, she won't feel so alone," she says.

Honestly, there are no words to describe the sense of isolation I feel at this moment. I've told so many lies and played so many games with my wife, I'll never turn things around between us. I've dug myself a hole—a deep one, and I don't know how to climb out of it. I turn and face the railing. While there are at least two hundred meters between me and the sidewalk below, it still wouldn't be enough to create the velocity I'd need for an object of my size and weight to annihilate itself upon impact.

33
ANA

Tony surveys the skyline. His body shudders, then he backs away from the railing. He turns and studies me, but he remains quiet.

I return to the couch and sidle the edge of the cushion to buttress the girl. Once again, I refrain from placing my feet anywhere near the trampled stretch of rug. A cashmere shawl hangs over the back of the couch, and I unfold it and lay it across Aasia's chest. Her head lists to the side, and I trace my fingers along her cheek. I can't keep my hands off her.

Tony returns to the living room. "You don't fool me for a minute," he says. "Not with any of this."

He stations himself behind his chair and mutters. He's working himself up into quite the tantrum. "I don't buy an ounce of this grandchild stuff," he says. "It's all nonsense. It's another one of your bizarre stunts to get your own way."

"Tony, I'm not—this is not a scheme."

He maneuvers himself to the front of the chair, lifts the seat cushion, and rustles his hands beneath it. He pounds it back into place with his fist, then hurls himself into it and lets out a long, low sigh. He lets the palm of his hand drift lazily across what's left of his hair. "Please tell me you didn't spend your afternoon mobilizing all the various ways you could manipulate me with this child," he says.

My husband's comment bounces off me like rain water. I can't explain everything that happened to me today, or the epiphany I experienced, but what I do finally understand is how I closed my eyes to this marriage and allowed it to break apart. How I lied and maneuvered him, and all so I didn't have to be alone. I wish I could say our relationship had been forged out of love, and grounded in intimacy, but Tony and I weren't capable of this. Instead, we aimed for a union steeped in secrets and power struggles, then we centered it around division and withdrawal. So, rather than face the world together, we chose to disappear.

From the world. From each other. From ourselves.

I don't want to hide anymore.

I want a divorce.

"Tony," I say, "what I said in the car about Aasia. And us. I was wrong. I never should've used our granddaughter as a ploy to hold on to you."

He snorts.

"Listen." I sit back and jiggle my foot. It's weird, I'm nervous but not itchy. "I need to tell you something."

He raises an eyebrow.

34
TONY

I cross my legs, left over right, and flex my left foot upright. While it may be an image of repose, I'm anything but. I've latched on to my chair so tightly, my knuckles have turned white. My oldest is asleep in the other room, and I'm the one who now finds himself on the outside of this family's circle, even though the one person responsible for all of this is my wife.

I refuse to let her get away with it.

"A lot of people would give their right arm for what we had," I say.

Ana stops jiggling her foot. She doesn't bother to look at me.

Oddly, she's quite composed. She's too composed. Why isn't she upset? When is she going to beg me to stay? Not that I give a damn, but it *is* what she does. It's what I've come to expect. I count on it in the same way I depend on the sun rising in the east and setting in the west.

"How many years do you plan to rehash this argument?" my wife asks. She keeps her focus on the child.

"Can you blame me?" Rather than do the right thing and drop it, I continue to engage her. I can't seem to stop. While Ana appears to be making changes in her life, I'm still beating the same old, ramshackle drum.

"You will never forgive me for what I did to you." Ana drags her fingers through her hair, then fiddles with her shirt. I wait for her to scratch or claw at herself, but she refrains. "Even though you did the same thing to me," she says.

"It's not the same thing," I say. "You didn't want me."

Our eyes meet. I turn my head. "I fell head over heels for you," she says.

"You were young," I say. "You wanted to rebel, and you knew it'd piss off your father if you married a poor boy from suburbia."

"You're always so ready to point out other people's short-comings." Ana lightly pats the child's back. "I guess, that's one way to ensure you never have to face your own childhood baggage."

The temperature in the room skyrockets, and I sit up straighter. I didn't expect this retort. Nor am I prepared to address it. Am I sweating? I'd give my right arm for a glass of ice-cold water right now. Honestly, I don't need Ana to remind me how poorly I treat people and how miserably I've treated her throughout this marriage. It's a skill, and I've spent my life polishing it. Degrading others permits me to retain an illusion of control over my world.

"I never said I was beyond reproach." I clear my throat, then dig my hands beneath me, into the folds of the cushion, but the remote remains elusive.

"Thank God for that," Ana says.

"You don't think I regret that I've caused you so much anguish?" I lower my chin to my chest.

My wife doesn't say anything. She rises from the couch and

crosses the living room. She looks out onto the city for a while, then turns to face me. Her expression is intense, yet tranquil. On the street below, someone blows a horn. It goes unanswered for a change.

I want to apologize. I do. I want to tell her how I never meant to hurt her and how there were too many times during this marriage that I struggled to be a good husband, but I failed. I smack my head against the back of the chair. I'm certain a muscle pops in my neck.

I return my attention to the rug, and wouldn't you know it? There's the remote. I retrieve the damn thing and hold on to it for all it's worth.

35
ANA

I appreciate Tony's comment, his apology of sorts, but I don't want to dredge up the past and dissect how it relates to our crummy marriage. Not again. Not tonight.

My husband is comatose. He fixates on the blank television screen. I can't imagine what he's thinking.

We need to change this scenario.

"How about some music?" I wander over to the stereo. When we were newlyweds, Tony and I drank wine and listened to records almost every night after dinner.

"I don't want to listen to music." He keeps a tight grip on the remote.

"Do you remember our wedding song?" I kneel in front of our stack of old LPs and pan through them. It's like being on a musical paleontological dig. Specs of dust float through the air and stick to my hair, my lips, my eyelashes. I keep sifting until I find it—a vintage album I found in an antique shop in the Village long before Tony and I met. It's Bessie Smith's 1972 album *Nobody's Blues But Mine*. It meant so much to me, I played that thing until I nearly wore it out.

That was a long time ago.

I'm not that same girl.

"Do you remember how we danced?" Tony and I were married in the living room of our apartment in Belleville. "Or how you held me?" We exchanged our vows under an arch of white gardenias. Chace and Médée were the only ones in attendance. Although we invited both of our families, neither my parents, nor his dad, nor any of his brothers joined us for our special day. We didn't care, though. We clung to each other and promised we'd never let go. We thought we'd found everything we'd ever need. We thought we'd found true love.

My husband sits back. He loosens his hold on the remote.

"Or the dress I wore?"

"It was the most beautiful gown I'd ever seen." He closes his eyes. "And you were the most beautiful woman in it."

I slide the vinyl record out of its cardboard sleeve, balance it between my fingers, and gently place it on the turntable. I lower the needle until its diamond tip skims the record's high-gloss surface. The speakers crackle, then the room fills with the keystrokes of an upright piano and the cool, laid-back tempo of the American blues. I patter over to Tony's chair.

He peeks at me, then looks away.

"We couldn't get enough of each other." I stand in front of him and sway to the music. I hold out my arms and encourage him to dance with me, but he doesn't budge. So, I hop into his lap and straddle him.

"I don't want to dance." He reaches around me and points the remote at the television.

I take his hands.

He pulls them back, scratches his nose, then drops the remote. It lands on the floor in front of him.

I take hold of him again, place his arms around my waist,

and as Bessie Smith belts out the words, so do I. *"I'm sad and lonely, won't somebody come and take a chance with me?"*

Tony inches his foot across the rug. He stabs at the remote with his toes.

I move my body to the beat. *"I'll sing sweet love songs, honey, all the time."*

My husband angles his head and peers around me.

"If you'll come and be my sweet baby mine?" I attempt to dip us, which isn't easy when two people are seated in the same chair. It doesn't go well.

Tony laughs, at last. He rests his head back against the cushion. His eyes beam. They're again a bright cobalt blue. It's nice to see him smile after everything we've put each other through.

"It's time we both move on," I say. "You know that, right?"

Then, just as fast, the color dissipates, and my husband sinks back into his usual moroseness. He pushes me away.

36
TONY

The song ends. It plunges the living room into an awkward silence.

"It wasn't *all* bad, was it?" Ana asks.

"No."

"We had some good times together, didn't we?"

I can't believe my wife intends to end our marriage. Does she actually want a divorce?

"I caused my share of disappointment," she says. "That's for sure."

"It wasn't all you," I say. "I generated a decent amount of aggravation." A groundswell of grief descends on me, and I resist it and push it into the farthest recesses of my mind.

"I guess we're just trouble together." She smiles tenderly at me.

I forage for the remote with my toes.

"I spent so much of this marriage clinging to you," she says, "It nearly killed us both."

I've never heard my wife speak this way. It's like she's on

some kind of psychic journey—without me. It makes me see red, and I exchange my regret for belligerence and regenerate the battle between us all over again. "Maybe you should've made better decisions," I say.

Ana rolls off my lap, crosses the room, and hovers over the girl again. She's unperturbed by my outburst. "I made a lot of mistakes when I raised Chloe," she says.

"Is that what we're calling them now?"

"I did the best I could with what I had." She catches my eye. There's a layer of remorse in her face. "I made the same mistakes my mother made with me."

"This is a do-over for you, then."

"I've waited years for my mother to tell me I'm a good person, but it never happened, and it probably never will. It's time I let it go."

I swear, she's crossed some proverbial bridge.

"I need to stop blaming her," she says. "It's not her fault."

I should cross it with her. I should do *something* to change the trajectory of our marriage.

"My mother's lack of faith in me isn't about me at all; it's about how she sees the world. My mother doesn't have faith in *anyone* because the people who were supposed to love her and keep her safe when she was young, didn't do it. It makes her unhappy, and no one can make her happy except her."

My face smarts from gritting my teeth. I exercise my mouth to loosen my jaw, but it doesn't help. There's no denying it. I've made my bed. My wife is giving me the heave-ho.

I *am* a dumb-ass.

"My mother loves me," Ana says. "She loves me the best way she knows how. You can't pass something on to someone else if it wasn't passed to you in the first place."

Who is this woman? I rotate my neck, but I swear something seizes in the back of my head.

"Which reminds me," she says. "I should call her tomorrow. It's been too long, and I know she'd enjoy hearing from her granddaughters—and her brand new *great*-granddaughter."

Dear God, I'm about to have a stroke.

37
ANA

Aasia looks adorable in one of Meadow's old shirts. The fit isn't the best, but it's better than any of the oversized clothing I found in that vacant house. I straighten it, but she's waking now and willing to tolerate only so much of my handling. She repels her way out of the cashmere's death grip and hops off the couch. She speeds over to where the dogs are lying butt-to-butt on the rug, drops to all fours, and places her face inches from Kook's nose. I brace myself for the outcry.

"I thought we'd be together forever." Tony hasn't budged from his chair. He looks small, pale. The remote lingers at his feet.

"Never say never."

"You were the love of my life," he says.

"As you were mine."

My husband rises from his chair. He groans and makes a production of stretching out his lower back. He extends his arms toward the ceiling, wiggles his fingers, and crosses the living room. He treads softly down the hall toward Chloe's room. The door creaks as he opens it. A few moments later, it closes. Then he returns to the living room. Meadow follows him. She keeps a safe distance, but she's right on his heels. Tony stops, and she slips past him and sits on the couch. She curls her legs underneath her, opens a book, and makes like she's losing herself in its pages.

"I'll come back next week and box up some of my effects," my husband says.

"Sure." I leave it at that. Tony may talk a good game, but given he's prepared to move out this fast, it's safe to say he was never truly invested in a family reunion. I'm not surprised. I wish his mistress the best, she's going to need it. Now she's the one who'll have to withstand his indignation, sanctimousness, and greed; steel herself against his tireless resolve to expose all her flaws; and comfort herself with being kept at arm's length as he works to protect his fragile ego.

"Come back whenever you like," I say.

Tony strolls over to where Aasia is busy head-butting Dharma. He stoops to her level and touches the girl's cheek. He holds her chin in his palm, and for the first time this evening, he looks straight into her eyes. Then he searches out mine. "When I return," he says, "maybe I can put the girls' old crib together? You know, for the kid. Would that be all right?"

"That'd be great." I jump up from the couch and stop Aasia from pulling on Dharma's ear. I lift her and brace her against my hip.

Dharma rises and shakes her tender frame. She forces her snout into Tony's hand. My husband pats her on the head, stands erect, and looks around the living room. Then he plods out. Dharma watches him go. She doesn't follow him. Neither dog does.

As Evelyn tinkers with the espresso maker in the kitchen, Aasia and I sit and listen while Tony packs his things. He moves about in his usual methodical manner. He tosses some clothes and toiletries into his duffel, then heads for the kitchen where he rustles papers and assembles books, then dumps it all into his briefcase. Then the front door opens, closes, and he's gone.

He's *gone.*

The stillness perforates my eardrums.

I cross the living room and stand in front of the open window. As the horizon converges with the sun, it yields a halo that's rich with hues of wild watermelon and periwinkle. It frames the Eiffel Tower, which is deep into its five-minute light show. The steel structure dazzles with twenty thousand lights, and its beacon crisscrosses the neighborhoods of Paris. Tourists wildly take photos beneath it, but they can't capture such beauty in a photograph. The tower is one of those Parisian wonders that has to be experienced to be appreciated.

I breathe deep and drink in the loose evening breeze whispering into the room. It wafts across the dogs' backs, hips, and the tips of their tails. Neither one stirs. They're content, wanting nothing more than to laze around the house with the ones they love.

It's taken me a long time to appreciate contentment, to recognize I'm not a bad person, and I'm not defective because my mother wasn't able to care for me. Or because I have BPD. These are only parts of my story. I may have a long road ahead of me before I can be the woman others believe I can be, but I've got plenty time to fine-tune her. Besides, I don't need to fix anyone else in this world except me.

Aasia jumps to her feet and makes a beeline for the balcony. Kooks gets up and follows her. I race after both of them and overtake the child before she gets to the terrace. Kooks moseys past us and inspects the railing planters. He's looking for rogue birds that don't belong in the warbler's garden.

"Do you miss your friends?" I sing to him. "It's okay, buddy. They'll be back again next year." He smiles at me with a soft, open mouth, then plants himself on the terrace, facing the window boxes.

I redirect Aasia back inside and steer her toward the couch. The child mounts the furniture like she's climbing Everest. I hold out my arms, but she rejects my help, so I sit back and marvel at her tenacity. Herbie Hancock's electric piano percolates through the walls from our neighbor's apartment, and I hum along. Chloe stirs in her room, and the legs of her poster bed creak against the antique wood floor. I stop and listen, anxious for her to wake, anxious for me and my girls to be together once more. It's been a long time, but this place feels like a home again.

Kooks returns to the living room, flops down on the rug in front of us, and stretches. It's another one of his wonderful four-leggers. Aasia scrambles off me and drops to his level. She pokes her fingers at his creamy muzzle. He lifts an eyebrow and looks at me. I get up from the couch to rescue him, but my second eldest intercepts me.

"I've got her." Evelyn scoops the girl into her arms. The child fails to emit her usual falsetto screech, and we're all grateful.

"You know," I say, "your father and I had plans to celebrate Chloe's return last night with a seafood casserole and some wine, but we never made it to the casserole. How about if you and I have it tonight? I'll reheat it and make a salad. Mac and cheese tastes better the next day anyway."

"Sure," she says. "That sounds good." She makes a game of bouncing Aasia on her hip.

"So," I say, "it'll be me, you, Chloe, and Meadow." I turn to my youngest. "Would you like Aurelien join us?"

"He's a jerk," she mumbles. She doesn't look up from her book.

Evelyn and I exchange glances. Her expression is warm, motherly.

"Maybe there's someone you want to invite?" I ask. "I'm just saying, you know, if there's someone special you'd like us to meet?" I stop myself. I don't want to sound like I'm chastising her for not sharing her life with me. I want her to trust me, to know she can confide in me.

My daughter looks away. "Sneaky, Mom." She smirks, but it's forgiving. "Sure," she says, "but how about another time? Maybe tonight we could keep it to the five of us. You know, just us Sutton women."

Sutton. She uses my mother's maiden name in a loving way.

Then, she turns, steers around both sleeping dogs, and carries her new niece down the hall toward the kitchen. She asks the child if she'd like some Cheerios.

I go to follow them when my cell phone dings. It's a text from Adel. She asks if I'm all right.

I'm good. Real good.

I put the phone down, then pick it up again and type out a reply.

How are you doing?

I add a yellow heart emoji. Then I delete it and insert a red heart instead, add the little guy with the smiling face and the smiling eyes, and hit send. It's about time I kept up my half of this friendship.

I enter the kitchen. It's dark, but for the last few rays of sunlight. The light show has ended, and neither Evelyn nor I have bothered to put on any lights.

My daughter sits Aasia in her lap, opens the girl's palm, and spills a handful of Cheerios into her hand. It takes the child a whole second to hurl them across the floor. She hoots and claps at her achievement.

I laugh at the scene. It's pure and straight from the belly.

"Whoa," Meadow now enters the kitchen. "Someone's made a mess." Her face lights up, and she retrieves some of the Cheerios. She hands them to Ev, then hoists herself onto the counter. She's done hiding in her books. I don't know what happened between her and Aurelien, but I'm glad she's home tonight.

"Hey, you," a voice calls from the archway.

I turn to see Chloe enter the kitchen. She looks better; she's glowing. She's had a couple of hours of sleep, and the color's returned to her cheeks. She folds her arms across her chest. "What have we here?" she asks. Then she grins. It's good to see her at peace with us. With me. It's a dramatic change from the girl I knew seven years ago, and it's on me to make sure it continues.

Ev stands with the little one as Chloe makes a playful face and holds out her arms. But before Evelyn can pass the toddler over, Meadow hops off the counter and ambushes her big sister. She throws her arms around Chloe, and my oldest lets out a whoop. Years of secret-keeping wash away, and the sight of them joined in an embrace brings me to tears. I wipe my face before they catch me.

"All right, you two," Evelyn says. She steps between them and passes Aasia to her mother.

The girl's face stirs with excitement, and her eyes sparkle

like a million points of light cresting the surface of the
Mediterranean. She lets out another hoot and throws her arms
around my oldest daughter.

Life doesn't get more perfect than this.

THE END

RESOURCES

If you or someone you know expresses an interest in hurting themselves, or if you or any of your loved ones believe they are suffering from symptoms of borderline personality disorder, please consider contacting any of the following for assistance:

988 Suicide and Crisis Lifeline

Self-Injury and Recovery Resources (SIRR)
    http://www.selfinjury.bctr.cornell.edu/resources.html

McLean Hospital BPD Programs
    https://www.mcleanhospital.org/search?text=bpd

National Education Alliance For Borderline Personality Disorder (NEABPD)
    https://www.borderlinepersonalitydisorder.org

National Alliance of Mental Illness (NAMI)

https://www.nami.org/About-Mental-Illness/Mental-Health-Conditions/Borderline-Personality-Disorder

Helpguide.org
https://www.helpguide.org/articles/anxiety/cutting-and-self-harm.htm

Sorry My Mental Illness Isn't Sexy Enough For You
https://www.livesnotlabels.co.uk

ACKNOWLEDGMENTS

I would like to express my deepest gratitude to the late John Gunderson, M.D. who provided me with a wealth of opportunities to improve my understanding of borderline personality disorder (BPD). It was a privilege to work beside him. I'm also grateful to the many patients at McLean Hospital who graciously shared their stories with me during the time I was there and engaged in research.

Much thanks to Dave King and the Marion Writers Group for reviewing very early drafts of a manuscript.

I wish to thank the many wonderful book coaches and independent editors I've worked with these past ten years including Joan Dempsey, Carrie O'Grady, Shelley Singer and Writers.com, Dina L. Relles, Mary Kole, Jennifer de Leon and the creative writing center at GrubStreet, Betsy Ellor, Starr Waddell and the beta readers of Quiethouse Editing, and Vicky Brewster. Each of you taught me about the craft of writing and contributed something meaningful to the story, and I'm grateful.

Many thanks to the Women's Fiction Writers Association (WFWA) for the countless writing opportunities and for the incredible beta readers I had the pleasure of meeting: Nina Simon, Nicole Jeffries, Lisa LiDieuelene, Jill Caugherty, Jennifer Craven, and Kim O'Brien. I thank you all for your honest feedback. Heartfelt praise goes to Lidija Kljenak Hilje and the amazing women of the WFWA Writer's Book Club and to the

Women's Fiction Indie Author Support Group for your contributions. I'd also like to extend a warm thank you to Ralph Walker and his Virtual Donut Parties (so many conversations on writing skills!), and to both he and Tif Marcelo for introducing me Twitter's #5amwritersclub. Such an amazing community of writers.

Still, there are some who deserve additional recognition, and I'd like to offer my deepest appreciation to Jennifer de Leon for challenging me to stretch myself creatively, Starr Waddell for taking an editorial machete to this story and pushing me to make it better, and to my friend Swati Mukerjee for not only reading the full manuscript, but for rereading multiple versions of chapter one until I got it right.

While Ana Storm is a work of fiction, her character and that of her mother were informed by a number of academic publications related to the onset of BPD in women. I'm particularly grateful for the following books: Dana Becker's Through the Looking Glass: Women and Borderline Personality Disorder; Armando R. Favazza's Bodies under Siege: Self-mutilation, Nonsuicidal Self-injury, and Body Modification in Culture and Psychiatry; Jean Baker Miller's Toward a New Psychology of Women; Women's Growth in Connection: Writings from the Stone Center authored by Judith V. Jordan, Alexandra G. Kaplan, Irene P. Stiver, Janet L. Surrey, and Jean Baker Miller; Harriet Lerner's Women in Therapy; and Laura S. Brown and Mary Ballou's Personality and Psychopathology: Feminist Reappraisals. I'm also grateful for the academic journal Feminism & Psychology. I read through many volumes.

I'm indebted for the abundance of free material presented online by MentalHealthAmerican.ca; Themighty.com; PsychologyToday.com; BPDCentral.com; BPSResearchDigest.com; AJMahari.com; and the National Library of Medicine's National Center for Biotechnology Information through the National

Institute of Health. I also owe a world of gratitude for the countless online blogs I visited that are written and maintained by those diagnosed with BPD. Their stories gave me a direct window into the day to day experiences of those who live with this disorder.

Thank you to Laura Boyle for her work on the cover design and to Shutterstock for the bird silhouette.

A deep sense of gratitude goes to my loving parents—my mother and late father, Nellie and Thomas Daversa, for how they encouraged my love of reading and writing—way before I started school. I took their excitement for education and ran with it.

A heartfelt thank you goes to my husband, David Gulley, who's been my biggest cheerleader and who believed in this project from the start. I love you. *Family.*

Lastly, and far from least, I want to recognize the faithful companions who've patiently sat beside me these past ten years as I typed out draft after draft (after draft) while they waited for me to take a break so we could go for a walk, or get a snack, or have dinner, or toss the squeaky ball. The names of these beautiful four-legged creatures were Rayne, Delilah, Kaptain, Simba, and Cody. Bono continues to sit with me. And wait. Good boy, buddy.

ABOUT THE AUTHOR

Maria Daversa is a licensed clinical psychologist whose distinct career included working with antisocial adolescents, and later, with women diagnosed with borderline personality disorder (BPD). She's published numerous articles on various personality disorders including BPD. *Sweet Baby Mine* is her debut novel. Maria lives in the US and shares her home with her husband and two rescues. If you would like to find out more about her, please check out her website at https://maria daversa.com. You can also follow her on social media.

Please Review This Book!

Reviews help authors more than you know. If you enjoyed reading *Sweet Baby Mine*, please consider leaving a review on Amazon. It would be very much appreciated!

Sweet Baby Mine